BRUSH FIRE

OTHER BOOKS AND AUDIOBOOKS
BY CLAIR M. POULSON

* Novella

BRUSH FIRE

A SUSPENSE NOVEL

CLAIR M. POULSON

Cover image: *Man in Woods* © *hsyncoban* / istockphoto.com, *Fire Sparks* © DKosig / istockphoto.com

Cover design by Kevin Jorgensen
Cover design copyright © 2023 by Covenant Communications, Inc.

Published by Covenant Communications, Inc.
American Fork, Utah

Printed in the United States of America
First Printing: October 2023

29 28 27 26 25 24 23   10 9 8 7 6 5 4 3 2 1

To my wife. I couldn't do it without Ruth.

PROLOGUE

THE FIRE BURNED BRIGHTLY, CONSUMING grass, brush, and trees. It had been a hot, dry summer. Fire crews were overworked as one fire after another burned throughout the state of Utah and beyond. Fire investigators were frustrated because they were having a hard time figuring out the cause of many of these fires. Some were obviously caused by humans: campfires left unattended or not properly extinguished, cigarette butts tossed recklessly from vehicles, and fireworks that had been banned even for the July holidays.

There had been fewer thunderstorms than usual, so lightning could be blamed for only some of the fires. People were tired of the destruction, the ever-present smoke that hung in the sky day and night, and the ashes that covered everything. Anyone with lung problems was encouraged to stay indoors.

One man in his late twenties loved the fires, the flames, and their color and intensity, and he took great delight in watching things burn. He traveled around the state in a pickup, watching the worst of the fires as they consumed everything in their paths. He even volunteered to fight fires and was in his glory when he was on the front lines of the destruction. No one suspected he had been the cause of any of the fires. After all, he often mentioned how sad he felt about the devastation each blaze caused.

His remorse was, of course, a lie. He was an arsonist of the worst kind—or in his mind, the best kind—and he was good at what he did. He started fires using the same methods that careless people were accused of. Of course, when he let a campfire burn out of control, he did it under the cover of darkness, making sure he left behind no evidence that could tie the fire to him.

The man was a heavy smoker, and he often threw his cigarette butts into dry grass, hoping sparks would catch and spread. Sometimes it worked, and sometimes it didn't. This year was not the first time he'd fed his insatiable love of fires by lighting them himself, but in previous years he'd resorted to the use of matches and gasoline. He didn't need to do that in this super dry summer, which made it less likely that he'd ever be caught.

Some people said he had a "drinking problem." Sure, he loved to get drunk, but he wasn't an alcoholic or anything close to it. More times than not, he was able to avoid being arrested, but he did have a couple of DUIs on his record over the past three or four years. And he'd been jailed for intoxication on several occasions, but that hadn't happened so far this year. He swore that if anyone arrested him again for drunk driving, he would get even. In the past, he'd cut the officers some slack, but that would never happen again.

He hated cops with a passion, but he *loved* fire—the bigger, the better. So far this summer he'd started about a dozen fires and helped fight at least half of them just so he could enjoy them up close and personal. He was living his dream.

***

Bentley Radford, a twenty-three-year-old stocky, brown-eyed trooper with the highway patrol was also living *his* dream. He enjoyed his job, patrolling the highways of the Uintah Basin and finding and arresting lawbreakers, especially drunk drivers. He gained satisfaction from making the highways safer for the public he served.

But that was not the only dream he was living. No, his greatest dream was his recent marriage to beautiful Evie, an experienced emergency-room nurse who was employed by the hospital in Roosevelt. She was smart, driven, and worked well under pressure, which Bentley appreciated every day. She was also slender, blond, and had the brightest blue eyes Bentley had ever seen. Bentley towered over his new bride with an eight-inch difference between them. As newlyweds, they were busy decorating the house they rented in Duchesne, Utah, making it into a home, basking in each other's company. They both worked jobs that kept them in contact with folks who had troubles of one sort or another, but those jobs only made the time they had together sweeter.

CHAPTER ONE

FIVE WEEKS AFTER HIS MARRIAGE to Evie, Trooper Bentley Radford was working a night shift, patrolling a few miles east of Duchesne, when the lights of an oncoming vehicle veered into his lane and then back the other way. He pulled over, waited for the vehicle to pass, and then turned to follow it. It was an older-model Dodge Ram with a huge steel grill on the front and oversize tires. In fact, the entire truck appeared to have been beefed up. The driver continued to veer from one lane to another, and Bentley had seen enough; it was time to stop the truck before it caused an accident. He activated his bar lights. The truck didn't stop. He hit his siren. The truck still didn't stop.

Finally, he pulled up alongside the truck and honked his horn. The driver looked over and shook his head when Bentley pointed to the side of the road. The driver picked up speed, and Bentley stayed right with him. A couple of times he had to swerve when the truck veered toward him. They entered Duchesne at a high rate of speed, blew through the red light at the center of town, and continued west out of Duchesne.

Bentley contacted his dispatcher, then called in the license plate number and found that the truck belonged to a man by the name of Silas Villard from Myton. Bentley had heard the name and recalled being told that the guy had a couple of DUIs from a few years past. They continued for several miles before the driver finally pulled to the side of the road and stopped. Bentley got out of his patrol car and proceeded toward the back of the Ram. The driver suddenly jumped out of his truck and ran toward Bentley, shouting threats and obscenities.

Bentley attempted to calm Silas down, but the guy threw a wild punch, which missed Bentley. At that point, Bentley took the driver down and slapped cuffs on him.

"You'll pay for doing this, Trooper," Silas shouted. "You got no right to hassle me."

Bentley ignored him, placed him in his patrol car, and waited while a wrecker came to get his truck. Silas refused to do any field sobriety tests, take a breath test, or answer any questions. Bentley requested a blood-draw warrant, and blood was drawn. Silas was then locked in a jail cell, facing charges of felony DUI and a handful of misdemeanors. During the entire process, Silas continued his verbal threats against Bentley.

CHAPTER TWO

Evie was on day shift while Bentley was working nights. Despite arriving home in the wee hours of the morning after his tumultuous arrest of Silas Villard, Bentley got up to see Evie off to work, kissing her just before she walked out the door to drive to her job at the hospital. As they walked hand in hand to her car, she said, "You promised you'd get me a horse after we got married." She grinned. "Well, we've been married for a little over a month now, and still no horse."

"We can't get just one horse," he reminded her, also with a grin. "If you have one, then I need one too."

"Of course." She sighed. "I expected that. I don't want to ride alone. I want to ride alongside you."

"We need a place to keep them when we get them, and we need feed for them," he reminded her as he leaned in for another kiss.

"That was nice," she said. "I guess I better get going. Are you going to look for a place to keep our horses today? You are starting your days off, aren't you?"

"I am, and that's a good idea. I've been thinking about it and have someone in mind who has property for boarding horses."

Bentley looked adoringly at his young, petite bride. She looked like a million bucks in her nurse scrubs. She smiled up at him and asked, "Did you have a good shift last night? You haven't mentioned it since you got up."

"It was a busy one," he said with a frown. "I arrested a drunk driver. It's always a good shift when I get a drunk off the road, and the guy I arrested was so drunk he was staggering. He tried to punch me, but he missed." Bentley chuckled. "When I got him to the jail, he refused to take a breath test. He wouldn't even do the standard field sobriety tests for me, and he refused to answer questions."

"So, you got a warrant and drew blood," she said knowingly.

"That's right," Bentley said, "and he fought like a crazy man while they were drawing his blood. I've got a knot on my shin from where he kicked me while we were trying to hold him still. I'm afraid we'll see this guy again. I ran a records check and learned that he had priors. This was his second DUI in just over a year and his third in three. I'm charging him with felony DUI, assault on a police officer, and a few other charges.

"His language was horrible. At the hospital, where I took him to have the blood drawn, the drunk said, 'I will make you regret you ever touched me, Trooper,' for about the tenth time. When I pulled into the sally port at the jail, the guy said, 'You will remember me when I get through with you. You've made a huge mistake,' and the threats went on until we finally booked him into jail."

Evie shivered as Bentley described the arrest and the man's atrocious behavior. It would have been worse for her if he'd told her about the full nature of the threats, but he left that part out. Threats came with the job, and he didn't need to worry her needlessly with that kind of information.

"I hate it when they bring victims of drunk driving accidents into the emergency room," she said. "It is so sad and so senseless. But seriously, I need to go. I hope it's a slow day today. I'll call you when I get to the hospital."

"I'm glad you weren't on duty at the hospital last night when I took him for the blood draw. I wouldn't want the creep to see you. Be careful driving," he said.

They kissed again, and he opened the door of her car for her, shutting it once she was inside. He watched from the driveway as she drove onto the street. She looked back at him and waved, a big smile on her face.

He waved back. Bentley felt like he'd won the lottery when Evie had agreed to marry him. She was an amazing young woman. After she'd driven out of sight, he went back to their bedroom to finish getting ready for the day. He'd only had a few hours of sleep when it was time for his wife to get up and get ready for her twelve-hour shift at the hospital. As a result, he fell asleep in their recliner, but woke up when Evie called to tell him she was at the hospital. "Were you asleep?" she asked. "You sound like it." She chuckled.

Sheepishly he said, "I was in the recliner. But it's okay. I never want you to not call just because I've had a late night at work."

"I love you, and I'll see you tonight," she said, making him smile as he echoed her expression of love.

***

That morning, Silas Villard called his grandfather and asked him to come bail him out. The old man told him he could just sit in jail. "You'll regret not helping me," Silas threatened. It was noon before he found a friend who owed him a favor and reluctantly agreed to bail him out.

His friend also helped him get his truck out of impound, and then Silas drove to his home in Myton, where he began to drink. The more intoxicated he became that afternoon, the angrier he felt toward the trooper. If Trooper Radford hadn't harassed him and accused him of driving while he was drunk, he wouldn't have been arrested. And he wouldn't have needed to ask his grandad to bail him out of jail. He'd lost his cool when his grandad refused; the old man had no right not to help his own grandson. As Silas continued drinking, he considered what he might do to make the old man pay for refusing to help him and how he could get back at the trooper for arresting him. Getting revenge on him would be payback for all the other lousy troopers who had harassed him over the years too.

Later that afternoon, he had a flash of brilliance; he drove past his granddad's house and stopped beyond a large area of dry brush, weeds, and grass that led right up to the back porch. He felt giddy at the thought of how quickly the house would burn down. He lit a torch of rags soaked in gasoline from a can in the back of his truck, and without even looking around, he threw it into a thick patch of tall dry grass. To his morbid delight, there was a breeze blowing right from where he started the fire toward his grandad's house.

He left the area for a few minutes and then returned to watch the fire burn. He moved farther away as the fire grew, and he watched through his binoculars. As it approached the house, he expected to see his granddad come running out.

But he did not. After a few minutes, a fire truck sped up the street. A pair of firemen entered the burning house and came out carrying what Silas figured had to be the old man. Moments later, Grandad was whisked away in an ambulance. Silas had not intended to injure him, just burn his house down, but he was quite sure his grandad would survive.

He returned to his rundown house in Myton. His grandad would probably ask to live with him now that his house was gone. His junky house wasn't too far from where his grandad lived, or had lived, until the fire had pretty much destroyed his house. But there was no way. As he thought about his grandad, he wrinkled his nose in disgust and drained the last few drops of whiskey from the bottle he hadn't finished when he'd left to start the fire. He tossed the bottle into a growing pile of bottles and cans in one corner of his living room.

He wished it had been Trooper Radford in that house because he deserved to be burned even more that his grandad did. That thought got him to thinking that there must be some way he could get his revenge. Maybe another fire— one during the night at Trooper Radford's home would be perfect.

That cheerful thought called for opening another bottle of cheap whiskey. He took a swig and then decided it was time to figure out where the trooper lived, then scout the place out. Revenge would be so sweet, and he could watch another fire burn the next night. Two in as many days, Silas thought. How sweet was that?

***

Late that afternoon, Bentley was cutting the grass in his backyard while his Australian Shepherd dozed in the shade. Bentley heard a siren, then another. Curious as to what was occurring, he went to his patrol car, turned on the ignition, and listened to the traffic on his police radio. It seemed there was a large brush fire in the east end of the county not too far from Myton. He wasn't surprised. It had been a very dry summer, and there had already been a number of wildfires in the state, including some right here in Duchesne County.

He sat in his car with his left foot hanging out the door and listened to the radio traffic for a few minutes with his faithful dog's paws on his leg. He patted Twy's head even as he wished he could do something to help. He knew that if he was needed for traffic control or anything else, he'd be called. He didn't expect that to happen as there were probably enough officers on duty to handle traffic control if it was needed. Firefighters would take care of the fire.

After a couple minutes, he shut his car off and went back to mowing his lawn. He wondered what had ignited the brush fire. Probably a farmer who was burning something and allowed it to get away from him. As dry as the past few months had been, this wasn't a good time to be starting fires. A few minutes later, he went into the house to get a drink and grab a snack. He turned on the TV to see if there happened to be anything on it about the fire, although he doubted it. As he expected, there was nothing about the fire, even though he flipped through several channels. Hopefully that meant it was out by now.

When he had finished his short break, he went back outside to his pickup. He opened the passenger door and said, "Hop in, Twy." His dog was a registered Australian Shepherd with a mostly gray coat with some black and yellow fur mixed in. He had one brown eye and one blue eye. Thus his name, which sort of meant "two-colored eyes" or "two eyes" for short. The dog jumped in. He had to ride in the back seat when Evie was with them, but when it was just Twy and Bentley, he got to ride up front where he'd sit with his paws on the dashboard and look out through the windshield.

Bentley decided to check the place he'd planned to visit about boarding horses when they got some. Mowing the rest of the lawn could wait until he was back. He was in no hurry. It would be after eight before Evie got home from the hospital, and he was off tonight.

More sirens sounded in the distance. Either the fire was a really nasty one and more fire equipment was needed, or there was some other emergency. He'd hoped that they'd have the brush fire under control by now.

Before starting his truck, he stepped back out and got in his patrol car again, Twy following along, to listen to the radio traffic again.

The fire had grown rapidly and had spread to a house, eventually burning it to the ground.

Bentley silently prayed that there had been no one in the house or that they'd gotten out safely. He listened a while longer, then returned to his truck.

He didn't have far to drive to the place where he planned to inquire about boarding horses. He had the radio tuned to a local country-music station and enjoyed the music and his dog's company as he drove out of town. The music was interrupted by a news bulletin about the fire. It was reported that there had been an elderly gentleman inside whom the fire fighters had rescued when he had failed to come out on his own.

More upsetting, the fire had reportedly been started by an arsonist, a man who was seen by a passerby throwing a burning torch into the grass. Apparently, the arsonist was driving an older white truck with Utah plates. A partial plate number was given, and the public was asked to be on the lookout for the truck.

Bentley suddenly realized that the truck fit the description of the one driven by the drunken Silas Villard the evening before. Surely the arsonist wasn't the man he'd arrested for drunk driving. He'd impounded the truck and jailed the driver; however, he knew the man might have been bailed out and retrieved his truck from impound.

Now he really wished he was still home so he could listen to his police radio again. But since he was almost to his destination, he kept going. Unfortunately, when he reached his destination, no one was there. Frustrated and wishing he'd called ahead, Bentley returned home, deciding to try the place again in a few hours. Back at home, he once again listened to the police radio in his patrol car, and while doing so, he checked his notes on the arrest he'd made the night before.

The three letters from the reported license plate matched the plate of the truck he'd stopped. He was almost certain that the arsonist was indeed Silas Villard. The man deserved to sit in jail for a while, but it seemed like there was always someone who would help guys like him bail out. The dispatcher from Central Dispatch in Vernal made a call to all cars to be on the lookout for an older-model white Dodge Ram with oversize tires and a huge steel grill on the front. It was registered to a man by the name of Silas Villard.

"That's him. I knew it!" Bentley exclaimed to Twy when he heard it. "He's a seriously disturbed guy."

Embarrassed by his outburst, he shut his mouth, patted the dog's head, and listened to the dispatcher again as she said, "The house that burned down is owned by Silas's elderly grandfather, Elijah Villard. Consider Silas Villard to be very dangerous."

Considering that the house and the brushy area surrounding it belonged to Silas's grandfather and that Silas had reportedly intentionally started the fire, Bentley wondered if the act was intended to cause the old man harm. It certainly wasn't out of the question. Silas was a very nasty piece of work.

At that moment, Bentley received a call on his cell phone.

"Bentley, this is Sergeant Cannon. If it's at all possible, we'd like you to come back on duty. There's been a fire, and it was apparently started by the man you arrested last night for DUI. The lieutenant and I thought it would be best if you joined the search for him since you are familiar with both him and his truck."

"I'll put my uniform on and be right out," Bentley said, happy to be asked to help. He'd like nothing more than to arrest Silas again after all the threats he'd spewed at him last night. The man should be in jail with bail so high he could never get out. Of course, Bentley knew that would never happen. Lately the laws seemed to favor perpetrators over victims. It was a bad situation caused by politicians who caved to the pressure of do-gooders who either didn't appreciate the harm they were causing or didn't care.

Within five minutes, Trooper Radford was in his patrol car, searching for the arsonist.

CHAPTER THREE

DETECTIVE HANK PARKER LOOKED TOTALLY worn out when he walked into the emergency room. He said hi to Nurse Evie Radford, whose trooper husband had just come on duty to assist in the search for the arsonist who had burned his grandfather's house to the ground. The old man had been badly burned when firemen, risking their lives, pulled him out of the burning house. Hank had been assigned to investigate the case as an attempted murder with the old gentleman's grandson as the suspect.

Evie and Bentley were in the same church congregation as Hank and his family, and they both thought very highly of him. Evie smiled at Hank. "You look like it's been a hard day," she said.

"I'll say it has. I'm guessing yours hasn't been easy either," he replied, returning her smile. "I suppose you saw Mr. Villard when he was brought in a few hours ago."

Her expression clouded over. "I'm afraid so. It's horrible what happened to him," she said. "Are you investigating his—ah—his accident?"

He looked around, and when he didn't see anyone else in the waiting area, he said, "It was not an accident, Evie. His grandson started the brush fire that burned right to his house and caught it on fire."

"Oh no! I didn't know that. Did he do it intentionally? Surely not."

"It's my job to figure that out, Evie, but I think it might be the case. I talked to a witness who claims to have seen him throw a burning torch into the grass next to the road. She was a fair distance away but is sure of what she saw. She even stopped her car and was able to get a partial license number and a description of his truck as he was driving off."

"That's horrible, Hank! I'm glad my husband is on his days off now. He had to arrest a difficult man last night for DUI."

"He's actually been called out to help in the search to find the arsonist," Detective Parker said, "because he knows the guy and his truck. It's apparently the same man Bentley arrested last night for drunk driving."

"That's just awful!" Evie exclaimed. "Bentley said he was a really bad guy." She looked around, concerned, then pointed a thumb behind herself. "I guess I'd better get back there. There's a patient I'm trying to keep an eye on for the doctor."

"It's not Mr. Villard, is it?" Hank asked.

"Didn't you know? He passed away a couple hours ago. The mortuary has already taken his body away."

"That's terrible, Evie." Hank tapped on his leg in agitation. "I was hoping to speak with him, to see if he could tell me if his grandson had a vendetta against him for some reason."

"Thankfully, I can answer that," Evie said. "He was talking to me a little bit when they brought him in. He said that his grandson had called him to bail him from jail early this morning, but he said there was no way he'd do that—the young man was right where he needed to be. He was having a hard time talking, but he said something about his grandson threatening him."

"Oh boy, that tells me this could be a case of murder," Hank said with a groan. "That's all we need."

"I had no idea it was the same guy my husband arrested. I hope you guys catch him soon," she said with a shudder. "I need to go. Sorry to give you the sad news."

"I don't suppose if the old man had lived, burned as seriously as I was told he was, that his quality of life would have been very high," Hank said sadly. "Thanks for the information, Evie. I'll see you at church on Sunday if not before."

***

After making sure her patient was comfortable as they waited for Dr. Steinhart to come in and examine her, Evie stepped out of the room and called her husband. She seldom did that when he was on duty, but with him out looking for a very dangerous man, she felt the need to do so now.

"Hi, sweetheart," he said when he answered her call. "Is something wrong?"

"No, but I'm worried about you. Detective Parker was just in here hoping to interview the man who was burned, but the old gentleman died a couple hours ago," she said. "Hank told me you'd been called out and asked to look for the guy you arrested last night. I can't believe it's the same guy."

"Apparently it is," Bentley said. "There are a lot of us looking for him, but we aren't having any luck. I'd really like to throw him back in jail. But don't worry about me. If I find him, I can handle the guy, and I'll call for backup as well."

They talked for a few more moments after that, then Evie said, "Be careful. I love you, Bentley."

"I will be careful, and I love you too. See you at home later this evening. Don't worry about me if you get home first, although I don't really expect to be on duty too long."

Evie had a bad feeling, and even after talking to her husband and hearing him say he'd be careful, the feeling didn't go away. Just then another patient came in, so she had work to focus on, for which she was glad. It would help to keep her mind off her husband's dangerous job.

***

By the time Bentley got home late that evening, his wife had dinner on the table. "I'm sorry you had to work on your day off," she said. "I'm guessing you guys never found that despicable Villard guy."

"No, but someone will, unless he's left the state, which could be the case," he said. "Of course, since this is now classified as a murder, cops all over the area, including out of state, will be looking for him. I sure hope someone catches him before he hurts someone else."

"I hope so too," she said. "I can't believe he would be so wicked that he would burn his own grandfather to death just because he wouldn't bail him from jail."

"How do you know that, Evie?" Bentley asked with a cocked eyebrow.

"Mr. Villard was able to talk a little bit before he died. He told me that his grandson had threatened him," she replied.

"So you saw Mr. Villard and talked to him," Bentley said with a frown.

"When they brought him in, I was assigned to take his vitals and keep him comfortable." Tears leaked from her pretty blue eyes. "He seemed like a nice guy when he talked to me. Bentley, it was awful. Today was the worst day I've had in the ER."

"I'm sorry you had to go through that. How long did he live after he was brought in?" Bentley asked.

Evie stifled a sob. "Not more than an hour. He died while Dr. Steinhart and I were trying to treat his burns. I'll never forget when he took his last breath. For a minute, Dr. Steinhart and I just stood there by him, and then the doctor said the man would have suffered greatly from the effects from his burns for the rest of his life. I know he was right, but I sure hated to see the old man die."

"I'm so sorry, Evie." Bentley thought for a moment. "I can't believe someone helped Silas get out of jail. If he hadn't been released, his grandad would still be alive. Did he say anything else to you?"

"Yes, but it was a little hard understanding him. He mentioned how much he was hurting, and Dr. Steinhart told him he was giving him something to help with the pain. He also said that he wished his grandson hadn't become a drunk. He used that word, Bentley. He called him a drunk."

"That's exactly what he is. We've got to catch him again, even if it's someone from out of state who finds him. Since his grandad died, there has already been a warrant for murder issued for his arrest. I wish I—"

Evie touched a finger to his lips. "You did your job, Bentley. I'm proud of you for that. And I'm so glad you're here with me for dinner tonight, even though it's late. Let's eat before it gets cold."

As they ate, they avoided the topic of the killer Silas Villard. But they did talk about how exciting it would be to have their own horses.

"I haven't found a place to board them yet," Bentley said. "I'll try again tomorrow."

"There's no hurry," she said. "But it'll be fun when we can go riding together."

"How are your sister and little brother?" Bentley asked at one point during their dinner conversation.

Evie was a twin. Bentley had met her twin sister, Ember Skeed, several times since he and Evie had started dating, and they had spent some enjoyable times together. Like Evie, she was sweet.

Evie's little twelve-year-old brother, Cedrick Skeed, was living with an aunt and uncle. The parents of the three Skeed siblings had both died a couple of years ago in a catastrophic car crash. Neither Ember nor Evie was in a position to care for Cedrick at the time of the crash. Ember was in college hoping to go to law school after she finished her bachelor's degree. Evie was also unable to care for Cedrick. So he had really had no choice but to live with the uncle and aunt whose own children were all grown and living elsewhere. He was not happy there, constantly feeling the ire of his Uncle Claude. Evie kept in close contact with both her siblings, but she was deeply concerned about Cedrick. She and Bentley had spoken a few times about how unhappy Cedrick was and had wondered whether they should take him in, but to this point, all they had done was talk about it.

"I talked to Ember right after I got home, after I called you to tell you I was here. She says law school is hard. She's having second thoughts about being a lawyer. But when I told her about my day, she said, 'Then I sure don't want to be a nurse. Maybe I should stick with law school and become a prosecutor so I can help put people like that scummy man who killed his grandfather in prison.'"

"You know, I can see Ember as a prosecutor. I hope she does that. We cops arrest the crooks, but it takes a good prosecutor to see that they are convicted and a good judge to send them to prison. What about Cedrick? When did you talk to him last?" Bentley asked.

"I also called him tonight while I was waiting for you to get home, but I didn't tell him about the Villards. He's a good kid, but I wish Uncle Claude would treat him better. Cedrick seems quite sad. He says it's getting harder for him with Uncle Claude. I'm worried about him, Bentley. He's a good boy and deserves to be happy."

"We've talked about this before, and I don't know how we would manage it, but maybe we should see if he could come live with us," Bentley suggested after he'd pondered his wife's words for a few moments. "For Cedrick's sake, and considering Claude's problems, we need to seriously decide—sooner rather than later—whether we could make it work."

"Are you serious?" Evie asked. "I'd love that! So would Cedrick."

"Of course I'm serious. Like you said, Cedrick is a good kid. He needs to be where he's loved."

"Aunt Faye loves him, but Uncle Claude . . . doesn't," Evie said. "Cedrick says Claude is mean to Faye too and that it's getting worse."

"I'm not surprised. That's not a good environment for Cedrick."

"We could make it work, but then we'd have to have three horses," Evie said with shining eyes. "I think we should seriously consider it. I could cut my work back to part time, and that would give me more time with Cedrick."

"We can do that. We're in good shape financially," Bentley said. "But I know you love your job, and I hate to see you have to cut back on your hours."

Evie smiled at him. "I love my brother more than my job. And like you say, we're not broke—far from it. We haven't touched the insurance settlements I got from my parents' deaths. We could use that to help care for Cedrick."

"We can do this, Evie," Bentley said with a smile. "I really think we should seriously consider it."

"I agree. Cedrick got the same amount that Ember and I did from the insurance settlements, although I have a feeling Uncle Claude is dipping into Cedrick's money to take care of his own expenses," Evie said. "I just hope he's not taking more than is necessary, but I can see him doing that. He's really a creepy guy, and I don't think he's honest. I feel bad for Aunt Faye. She's such a sweet lady."

Bentley was thoughtful for a moment. "Claude might be glad if we take Cedrick. On the other hand, if he's being greedy with your brother's money, he might not be too happy to let the money go."

"I never thought about that, but if we insist, I don't think there will be much choice for him and Aunt Faye. After all, we are his closest relatives. I'm not so sure about how my aunt would feel about it though. She and Cedrick get along pretty well."

"We'll pray about it, Evie. Something will work out if it's the right thing to do."

***

Evie was scheduled to work another twelve-hour shift the next day, so they went to bed early, but she did not sleep well. She couldn't get her mind off seeing Mr. Villard draw his last breath. And the same sense of concern she'd felt at the end of her shift the day before still disturbed her. She hoped and prayed that her husband would be safe. She was glad he was off duty for another day, and she hoped he wouldn't get called to go to work again. She wanted him to be right about Silas Villard—that he had left the area and wouldn't return unless he was in custody with no chance of getting out of jail again.

Twice during the night, after finally falling asleep, she'd dreamed of the guy, or at least she thought it was him, even though she'd never seen him. What she saw was an evil face with eyes that blazed with fire and a beard that burned, orange and yellow flames surrounding his face. He was looking directly at her, and she could feel heat from the fire in his eyes and beard as it scorched her face.

She woke up in a sweat the first time, thinking it was a reflection of the brush fire that she'd seen in the evil eyes of the character in her dream, and yet the heat had felt real. The second time, she dreamed the angry man was glaring at her again, but this time there was no fire consuming his beard or shooting from his eyes, just anger distorting his features. He said something about her husband and how Trooper Radford would regret arresting him. She woke up, trembling with fear, knowing now that it was Silas she'd been dreaming about. Evie didn't usually have nightmares, so it shook her.

When she got out of bed a couple hours later, Bentley said, "I'll fix breakfast for you this morning. Is French toast okay?"

She smiled at him. "You know how much I like French toast. Of course it is. I'll get showered while you fix it. You are such a good guy, Bentley. I sure am lucky to be married to you."

"I'm the lucky one, Evie." He gave her a kiss, and she smiled and headed for the shower.

She'd considered telling him about her bad dreams but decided not to. It might make him worry, and she didn't want that; he had enough on his mind. Anyway, she was quite sure the dreams were related to the horror she'd felt while treating Mr. Villard's injuries and of watching him die while suffering so much pain, more than she could even imagine. She prayed that she would have a much better day at work today.

As they knelt at the table before breakfast, Bentley asked her to pray. She struggled with her prayer, as worry made her shoulders tense. She asked the Lord to watch over Cedrick and to help Uncle Claude be nicer to him. She also prayed that if it were possible, she and Bentley might find a way to take him into their home. After she'd finished, Bentley tenderly asked, "You're really worried about Cedrick, aren't you?"

She nodded. "I am. I have a feeling that things are really bad for him."

"Even worse than he tells you?"

"I think so," she said.

"Are you okay, Evie? You seem down this morning. Is it because of your worries about Cedrick?"

"Well, yes, but I'm fine. I just hope I don't have a day at work today like I had yesterday." Again she didn't mention her nightmares. She just smiled at him, and they kissed before getting off their knees and sitting at the table.

Evie told Bentley that the French toast was perfect. Then as he stood at the door with her a few minutes later, just before she was to drive to Roosevelt, he said, "I love you, Evie. Drive safe."

"I love you too." She wrapped her arms around him and hugged him. It was a longer-than-usual hug, followed by a passionate kiss. "Are you planning to look for a place to board horses today?"

"I sure am," he promised.

"Look for a place to keep three of them," she said. "My brother loves horses as much as we do. I really think Heavenly Father wants him to be with us." With that, she hurried to her car. She looked back as she started to drive away. Bentley was watching her from the doorway, like he so often did. She waved, and when he waved back, her heart surged with love for him. She made sure he didn't see her wiping tears from her eyes.

CHAPTER FOUR

BENTLEY FOUND A PLACE THAT would board horses for him at a reasonable price. Even though he and Evie hadn't actually made solid plans about trying to get Cedrick to live with them, he spoke to the rancher about three horses, not just two, because he and Evie both wanted her brother to live with them, and he planned to make it happen if he possibly could. He did clarify that he didn't yet have the horses.

He was excited about the place and couldn't wait to tell Evie about the arrangements he'd made when she called him to tell him she was ready to head home at the end of her shift that evening.

Now that he'd secured boarding, he was anxious to see what it would take to find horses at a price they were willing to pay. He sat down at his computer when he arrived home and searched. He found several possibilities but knew that any decision would be his and Evie's together. After all, some of her insurance money might be needed to buy them. He knew she would not object to that. He was excited, thinking about how thrilled she would be.

***

Evie was having a decent day at work. The emergency room had been busy, but it was all fairly minor injuries and illnesses. She could deal with days like this. In fact, she enjoyed them. She could do what she'd been trained to do and not have to see anyone die a painful death. Yesterday had almost been too much. She didn't want a repeat of that, although in reality, she knew that, given the nature of her work in the emergency room, it was bound to happen again. People had died in the emergency room when she'd been on duty before, but it had never been quite like Mr. Villard's death. Maybe it was because he'd spoken to her in such a confiding voice and that she had actually seen him draw his last breath.

Her shift ended at eight, and she pulled out her cell phone as she headed for her little white Saab. She dialed Bentley's number, and when he answered right away, she said, "Hi Bentley. I'm on my way home. It's been a good day today."

"I'm relieved. I'll tell you about my day when you get home," he said.

"Tell me now," she begged.

"You need to drive, and I don't want to distract you."

"I'm not driving yet. I'm sitting in my car in the parking lot. So tell me what kind of day you had. Specifically, tell me if you found a place to board horses."

"Yes, I did," he said, "but I'll tell you more when you get home. Drive safe. I can't wait to see you. Hugs for you."

"Hugs right back," she replied with a smile. "I'll start driving now."

***

Silas had spent two hours trying to find where Trooper Radford lived. He thought he was from Duchesne, and he'd finally been able to confirm that on social media. But he hadn't found an address, so he'd driven all over Duchesne, not once thinking that he could be arrested again for DUI. After all, he didn't consider himself drunk. He didn't think he'd been drunk two evenings ago either. He'd been falsely harassed and arrested, and the trooper would pay.

After asking a few casual questions at the local grocery store, he finally figured out which house was Radford's. After he'd driven past it several times, a plan began to form in his mind. In his mind he could see it burning. He couldn't wait.

***

Evie's sister, Ember, called just as she pulled onto Highway 40, so she put her phone on speaker, sat it beside her, and the two of them visited. She told Ember about Bentley finding a place to board horses. "I am so excited about getting horses. You and I always loved to ride."

"You're lucky you found a guy who liked horses as much as you do," Ember replied. "You got a good man when you got Bentley."

"I sure did," Evie replied. Ember was a wonderful, attractive woman, and she'd find someone. Evie honestly hoped that when she did, he would be as good a guy as Bentley.

Ember spoke again, and when she did, Evie detected a note of anxiety in her sister's voice. "What I really called about was our little brother."

"What's the matter?" Evie asked. "Did he get hurt?"

"It's Uncle Claude. He's upset Cedrick again, worse than ever before, and Cedrick called me a few minutes ago. He was crying. He said that when he got home from school he could hear Aunt Faye and Uncle Claude arguing in the kitchen. When he heard Uncle Claude mention his name, he stopped and stood out of sight and listened."

"Were they arguing about him?" Evie asked as she put her blinker on and began to pass a slow-moving truck. "Did Uncle Claude say something that made Cedrick feel unwelcome there?"

"I'll say he did. Uncle Claude said something about having raised his sons, and really didn't like being tied down with someone else's kid."

"That's just dreadful," Evie said as she pulled back into her lane after completing the pass. "Bentley and I were talking about Cedrick last night. Bentley suggested that maybe we should consider letting him live with us."

"Bentley said that?" Ember exclaimed. "But could you guys manage it with your jobs and all? I know I can't take him, but I would if I could. It breaks my heart that Uncle Claude doesn't like him. I think Aunt Faye loves him. Cedrick said that he heard her say so to Claude, but that Claude said something about she could love him just as much if he lived somewhere other than with them. He wants the boy gone. And get this, Evie: He even said that Cedrick's insurance money wouldn't last forever and that he was not willing to spend a dime of his own money on him. Evie, I think Uncle Claude is using Cedrick's money for more than it costs to take care of him. That's a lot of money to be gone so soon. In fact, for just Cedrick's upkeep, that money should last ten to twenty years!"

"You're probably right. Uncle Claude is greedy, and I don't think he's honest. I've never felt comfortable around him. Bentley and I will talk about it some more tonight. I don't know what we'll do, but we have some ideas. We'll figure something out."

"Oh, Evie, I was praying that you'd say something like that. It would break my heart if he had to go into foster care, and that's what would happen. Not that that's necessarily a bad thing, but he needs to be with family if possible. I know none of Uncle Claude's and Aunt Faye's kids would be willing to take him, even if they got his money in the deal."

"Thanks for calling me about this, Ember."

"You were the first person I thought of when Cedrick called me. I think Cedrick's going to call you too, and if he does, you can tell him that I told you what happened and that both of us are concerned," she said. "Oh, guess what. I have a date with a really cool guy."

Evie thought of her little brother. She and Ember had been devastated at the loss of their parents, but they were grown, had already left home, and were able to care for themselves. Cedrick had been only ten at the time and needed their parents badly. Aunt Faye had immediately offered to give him a home, and the sisters had been grateful, because they weren't in a position to care for him. Yet they had both known from the first that Claude had not been happy with the situation, and he had never been kind to the sweet boy, despite the fact that he was able to tap into the insurance money to cover Cedrick's expenses.

Both twins talked to Cedrick on the phone several times a week and visited him when they could. They were both single girls in college at the time of their parents' deaths, and because they had roommates, they didn't even have a place where Cedric could stay with them for overnight visits.

Evie was determined to do whatever was necessary to allow Cedrick to live with them. Cedrick needed her. Not only that, but Cedrick also needed a good man like Bentley in his life.

CHAPTER FIVE

Evie slowed to fifty miles per hour when she entered the outskirts of Myton. She was aware of her surroundings, driving carefully like she always did.

A white pickup approached the intersection of Highway 40 and Myton's Main Street. It appeared to be slowing for the stop sign there, so she continued on, but suddenly it sped up, blowing through the stop sign.

Evie tried to swerve, but it was too little too late. The pickup rammed into the side of her driver's door. Her car was plowed off the road.

Evie felt a fraction of a second of panic, then pain, and then she seemed to be floating. Looking down, she could see her crumpled car with her body inside.

She looked up and saw her mother and father. They were beckoning to her.

***

Silas Villard's old Dodge Ram had a solid steel grill with a winch on the front of his truck. It rode high above the ground because of his large tires. His drunken brain told him that he'd hit someone's car. He looked around as dust settled from the collision. He sat there, dazed for a moment. Then he examined himself. His chest hurt from when he'd slammed onto the steering wheel, but he didn't think he was injured badly. He opened the door and stepped out onto the running boards and then to the ground, leaving his truck engine running. He walked around to the front of his truck.

He examined it, looked at the other car, and cursed the blonde lady he saw slumped against the far door of her car. His huge steel bumper had struck the small car high on the driver's side. There was very little damage to his truck, but the car was a crushed mess.

"You stupid woman!" he shouted. "You ran right in front of me. You got what you deserved."

Silas climbed back into his truck, shifted into reverse, and stomped on the accelerator. It shot backward, dragging the white car with it for a few yards, but then his grill came free of the car. He turned and sped back into the little town, driving rapidly from the scene, still cursing the blond lady for causing the accident. He found it a little hard to drive with the bumper touching the front tires, but he managed.

Not once did he feel any concern for the young woman in the car. He blamed the crash on her, and yet, he instinctively knew he had to get away because the cops would blame him. And there was no way he was going to jail again.

He knew the back roads of the area very well, and he drove one mile after another as he fled from the scene of the accident.

It was getting harder and harder to drive, and suddenly one of his front tires blew, and he continued for a few yards on the steel rim, scattering sparks into the dry grass along the road. He tried to keep the truck driving straight, but it was pulling hard to the left, and it finally veered off the road into some grass and brush. After it came to a stop, he jumped out. The front left tire was burning. He ran around to the other side and opened the door. He grabbed his rifle and headed away from the truck, once again cursing the blonde woman who had caused him to wreck. Silas had walked for about a hundred yards before he heard loud crackling noises behind him. He looked back and paused when he saw flames shooting up along the side of the road and around his truck.

A fire! He watched in fascination as it grew larger, and soon it was a raging wildfire. The flames engulfed his truck, and a moment later there was a loud explosion. His truck blew apart as the gas tank exploded, followed by a secondary explosion that he assumed must have been from the can of gasoline he had in the back, the one he'd planned to use to set Trooper Radford's home ablaze that night. Revenge would have to wait. He needed to get away before fire trucks and cops showed up, even though he didn't expect that to happen anytime soon as he was far out into the wild countryside.

Silas would have loved to watch the fire burn a lot longer, but through the drunken fog of his mind, he decided he had to save himself, because the cops would blame him even though he hadn't done anything wrong.

The blond lady in the white car was to blame for his troubles. It was her fault. She'd driven right in front of him, not even giving him time to hit his brakes or swerve. For now though, self-preservation was his primary objective. He ran toward the juniper trees a few hundred yards away. Once there, he felt safe, so he stopped and watched, enthralled, as the fire spread rapidly through the dry brush and weeds and then into the trees. Even though he was now a half-mile or so away, the burning fire was still fascinating to watch. He felt safe. No one could find him or bother him.

***

Bentley had decided to work in the backyard of their rental house while he waited for Evie to come home late that evening. He started the lawn mower and began to cut the grass around the edge of the fence. It was a beautiful late summer day. He loved being outside working on days like this.

Over the noise of the mower's engine, he thought he could hear sirens coming from Main Street. He was curious but also glad to be off duty this evening. Others could deal with whatever was happening. He looked forward to a relaxing evening with his sweet wife.

He got so busy with the lawn that he never thought about the time, but when he shut the mower down to empty the bag of clippings, he glanced at his watch. It was getting dark. Evie should be here anytime now. In fact, she should have already been home. Assuming she must have stopped at the store to buy a few groceries as she often did, he emptied the grass in the back of the yard at the compost pile he was making and then put the mower away before beginning to pull weeds growing next to the fence.

The time flew as he worked. He checked his watch. Evie should have been home long before now. Even if she stopped at Al's Foodtown for groceries, she wouldn't be this late. He felt a pang of worry in his gut.

He pulled a few more weeds, glancing up every few seconds to see if Evie was pulling into the driveway. It was getting dark. He finally stopped and went into the house, and with slightly shaking hands, he pulled out his phone and called her. It rang and rang but finally went to voice mail. He looked at his phone as his worry increased. She'd never been this late coming home from work before. Where could she possibly be?

He considered going to his patrol car and driving toward Roosevelt to see if her car had broken down along the way. But she would have called him if that had happened. Maybe her phone had died, and she couldn't call . . . He walked to his patrol car, got in, and turned the engine on. He sat there undecided as to what he should do as he listened to the police radio.

After listening for two or three minutes, he learned another wildfire had caught in a remote southern part of the county. Many firefighters were heading out there; it must be a big one. Apparently it was several miles from Myton. Two major fires in two days seemed a bit much, even for this busy fire season. He just hoped no one got hurt in this one. At least Evie wouldn't have to deal with it, since she was off shift.

But where was she? He again considered driving toward Roosevelt, but as he prepared to back out of his driveway, a patrol car just like his and another vehicle, one he recognized as his bishop's pickup, stopped on the street in front of his house. His sergeant stepped out of the patrol car. Bentley shut off his car and got out as he felt his heart sink with despair. This could only mean one thing, and that one thing was inconceivably dreadful.

The two men walked together toward him. The grim look on both their faces told him they had terrible news for him. Evie! Surely it wasn't about her, the love of his life.

Bishop Green reached him first, followed by Sergeant Carter. Before either of these men could speak, Bentley asked in a strained voice, "Is Evie okay?"

It was Bishop Green who delivered the worst news Bentley had ever received. "I'm so sorry, Bentley." Tears filled the good bishop's eyes, and his voice quavered as he uttered the terrible news.

Bishop Green was a tall, gentle man of about fifty, and as Bentley felt his knees go weak, the bishop wrapped his arms around him in a giant hug and kept him from falling. Both men cried together.

Sergeant Carter, a man he respected a great deal, stepped close and put a hand on Bentley's shoulder. "She didn't suffer, Bentley. She was killed instantly."

Bentley pulled back as he felt strength return to his legs. "What . . . what happened?" he stammered through his tears.

"Evie was just passing the main intersection in Myton when a pickup truck blew the stop sign and drove into her, shoving her car clear off the road. Two men who were gassing up at the Ute Petroleum service station saw it happen. They both ran across the road to see if they could help, but she was gone when they got there."

"What about the driver of the truck?" he asked.

Sergeant Carter shook his head. "The witnesses told us that as they were running toward Evie's car, the driver got out of his truck, a large white one with huge tires and a large steel bumper. He looked into Evie's car, and then he went back to his truck, got in, and backed away as they were shouting for him to stop. His bumper was hooked to Evie's car, and when his oversized bumper came free of her car, he sped away, nearly striking one of the men."

Bentley was stunned, but he did manage to ask, "Did they get a license number?"

"No, they didn't even get a good look at the driver because it all happened so fast," Sergeant Carter said. "The truck's description was broadcast. He'll be found."

Bishop Green spoke up then. "Bentley, let's go inside and sit down. We'll talk more in there."

He turned and led the way into the small, white frame house he and Evie were renting. Once the men were seated in his living room, Sergeant Carter said, "The truck that we believe was involved started a fire several miles out in the desert south of Myton. It blew up and burned. The driver hasn't been seen. He wasn't in the truck when it burned, but apparently there was damage to the front end that indicated it had been in a wreck before it burned. I was told that the bumper looked like it had been shoved back and could have rubbed the tires, but no one could be sure because the tires were gone, and the truck was largely blown apart."

Bentley dropped his head into his hands, sobbing. He heard little of what was said about the truck. All he could think of was Evie. She was gone. What would he ever do without her? No one spoke while he regained control of his emotions. Finally, he sat up straight. "Did you say it was a large truck with a steel bumper and winch?"

"I haven't seen the truck," Sergeant Carter said. "I was still at the accident scene in Myton when the truck was found by some of the firemen who'd gone out to fight the fire. But like I said, it does fit the description you just gave. I'll find out more, though. Detective Parker is out there. Should I call him and see what he knows about it?"

"Please do. I was wondering if the truck was the same one Silas Villard was driving when I arrested him for DUI. I know it's a stretch to think that. I'm probably wrong, but I . . ." He stopped.

"I know," Sergeant Carter said. "You could also be right, although I doubt it. I'll call Detective Parker right now."

CHAPTER SIX

Sergeant Carter stepped into the hallway while he spoke with Detective Parker on the phone.

Bishop Green asked, "Bentley, is there anyone I can call or anything I can do for you?"

"I don't think so, but thank you. I need to call Evie's twin sister, Ember, and her Aunt Faye. Evie's little brother, Cedrick, lives with her and their Uncle Claude. I don't know how I'll ever be able to do that as upset as I am. Maybe if I wait for a little while I can do it," Bentley said. "They are going to be devastated . . . all but Claude. Evie lost her parents nearly three years ago in—if you can believe this—a car wreck caused by a drunk driver. It's been a hard time for her and her siblings."

"I'm so sorry, Bentley. Are there others in either of your families that need to be notified?" Bishop Green asked.

"I was an only child, and my parents have both passed. They were quite elderly, and they didn't even have me until they were both in their late forties. Uncle Claude is the only one of my wife's family still living. He is Evie's father's older brother. My father's family will need to know, but they live back East. I haven't heard from any of them since my mother died about three years ago. Dad was a convert to the Church, and his family didn't take it well. So we've never been close to them," Bentley explained. "A few of them did come to my parents' funeral, but they left as soon as the service was over. They didn't even stay for the meal at the church. They left right from the cemetery."

"Oh, Bentley, I'm so sorry. Now, why don't we start with your wife's uncle and aunt and also your sister-in-law? Maybe, if you would like, I'll see if I can find out who their bishops are and ask them to go in person and tell them," the bishop suggested. "Do you have any idea what wards they're in?"

"Evie knows." Bentley stopped cold. "She knew." Reality was slow to sink in. It didn't seem like she could really be gone. Oh, how he hurt—oh, how he missed her. And he instinctively knew that the pain would be even worse later. He didn't know how he could ever handle it.

"I know this is hard for you, Bentley, but do you know their addresses?" Bishop Green asked, his voice filled with sympathy. "If you do, I can figure it out from there."

"Actually, I do. I have them in my phone." Bentley pulled it out, and by the time Sergeant Carter rejoined them, Bentley had texted the addresses and phone numbers to his bishop.

"I just spoke with Detective Hank Parker," Sergeant Carter said. "Incredibly, your guess was right. The truck that blew up and burned belongs to Silas Villard. Hank confirmed that the damage to the large front bumper and the winch has trace evidence that it is the truck that hit your wife's car. He was able to discern that, despite the additional damage it sustained when it blew up and burned. They don't have any idea where Silas went. He wasn't in the truck, so he got out of it before it blew up. I'm sorry, Bentley."

"I'd like to find him myself," Bentley said as a surge of anger raged through him. "First he burns and kills his grandfather, and then he . . . he . . ." He couldn't go on.

"I know, and he's started two serious wildfires. They still haven't controlled the latest one. Hank said it's burned several hundred acres already and is spreading rapidly," Sergeant Carter told him. "We'll find him. He's out there somewhere, and this time, no one will be able to bail him out of jail."

"I hope that's the case, but who knows what amount of bail the judge will set," Bentley said with a twinge of bitterness.

"Or the guy might just run and keep running. We may never see him again," Sergeant Carter said just as Bentley's phone began to ring.

He looked at the screen after pulling it from his pocket. He recognized the number. "It's my young brother-in-law. I can't tell him about Evie. I can't take this call right now."

"I'll take care of that," Bishop Green said. "I'll let you know after I've done so." Bentley let the phone ring until it finally quit.

As the bishop left, Sergeant Carter turned to follow him. "I'll get back with you," he said to Bentley. "Don't worry about work. I'll see that you have time off to deal with everything."

Bentley thanked him and walked the two men to the door. Then he went back to his chair and sat down. Bentley's phone rang again a few minutes later as he was sitting with his head in his hands, sobbing. He took a couple of deep breaths when he saw that it was Cedrick again. Reluctantly, he finally answered the phone. "Hi, Cedrick," he said, trying to sound normal, despite feeling an overwhelming weight in his chest.

"Hi, Bentley," Cedrick said. "How come Evie isn't answering her phone?"

"It's ah . . . it's broken," "Bentley said even as he realized that was certainly the truth. But it wasn't as broken as he was. He was worse than broken; he was crushed. His spirit was pulverized.

"Is she there? Maybe I can talk to her on your phone," Cedrick said. "I really need to talk to her."

Bentley choked back a sob before saying, "She's not here, but you can tell me what you want her to know."

"Okay, but will you tell her when she gets home?" Cedrick asked.

"Mmm," Bentley said, feeling helpless.

Cedrick seemed not to notice and said, "Well, Bentley, I need to tell her that I'm not wanted here anymore, and I don't know what to do. Uncle Claude told Aunt Faye that he'd raised his kids and didn't want to raise me too. It makes me so sad. I think he's spent most of my money from insurance, and that's the only reason he hasn't already kicked me out. It made Aunt Faye mad, but Uncle Claude doesn't care what she thinks. He is awful to her. He calls her terrible names and swears at her a lot. I think he even hits her sometimes. It makes her cry."

"How do you know he told Aunt Faye that?" Bentley asked, even though he knew that Claude didn't like having him there. He and Evie had discussed that just the previous evening.

"I heard him say it to Aunt Faye, but they don't know I did. They didn't see me around the corner in the hallway. Bentley, I don't know what I'm going to do. I feel like I should just run away."

"Don't do that!" Bentley said urgently. "Hang in there, and I'll see if I can figure something out for you."

"I can't stay here much longer. Uncle Claude glares at me whenever he sees me. I'm afraid he's going to hurt me. He looks like he wants to the way he clenches his fists whenever he talks to me."

"Have you called Ember and talked to her about it?" Bentley asked.

"Yeah, and she said she'd call Evie. I hope she has. Do you know if Evie knows yet?" Cedrick asked.

"I don't know," he said. Bentley thought about asking to talk to Aunt Faye, but there was no way he could do that until the bishop had been able to find someone who would notify her about Evie. It was all so ghastly. He spoke with Cedrick a little longer, trying to assure him that something would be worked out, although at this point, he had no idea what that would be. He and Evie had wanted to find a way to take him in, but now she was gone. He had to end the call. It was all he could do to keep from breaking down while talking to Cedrick. As soon as the call was over, he once again dropped his head into his hands and sobbed.

***

Silas was sobering up as he watched the fire from close to a mile away. It was still raging gloriously and growing by the minute, but the firefighters were doing everything they could to stop it. He hated them for fighting the beautiful blaze. Next to police officers, he hated firefighters the worst. They always spoiled his fun by doing everything they could to put out his fires. Yet ironically, he frequently fought right alongside them so he could be close to the magnificent flames.

He thought about the house he'd planned to burn that night. Thanks to the blonde girl who made him wreck his truck, his plans had been ruined. But he told himself that he would still burn down the trooper's house. He would just have to wait a few weeks, in case the cops were looking for him—for something that wasn't his fault. He also needed another truck to drive. His grandad had one, but it was parked by his house and may have burned. So even if he could get back there without being seen, it probably wasn't drivable. Again, he cursed the careless driver who had caused him so much trouble. He was pretty sure she was dead, and he took satisfaction in knowing that she'd gotten the punishment she deserved.

Eventually there weren't any flames close enough for him to watch, because it had burned far into the distance. So he turned his attention to the dilemma he was in. His truck and everything in it was destroyed. He was left with the clothes he wore and his rifle, which had a full clip of bullets, but nothing more. Of course, there were clothes and other supplies in his house, but he was afraid the cops would be waiting for him there. He was hungry and very thirsty. He needed to get to another road and see if he could find a ride.

He was terribly fatigued, but he pushed his way onward, walking slowly but steadily. Two hours later, he found a road, one he recognized and that he knew would have occasional traffic on it. He plopped down in the shade of a juniper tree near the road, so tired he didn't think there was any way he could go farther and wishing he had a bottle of whiskey. He sat there waiting for someone to come along. This was oil-well country, and he was certain that a worker would come along at some point. He hoped it was soon.

His head kept bobbing, and eventually, he fell asleep. He awoke with a start when someone shook his shoulders and said, "Hey, mister. Are you okay? You don't look so good."

He looked up with bleary eyes at a man in greasy blue jeans, a soiled tan work shirt, and a blue baseball cap. For a minute, Silas didn't know how to respond, because his brain needed time to fully wake up. It was dark out now with only a little bit of light from the moon. He would not begin to function for a minute or so, but when he did, that would be enough light to do what he had to do. He couldn't let this opportunity get away. He didn't respond as he tried to figure things out.

"Here, let me help you to my truck. You could die out here if you don't get some water. I have some in a cooler that I'll share with you," the man said. "My name is Leon Hawkins. I'm finished with the wells I take care of, and I can give you a ride to Myton or Roosevelt, or wherever you need to go."

Silas's brain was waking up. The guy had water. He had a truck. There was probably food in there as well. Maybe the guy even had a six-pack of beer or a fifth of whiskey. He began to scheme. The beginnings of a plan formed in his mind, and he finally said, "Can I have some water first, and then maybe I can make it to your truck?"

"Sure, I'll grab a bottle for you." The oil-field worker turned toward his truck, which was parked on the far side of the road.

Now was his chance. Silas picked up his rifle from beside him. "Hey, Leon," he called as he pointed the rifle at the man's back. The light from the moon and headlights of the truck was enough that he wouldn't miss at such a close range if he had to shoot the guy.

Leon turned. "What's with the rifle?" he asked, sounding angry.

"I need your truck. Start walking or I'll plug you," Silas threatened.

"Hey, I'm trying to help you," Leon said, fear in his voice as well as anger. That's exactly what Silas wanted. "I'll give you a ride. You don't have to threaten me. I'll let you off wherever you want, and I won't tell anyone."

"No, what you'll do is give me your truck," Silas said. He held the rifle in unsteady hands, pointed in the direction of the oil-field worker.

Leon's face drained of color. "It's not my truck. It belongs to my employer," Leon said as he looked around as if searching for someone to help him. There was no one, and Silas began to grin.

"Start walking that way!" Silas shouted hoarsely. He nodded to the trees and brush at the far side of the road. "If you don't, I'll shoot you right where you stand. Walk and don't come back to the road or you are a dead man."

"Let me get a bottle of water first," Leon said with a shaky voice, "and then I'll walk away."

"No, you won't. The water is mine now. You don't get none. Just go. Away from the road! Now!" Silas screamed, his voice hoarse but loud.

Leon did as he was told. Silas fired the rifle right behind Leon, throwing gravel at his legs. The frightened man took off running, his shadow from the headlights bouncing on the brush and trees.

Silas laughed and waited until the man was a fair distance away. The truck's lights went off, and the engine died. The man was swallowed up in the semi-dark night before Silas headed across the road to the truck. Just knowing he had something to drive and water to drink gave him unexpected energy. He reached the truck and opened the back door, because that was where he expected the water would be.

Sure enough, there was a cooler on the floor. He opened it, and then he laughed. There was not only water; there were also two cans of beer. Forgetting the water, he grabbed a beer, popped the top, and drank every last drop. Only then did he drink a bottle of water.

He needed to get going. He climbed into the driver's seat. At any time, another truck could come by, and he didn't want to have to explain who he was or what he was doing with this truck. As he looked around the cab, he saw a cell phone on the console. He grabbed it, thinking that was why the guy had offered to get him a bottle of water before leaving. He'd wanted his cell phone so he could call the cops. Well, too bad. Silas stepped back out of the truck and tossed the phone as far as he could. It wouldn't do him any good because he couldn't unlock it anyway.

Then he got back into the truck and looked for the ignition key. He cursed loudly. There wasn't one. This truck needed a key fob in order to start it. No wonder the truck had stopped. Leon had got away with the key fob. He should have shot that guy. In Silas's twisted mind, Leon had stolen the key fob. This truck belonged to him once he sent Leon running into the night like a scared rabbit.

CHAPTER SEVEN

SILAS CURSED AND POUNDED HIS fists on the steering wheel. He couldn't believe his luck today. It was nothing short of rotten. First that stupid girl drove right in front of him and caused a wreck, then his truck blew up, and now this!

It took Silas a few minutes to regain control of his anger and sort out his sluggish thoughts. Finally, he remembered that he knew a lot of things about vehicles, and one of those things was how to hot-wire a car to start it. He started to laugh again. Then he opened the door, thinking that he needed to be able to reach under the dash. This was a late-model truck, so it might not be as easy as cars he'd hot-wired in the past.

Before kneeling down, he looked up and then down the road for lights. Then he reached under the dash. That was as far as he got when a shot rang out and gravel peppered his pants and boots. He yelped and leaped into the truck, grabbing his rifle and scooting out the far door. Leon must have found help despite being ordered to stay away from the road. He'd pay for that!

Silas peeked over the top of the truck, and a bullet flew overhead. He heard Leon's voice. "We don't want to kill you, mister, but we will if we have to. My friend here has a gun, so you better run or come out from beside my truck with your hands empty and in the air. Leave your rifle. If you don't, it will only get worse for you."

Silas dropped to the ground and tried to think. Finally, he crawled into the brush, away from the truck, and then waited, watching to see if Leon and whoever was helping him would shoot again. Leon shouted, "If you aren't man enough to give up, then get up and run, like you made me do. Go, now!"

Silas fired a shot past the truck in the direction of Leon's voice before fleeing. He didn't go far though. The beer he'd drunk gave him courage, and it made him determined to fight back. He hid himself and peered through the brush as Leon and another man stepped out of the trees on the far side of the road opposite the truck. He could see them fairly clearly in the faint moonlight. Two men meant there was another truck somewhere up the road. That's why he hadn't seen any lights. They'd hid it and walked to where he was.

He knew what he had to do. He grinned and then fired a shot at the truck, aiming for the fuel tank. Even though there was only a little bit of light to guide his aim, his shot hit where he intended, and the truck exploded. It blew the oil-field workers to the ground in the middle of the road. Then he fired at them and heard a thump. He'd hit one of the men. He fired again, and he heard a scream. He'd hit both of them. It was time to find the other truck. It had to be close.

He had gone only a few steps when he remembered the key fob problem. He had to get one from the second man. He assumed it would be in a pocket of his work pants. He slowly approached them, veering around the burning truck. Both men were alive but bleeding. They had burned clothing, faces, and arms. They were moaning in pain. He ignored Leon and searched the second man's pockets. He found a key fob. He put it in his pocket, then stole the guy's cell phone.

The guy might have already called the cops. He dropped the phone on the ground and stomped on it, wishing he'd stomped on Leon's instead of tossing it away. It was too late now to worry about that. The pistol they had been shooting at him with was on the road several feet from the men. He grabbed if off the ground and shoved it inside his belt, behind his back. He paused to look at the two men. No need to waste another bullet; surely they would die before help arrived. So he walked up the road, lamenting the destroyed beer, sandwiches, and bottles of water that had been in the burning truck.

Silas glanced back occasionally to enjoy watching the fire burn before he crested the rise that now hid the burning truck. Around a sharp bend sat the other man's truck. Once inside of it, he grabbed a half-eaten sandwich and a bottle of water and finished them both before starting the truck. With the key fob in his pocket, it was no trouble. He was good to go, but he needed to drive the opposite direction from where he'd left the two bleeding, burned men. He turned the truck and drove north into the night.

***

Leon Hawkins pushed himself to a sitting position, fighting pain, weakness, and extreme nausea. He knew he'd been burned, but he had no idea how badly. It was certainly enough to cause extreme pain. His friend and coworker

Ellis Sharp was breathing but appeared to be in too much pain to move. Leon could see from the light of the burning truck that Ellis's face and arms were burned, and his shirt and pants were scorched but not on fire. Leon assumed that he must look the same.

"Hey, Ellis. We need to stop the bleeding. Can you hear me?"

He waited and was encouraged when Ellis moved his hands and arms ever so slightly. "Yeah, I hear you," he said in a croak after a half minute or so had passed. "Are you sitting up, Leon?"

"I am. I'm holding my hand on the bullet hole in my shoulder. Let me see if I can help you. Where are you shot?" Leon asked.

"My left thigh," Ellis responded through his pain. "If he didn't hit an artery, I should be okay. It just hurts an awful lot . . . I think we both got burned."

"Yeah, we did, but we gotta take care of ourselves until help arrives. You did get ahold of the cops when we left your truck, didn't you?"

"I did, but the connection was scratchy. I don't know if the dispatcher understood where we are. I think she understood that a guy shot at you and chased you off with his rifle."

The two men were silent for a moment as Leon scooted to where he could get a look at Ellis's leg. "The bullet didn't hit an artery. Let's see if we can help each other put some kind of bandage on our bullet wounds. There's nothing we can do about our burns. Can you sit up yet?"

"I think so," Ellis said and began making an effort to do so. "My phone is gone. That guy must have taken it." He struggled, and after a minute or two, Ellis was sitting upright next to Leon, his injured leg stretched out in front of him. For the next ten minutes, the two men ripped their scorched shirts and applied makeshift bandages to each other's bloody wounds as best they could. They managed to move themselves to the side of the road nearest the smoldering truck.

Leon finally spoke. "My wife will wonder where I'm at if I'm not home in an hour or two."

"Mine won't expect me for three or four hours. Will your wife call someone?" Ellis asked.

"I think she will. She'll try to call me first, and when she can't reach me, she'll probably call my boss," Leon said. "But maybe the cops will find us first. At least I hope so. I wonder where that guy is now."

"He could be anywhere. He took the key fob for my truck out of my pocket before he left. And that must have been when he took my cell phone," Ellis responded.

"The fool didn't get my key fob. I used it to turn off the truck so he couldn't see to shoot me as I was getting away."

Ellis moaned in pain. "Do you think the bullet broke the bones in my leg?"

"It felt like it when I was wrapping it. I'm pretty sure my shoulder is damaged badly too. It's getting cold. We need to get closer to the truck. At least there's heat coming from it."

They moved until they felt the warmth from the hot metal of the burned truck, then Ellis asked, "Did he get your phone too?"

"If he didn't take it, then it's destroyed." Leon shook his head. "It was in the truck."

"I guess we can hope the dispatcher understood what I was saying. I would have used the radio on my truck, but for some reason, it's on the blink. I couldn't even call my boss. We gotta hope for the best."

The men waited, both experiencing worsening pain as the minutes passed.

"There are so many roads out here that the cops could easily take the wrong one," Ellis said. He was quiet for a moment, then he said in a low moan, "I think I'm gonna pass out."

Ellis slumped over. Leon felt a jolt of serious concern. He touched Ellis with his damaged hands, and it appeared he had indeed passed out. Leon leaned down. Ellis was unconscious, but at least he was still breathing. Help needed to come soon, or they would both die. He felt what little strength he had left fading away, and he eventually slumped over next to Ellis, willing himself not to lose consciousness.

Somewhere a coyote called, and another returned the call. Fear stabbed into Leon. If the coyotes were near enough, they could smell them, and they might finish what that maniac had started. He continued to listen to their calls, but they did not seem to be coming any closer.

"Ellis, can you hear me?" he asked a few torturous minutes later.

He was surprised when Ellis answered. "Yeah, I must have passed out for a bit. Do you think those coyotes will get us?"

"I hope not. I wonder if my wife has called my boss yet. I wonder where the cops are."

"Will your boss come looking for you?"

"Oh yes, for sure. I hope he gets here soon. We're in pretty bad shape, Ellis."

"We are, and listen, the coyotes sound closer now," Ellis said. "We may be doomed."

"Hang in there, old buddy. We gotta have faith. We ain't dead yet, and that's something. Somebody will come soon."

CHAPTER EIGHT

EVEN THOUGH IT WAS GETTING very late, Bentley was sitting in his house surrounded by neighbors, the Relief Society president, his ministering brethren, and the bishop and his wife.

"I talked to both bishops again a couple minutes ago," Bishop Green said. "No one is home at Claude's house or at Ember's apartment. The bishops left notes on the door to call them when they got in. Their notes didn't give any hint regarding what they wanted to speak with them about."

"Claude and Faye have a landline," Bentley said. "Did you call it?"

"Yes, but no one is answering it or the cell phones for Claude, Faye, or Ember. They haven't tried Cedrick's cell phone because they didn't want to alarm him. I'm sorry, but all we can do is wait to hear back from the bishops involved. Bentley, the sisters have some food in the kitchen. Why don't you try to eat something?"

"I'll try, but I don't think I can eat much," he said.

He was right about that. He barely managed to eat a dozen small bites before he put his fork down and tried to swallow some milk. When Bishop Green's phone rang, he bounced up from the table and rushed into the living room.

"Yes, that's right. Does the boy know too?" Bishop Green asked his caller. The bishop listened for a moment, and then he said, "I'll let Bentley know."

"Know what?" Bentley asked, his voice breaking.

"The Skeeds are home, and they have been told," the bishop informed him. "But apparently your young brother-in-law is with Ember. He went to a late movie with her, and Faye Skeed told her bishop that when Ember's at the theater, she always turns her phone off."

"What movie did they go to?" Bentley asked.

"They don't know, but the two bishops and their counselors are going to go to every movie theater in the Salt Lake Valley that is playing suitable movies this late at night for boys his age and look for Ember's car. For now, that's all that can be done."

Bentley took a deep breath and said, "Thank you, Bishop. That's a lot." Then he sat in his recliner and dropped his head into his hands. Both Bishop and Sister Green knelt beside the chair, saying nothing—just being there for him. Bentley's phone rang, and he answered it.

"Bentley, this is Aunt Faye. We are devastated! This is the most horrible thing I've ever heard," she said. "We are so sorry."

"Thank you," he managed to say. "What time do you think Ember will bring Cedrick back?"

"She helped him pack a small bag and told me that she'd keep him at her apartment overnight," Faye said. "She doesn't have any classes tomorrow, so she'll see that he makes it to school, and she'll pick him up from school too."

"Is Cedrick okay?" Bentley asked.

There was a long pause on the line before Faye finally spoke. "You know how Claude is. He's been especially rough on Cedrick the last few days. I don't know what to do about the situation."

"When I hear from Ember, she and I will figure something out. Does he have his phone with him?" he asked.

"Yes, but he turned it off when they were leaving. Ember said she was turning hers off as well. She explained to me that she wanted to have a good time with Cedrick and didn't want phones interrupting. I'm sure you understand."

"I do. Thanks for the call," he said and pushed End. He was shaking with anger, not at Faye, but at Claude. He'd apologize to Faye later. Right now all he cared about was the need for Ember and Cedrick to know the terrible thing that had happened to someone all three of them loved dearly.

***

Nels Nielsen's cell phone rang around eleven. He was surprised when he answered to hear the caller say, "Mr. Nielsen, this is Fiona Hawkins, Leon's wife. He should have been home quite a while ago. I've been calling and texting for over an hour now with no response. Have you heard from him?"

"I haven't, but I'm sure he's fine. Something must have come up at one of the wells. You know that happens sometimes," Nels said.

"I know, but he always either calls or texts me when he's going to be late," she said. "The kids and I are worried that he's been in an accident." Her voice was strained, and Nels knew he needed to do something more than tell her Leon was okay, because he didn't know if that was the case.

"I'll call him on our company radio. I'll get right back with you," he said. When he went to his truck and tried to reach Leon, there was no response. Now he was worried. He was about to call Fiona back but decided to check with Central Dispatch in Vernal to see if there had been any traffic or industrial accidents reported.

"Central Dispatch, this is Kora speaking. How may I help you?" the professional-sounding woman responded.

Nels identified himself and said, "One of my employees, Leon Hawkins, is not responding to his phone or his company radio. He works on some wells way out in the oil field to the south. Have there been any sort of accidents reported over the past hour or two in that area?"

The response he got was chilling.

"Someone called in and said that his truck had been stolen at gunpoint, or at least that's what it sounded like. The call was breaking up, and we couldn't get a good location. We have a couple of officers out there looking, but they haven't found anyone yet. We've tried calling the number back a number of times, and it goes straight to voice mail."

"Did you get a name?"

"We think the caller was someone named Ellis. We weren't sure of a last name," Kora responded.

"Ellis Sharp works in that same general area for another company. I can give you the road both men would have been on." After he did so, he said, "Will you let your officers know and call me back when they learn something?"

"I will do that," she said.

After ending the call, Nels wondered what to do next. He should call Fiona Hawkins back, but he didn't want to frighten her, especially not if there was no cause for worry. He decided to call anyway but not tell her what he'd learned. In the meantime, he started his truck and headed in the direction of where Leon worked.

Fiona answered on the first ring. "Is that you, Nels? Do you know where he is?"

"I do, and I'm headed out to help him. Don't worry; I'll let you know when I reach him. There is no report of an accident of any kind, so you can relax," he said. "That's all I can tell you. You'll hear from me in a while."

When she tried to ask for more information, he told her to please be patient. Everything would be just fine. He wished he believed that, but he didn't, and he felt guilty for misleading her, but he thought it was best. He stepped on the accelerator and sped out of Roosevelt.

***

Ember and Cedrick left the movie theater a little after eleven. "Would you like to get something to eat before we go to my place?"

"How about a pizza? We could eat it at your apartment if you want to," he suggested.

"I'll call and have it delivered. What toppings do you want?" Ember asked as she turned her phone on.

"Pepperoni and sausage," he said. "When we have pizza, Uncle Claude says we can only have cheese on it. He's not very nice to me."

"I know, and we'll talk more about that later," she said as she worked her phone. As soon as she had ordered the pizza, she asked, "Did you like the movie?"

"It was great!" Cedrick said. "You're so good to me, Ember. You didn't have to come get me so late, but it sure is nice to be away."

"It's only because I love you," Ember said as she noted she had several missed calls on her phone. They were mostly from her bishop and a couple from Aunt Faye. She felt little worry bugs begin to stir in her stomach.

"Evie loves me too, and I guess Aunt Faye does, but Uncle Claude hates me," Cedrick said darkly. "He only lets me live there because of my insurance money."

"Cedrick, does Uncle Claude spend your money?"

"All the time. And he doesn't just spend it on me like we told him he could. He's says he earns it for himself for putting up with me."

"Do you have any idea how much of your money he's spent?"

"He won't tell me. And I don't know how to find out. He and Aunt Faye fight about it, but he tells her he's taking care of it, that she needs to quit bothering him about it."

Ember wondered if the money was gone now and whether that was why he wanted to be rid of Cedrick. If it was gone, that meant Claude spent a lot of money, because her little brother's share of the settlement was over a third of a million dollars. She felt a surge of anger. She'd ask one of her law professors what she should do about it, but for now, she wanted to move her conversation with Cedrick to a safer level. So she started talking about the movie, and that got him going. They talked and laughed all the way to her apartment.

Ember was surprised to see her bishop and his wife pull in behind her and park a few spaces away when she reached her apartment building. Her room-mate was away for a couple days, which was the only reason she'd been able to bring Cedrick home with her. She noted that Bishop Hunter had parked in her roommate's spot. She wondered whether they were here to see her or Kamryn. She knew he wanted to speak to Kamryn because her roommate had been a little spotty in church attendance the past few weeks, which was very uncharacteristic of her. But this late at night? It didn't make sense.

Ember was pretty sure the bishop was here to see her, and that made her stomach even queasier.

She and Cedrick got out of the car, and she grabbed his bag. Sister Hunter had waited for them, but the bishop had gone on ahead to her apartment. She thought she saw him pull a paper from the front door, but she wasn't sure.

"Is this the brother you've told us so much about?" Sister Hunter asked.

"Yes, this is Cedrick. Cedrick, this is my bishop's wife."

Cedrick, a very well-mannered twelve-year-old, shook hands and told her it was nice to meet her. Then the three of them walked to Ember's first-floor apartment. Cedrick was also introduced to Bishop Hunter, then the bishop said, "I think I parked in Kamryn's spot. Will she be getting home anytime soon?"

"No, she's with that guy I told you about," Ember said. "Bishop, I'm worried about her. He's not good for her. She's not the kind of person to do something wrong, but she has missed church occasionally because of him."

"I'll need to talk to her soon." The bishop shifted his stance, as if gathering his courage. "I know it's terribly late, but right now, would you mind if Sister Hunter and I came in and visited with you? Actually, with you and Cedrick both?"

"That would be nice," Ember said, worried about what such a late-night visit from them could possibly mean. It couldn't be good.

"We have a pizza coming. We'll share with you," Cedrick said.

"We don't need to eat, but thank you anyway."

Ember invited them in, asked them to sit, then put Cedrick's bag on the floor before she and her little brother sat down. The lateness of the hour and the look on the faces of Bishop Green and his wife panicked her.

CHAPTER NINE

THE BISHOP LEANED FORWARD. "I'm sorry to come here so late, but I've been trying to reach you for hours."

"My phone's been off. When I turned it on, I noticed I had some missed calls. I should have tried to call you back, but it seemed so late."

"It's fine," the bishop said, holding up a hand and shaking his head. "I have some bad news for you two. Your sister, Evie, has been in a very nasty car wreck."

Ember gasped. "Is she hurt badly?"

"I'm sorry, but she passed away," the bishop said.

Cedrick screamed and threw his arms around Ember. She was in shock, and it took a minute before the bishop's words sank in. Then she wrapped her brother in her arms, and the two of them cried inconsolably for several minutes. Ember only looked up when the doorbell rang.

"I don't want pizza now," Cedrick sobbed. "Evieeee." The name came out in a long, drawn-out, tragic breath.

Bishop Hunter answered the door, paid for the pizza, and handed it to his wife, who carried it into the kitchen.

Ember finally asked, "Does Aunt Faye know?"

"She and your uncle both know. Their bishop called me just before I arrived here to let me know he'd finally been able to contact them," Bishop Hunter said. "We've both been trying to find you."

"Uncle Claude won't care," Ember said, unable to mask the bitterness she felt over the way he'd treated her precious brother.

"Oh, I think he will," Bishop Hunter said.

"No, he won't. Believe me. He's a greedy, selfish man."

"Haven't he and your aunt been caring for Cedrick?"

"Aunt Faye has. She's a good woman, but Uncle Claude treats Cedrick badly."

"I think he stole all my money," Cedrick said as he looked up from where his head had been resting against his sister's side. "He only let me stay because of the insurance money. It must be gone now. I don't know where I'll go."

Ember made a sudden, life-changing decision. She pulled Cedrick close, looked down into his tearful eyes, and said, "I'll quit law school and take care of you."

***

Bentley's phone rang. "Hello, Faye," he said. "I guess you know."

"Oh, Bentley, I don't know what Cedrick will do without his sister. I don't know what I'll do."

"What do you mean?" he asked, puzzled at the angry tone he'd detected. "I'm sure you'll be okay."

For a few moments, Faye was silent. When she spoke again, there was a slight tremor in her voice. "I'm going to leave Claude. He's been horrid lately, treating sweet Cedrick like trash and threatening me. I'm afraid of him, Bentley. He didn't used to be this way, but he's a bitter, angry man lately. I don't know what I'll do about Cedrick."

Bentley was stunned. "I'm sorry, Aunt Faye. What else has Claude done?"

"I'm not sure exactly, but I checked our savings account today, and it's empty. Claude won't tell me what he's done with our money, but it's gone. I'm going to have to go back to work, and when I do, I won't be able to care for Cedrick," Faye explained, speaking slowly and emotionally.

"What about Cedrick's money?" he asked in alarm, having a sinking feeling that he already knew.

"Claude won't admit it, but I'm sure he's spent his money too."

"On what?" Bentley asked as anger mixed with his anguish.

"I don't know!" she answered, her voice full of sorrow.

"Let me speak with him," Bentley said. "Evie and I were going to take Cedrick, but now . . ." He couldn't continue for a moment. Finally, his anger overrode his tears. "Please, I need to talk to Claude."

"He's not here. We've been fighting since the bishop came by. He threw his phone at me and stormed out of the house just before I called you. I'm so sorry to drop all this on you at such a distressing time in your life." Faye broke down crying and could not go on.

"I'll call you later, Aunt Faye," Bentley said.

Faye attempted to mumble something, and then the call abruptly ended.

"Bentley, what's going on?" Bishop Green asked with concern.

Bentley explained this new information briefly. "I've got to talk to Ember and Cedrick. I hope they know by now." He rubbed his eyes. "I'll be okay now. Thanks, all of you, for coming and staying with me so long. I think I need to be alone."

His visitors all hugged him, told him to call if they could help him later, and then they left.

Alone.

With his beloved Evie gone, that's exactly what he was. It was just him and Twy now. As if sensing his thoughts, Twy padded over to him and laid his head on Bentley's knee.

Bentley hoped he hadn't hurt any feelings, but he needed time to figure out what he was going to do. Bishop Green and the others hadn't been gone more than five minutes, and Bentley hadn't moved from his recliner. He was bent forward, supported his aching head with his hands, when his phone rang.

He sat up and pulled it from his shirt pocket. He looked at the screen through bleary eyes, hoping it wasn't Faye calling back. No, it was worse: Claude.

He debated refusing the call but decided to see what Claude wanted. He'd wanted to speak with him anyway.

"You are a worthless soul!" Claude shouted into the phone as soon as Bentley answered. "First you force that bratty little brother of Evie's on me, and now you have convinced my wife to leave me."

"I have done no such thing. She just told me minutes ago that she was leaving you. I had nothing to do with her decision. She said you weren't even home," Bentley said, totally knocked off kilter by the anger and hatred in Claude's voice.

"I just got back. I found her packing. She told me she'd talked to you. You . . . You . . . You'll regret this, Bentley!" Claude shouted, and the call ended.

Five minutes later, Bentley was still holding his phone in his hand in stunned silence when it rang again. To his dismay, it was Faye again.

"I'm sorry about that, Bentley," she said around heart-wrenching sobs. "The devil seems to have taken possession of my husband. I'm in my car driving to a hotel."

At least that's what he thought she said. She was crying so hard that it was impossible to be sure of her words.

"I'm sorry, Aunt Faye," he managed to say. "You be careful now. I don't want you to get in a wreck."

He meant that sincerely. One dreadful wreck today was more than he could handle, and he truly did not want anything to happen to Faye. They were both silent for a moment. Finally Faye said, "If he took Cedrick's money, I'll find a way to pay it back even if I have to starve."

"You don't have to do that," he said.

"I feel like I must. Bentley," she said, her voice clearer now, "I loved Evie. Please know how sorry I am. I'll call you tomorrow."

That call barely ended before his phone rang again. He felt like screaming, until he saw that it was Ember calling rather than Faye or Claude. "Hello," he said as he felt the weight of the world crushing his very soul.

"Bentley, I'm so sorry. Cedrick and I will be there sometime tomorrow."

"You don't have to do that."

"Oh, but I do," Ember said. "Bentley, Cedrick and I are devastated. I can't believe Evie is gone. I don't understand how anyone could do that to her."

"I know who did it, and . . . well, there are evil people like that in the world."

"Who hit her?" Ember asked. "How do you know?"

"I just know. I'll explain when I see you. Is Cedrick okay?"

"Not really. Bentley, before we come out, I've got to go to Aunt Faye's and pick up some of his belongings. I also need to talk to our lawyer, the one who helped us get the insurance settlements from my parents' life insurance policies."

"Don't go to Aunt Faye's!" he said. "She's not there."

"How do you know that?" Ember asked.

He explained the calls from Faye and Claude.

"Oh, Bentley, how could Uncle Claude do such a terrible thing? Here, talk to Cedrick. He needs to hear you say you care about him."

A moment later, the soft, sad voice of his young brother-in-law came on the phone. "Bentley, I need Evie," he sobbed.

"So do I, Cedrick. I love you. I hope you know that. So did Evie. We will both miss her."

All three of us will, you and me and Ember."

"I love you too," the young man said. "What am I going to do now?"

"Ember and I will figure it out," Bentley said.

"She says she'll take care of me, that she's going to quit law school. She can't do that," Cedrick said through his tears.

"Cedrick, Ember says you guys are coming here tomorrow. I promise that we'll figure this out." Even as he said that, he was thinking about Ember being willing to drop out of law school for her little brother's sake and postpone her dreams. If anyone was to leave their dreams behind, it should be him. After all, he'd already lost the most important person in the world. His dreams had already been shattered. "Cedrick, Heavenly Father loves you. He will help us all through this."

"I know, Bentley. Ember wants to talk to you again."

"You don't have to quit law school, Ember," he said as soon as Ember came back on the line. "That's terribly drastic. We'll figure something out."

"Not as drastic as losing Evie," she said. "I'm the only person left besides Aunt Faye who cares about Cedrick."

"Ember, that's not true. I couldn't love him more if he were my own flesh and blood," Bentley told her.

"I know that, Bentley. I meant that no one left in my and Evie's family. Poor Aunt Faye. She doesn't deserve all this."

"No, she doesn't. None of us do, but the Lord will help us. You and I have got to be strong for Cedrick."

"Yes, we do, and if sacrifices need to be made, I am willing," she said.

"So am I, Ember. Thanks for calling. After that horrible call from Claude, it's good to hear a friendly voice."

"I'm so sorry, Bentley. I know how much Evie loved you and how much you loved her."

"I still love her. I always will. But oh, how I am going to miss her."

CHAPTER TEN

SILAS VILLARD SPENT THE NIGHT hidden deep in a forest of cedar and pinion trees. He'd sobered up enough to realize that someone might be able to trace the location of the truck he'd stolen, so he did what came naturally to him. He took what he could use from it, then set it on fire and walked away. He carried a blanket, which he used as a knapsack. It was filled with six bottles of water, a box of ammunition for the pistol, half a box of cookies, an almost-full bag of jerky, a small but very sharp hatchet, and his rifle. The one thing the oil-field worker didn't have in the truck was beer, and that irritated him. He craved alcohol.

He awoke in the morning after a rough night of sleeping on the ground curled up in the blanket. After starting a small campfire, he gradually warmed up. He knew how to start fires and took pride in that. However, he had no idea where he was. He'd driven mindlessly for miles after shooting the two oil-field workers. Then he'd walked for several hours after burning the truck he'd stolen. He'd only stopped when he was too exhausted to go on.

As badly as Silas wanted to get back to civilization and burn Trooper Radford's house to the ground with the trooper in it, he admitted to himself that he would have to wait for his revenge. He vowed that no matter how long he had to survive out here in the wilds, he would eventually complete that task. For now, he had to find a source of water, shelter if bad weather hit, and wild game to shoot and eat. He would live out here for a while and bide his time.

***

Detective Hank Parker of the Duchesne County Sheriff Department walked into the hospital in Roosevelt. He was both physically and emotionally drained. He'd not had more than two hours of sleep early that morning after spending many hours trying to figure out where Silas Villard had gone.

He'd spoken with Bentley Radford to let him know that he was determined to find the man who had caused the death of his wife. Bentley was an emotional wreck, but he'd assured Hank that he would find a way to move on, that Evie would expect him to.

Bentley had asked a lot of questions, and Hank had hidden nothing from him. So now Bentley knew about the two badly injured oil-field workers, about the fires, and about the fact that Silas was armed and considered extremely dangerous. But no one had been able to find anything indicating the direction they needed to go to find this dangerous man.

His purpose now in entering the hospital was to speak with the two injured men. Both were in very serious condition. He hoped they could help him focus the hunt for Silas Villard.

Both men, though in pain, were able to speak with him. He visited first with Leon Hawkins, whose wife, Fiona, was there with him. Leon briefly described the ordeal he'd gone through and then said, "I owe my life to this lady right here." Though his face was heavily bandaged, his eyes looked lovingly at Fiona.

"What did she do?" Hank asked, although he already knew.

"She is the one who convinced people to look for me," he said. "Had it not been for her, I have a feeling that Ellis and I would have both died out there."

"You are a blessed man," Hank said. "Are you sure you can't remember anything else that might help me find Silas?"

"I wish I knew more," he said, "but I don't."

"If you think of something, anything at all, no matter how trivial you think it is, please have your wife call me."

"We'll do that," Fiona responded for the two of them. "We won't be here much longer, though. They're going to move Leon to a burn unit in Salt Lake." She paused briefly, then she asked, "Do you have any idea how Trooper Radford is doing? His wife was such a sweet thing, and they had only been married for a short time. It's just dreadful."

Hank assured them Bentley would recover with time, and then he went to visit Ellis Sharp a couple rooms down the hallway. His wife and two grown children were with him, and hospital staff hovered in the room, getting him ready for his transfer to Salt Lake City, so Hank didn't stay long. The most important thing he hoped to learn from Ellis was what Silas might have stolen from his truck to use if he tried to hole up in the wilderness.

"Well, there were some bottles of water, some cookies, a sandwich, a bag of jerky, and a blanket," Ellis said. "Of course, I had a lot of tools too."

"That's good to know. Anything else?"

Just like Leon, Ellis's face was bandaged, so Hank could not read his facial expressions. But the man's eyes kept moving back and forth. They shut for a moment as he thought. "He probably found my spare box of .38 shells. Apparently, he took my pistol when he left Leon and me lying there on the road. Oh, and I had a hatchet under my back seat."

"If he left your truck somewhere, I suppose he would take some of those things with him," Hank said.

"Why would he leave my truck?" Ellis asked.

"Because once he sobered up, he may have realized that we might be able to find the truck, considering its GPS features," Hank explained.

"I never thought of that. Have you tried using that yet?"

"We have, and we're getting no reading at all."

"Any idea why? Even if he wrecked it, surely the GPS would still work," Ellis said.

"True, but if he burned the truck, then it probably wouldn't."

Ellis moaned. "I see, and that's probably something he would do, isn't it?"

"In my opinion, it is," Hank agreed. "I'd better go now. I hope you heal quickly at the burn unit. You are going there, aren't you?"

"I am," Ellis said.

"Well, good luck. If you think of anything else that might help me, please make sure your wife or someone else lets me know."

***

Ember took Cedrick with her to the law school where she notified the administration that she was considering dropping out. Her idea was not received well by anyone because she was a top student. One of her professors was especially upset and invited Ember and her little brother into her office.

Professor Kathleen Aldrich was a seasoned civil litigator, in addition to being a much-respected law professor. She was sixty years of age, a woman with boundless energy and a high degree of intelligence. She was around five eight with piercing blue eyes, long white hair, and a slender frame. She could be both intimidating and loving. Ember had become quite close to her, although she'd never shared the details of her personal life with her. Their discussions had always been about the law and the bright future ahead for Ember in that profession.

Professor Aldrich invited the two of them to sit down and then said, "I'm sorry to hear what you are considering. Is this young man your brother?"

"He is. This is Cedrick. Cedrick, meet Professor Aldrich," Ember said.

"It's nice to meet you," Cedrick said quietly. His eyes were red and downcast.

"Again, I'm sorry to hear that you are considering giving up law, Ember. You are one of my brightest and most ambitious students."

"Thank you. I'm sorry too, Professor," Ember said. "I really think I may have to do it. My brother needs me."

Today, Professor Aldrich did not appear intimidating but seemed very compassionate and concerned about Ember. "Why don't you tell me why he needs you now. I assume something has happened."

"He and I have suffered a terrible tragedy," Ember said. "My twin sister, Evie, was killed yesterday in a traffic accident. She was hit by a driver who left the scene and was almost certainly drunk at the time."

The mention of Evie's death got young Cedrick sobbing again. To Ember's surprise, the professor rose from her seat behind her large oak desk, walked around it, and pulled up another chair next to Cedrick. She put an arm around his shoulders and pulled him close. She didn't say a word as the boy sobbed. Ember was also sobbing. Cedrick's sorrow and Professor Aldrich's compassion had been more than her tender feelings could take.

Finally, without removing her arm from around Cedrick's shoulder, Professor Aldrich said, "You are a very lucky young man to have a sister who loves you so much she would give up her dreams for you."

He sniffled. "I have no place to live now. She says she'll take care of me."

"I'm sorry," she said. Then her piercing blue eyes caught Ember's. "Tell me about your family and why the loss of a sister, which is so very tragic, leaves this young man needing your care. Was Evie his guardian?"

"No, our Uncle Claude and Aunt Faye have been taking care of him since our parents were killed. Like Evie, they died in a car crash caused by a drunk driver. I don't understand why people drive after they've been drinking," she added in an undertone. "It makes me so angry."

"I understand how you feel. You and I have talked a lot, Ember, but never about your personal life. With the loss of your sister, I would think that an uncle and aunt would continue to care for him. Please, would you explain? And tell me about this sister of yours."

For the next half hour, Ember, with a few words from Cedrick, explained what had been happening in their lives, particularly in Cedrick's life. They both expressed their profound grief at the loss of their beloved sister and their concern for her widowed husband.

Professor Aldrich listened intently, sitting beside Cedrick the entire time. She did not ask a single question until the siblings had finished. Then she stood and returned to her seat. She looked compassionately across her desk at both siblings, and finally she said, "So do you believe that your uncle has stolen hundreds of thousands of dollars that were Cedrick's?"

"I do believe it, and so does Aunt Faye, but I guess there is nothing I can do about it. But as you can see, I must take care of Cedrick. Evie and Bentley had discussed taking him into their home in Duchesne, but that was only in the past few days that they'd considered it."

"You said that Evie was a nurse and worked in the emergency room at the hospital in Roosevelt. Was she going to give up her job? I suspect that she, if she was much like you, was very good at what she did and that she had a real passion for it."

"You're right, and I'm not sure what she and Bentley were thinking they would do. What she told me was that they would figure something out."

"They sound like good people," Professor Aldrich said. "On the other hand, your Uncle Claude is apparently a very evil man." She looked right at Cedrick. "Do you have a wallet with you?"

Cedrick looked very surprised, but he pulled one from his back pocket. "It's right here."

"Do you have a dollar in it?"

"I have several dollars, but I think that's all the money I have now," he said, rubbing at his eyes with one hand.

"Would you be willing to give one dollar to me if I were to become your lawyer and help you get your money back from your uncle, if he still has it? Or at least find out what he did with it?"

Without a word, Cedrick pulled out a wrinkled dollar bill, stood, and reached across her desk, holding it out to the kind professor. She took it and slipped it into a desk drawer. "Thank you. I am now your attorney. You may sit back down."

He did that, but with a puzzled frown on his face, he turned to Ember, who was barely able to keep her fractured emotions in check. "I thought she was a teacher, Ember. How can a teacher help me?"

Before Ember could explain, Professor Aldrich said, "I am both a lawyer and a teacher of the law. I am very experienced. Ember, is this okay with you?"

"Yes, of course. It's so kind of you."

The intimidating side of the professor suddenly surfaced. "Kind to you two but not to your thieving uncle," she said. "I will get to the bottom of this. I need to make some calls. Is that okay? I'd like you to wait while I do that."

"Of course," Ember said.

Professor Aldrich reached for the phone on her desk, but she paused before picking it up. "We'll talk shortly about your plans. I am going to call in a couple favors. Would you two wait in the hall while I make these calls? Then you may come back in." With that, she picked up the receiver.

CHAPTER ELEVEN

BENTLEY HAD NEVER FELT SO lost in his life; he didn't know what to do with himself. He was lonely despite visits from friends, neighbors, and ward members. Thanks to those visitors, he had more food in his fridge than he could ever use. People were so kind, but could anything relieve Bentley of his loneliness and terrible sorrow? Despite himself, he found that he was angry with God for letting this happen to Evie. He knew he had to get over that, but it would take time.

It was hard, but he made a visit to the mortuary that morning to pick out a casket and make other arrangements regarding his beloved wife. It was hard to look at her lying there dead, but he did it so that he could tell the mortician that it really was Evie. After that, he visited the Duchesne city office and purchased a couple of funeral plots, one for Evie and one for himself. Someday he would need one too.

At noon, the bishop came by to discuss the funeral.

Just after the bishop left, Ember called to remind him that she and Cedrick were coming later in the afternoon. As he thought about the pending visit, he realized that if anyone could help fill the loneliness in his soul, it would be those two. They were the closest thing to family he had left in this world.

With a few hours' wait looming over him, he acted on an idea that had occurred to him during the night. It was nothing he would have considered if Evie were still alive, but he considered it now. He drove to the office of a local realtor—Rachel Delaney—who also lived in his ward. He didn't want to continue living in the house he and Evie had been renting. There were too many memories there. Not that he could ever forget Evie, but he didn't want to be barraged with memories and lose hope every time he entered the house.

He wanted a private place out of town.

After expressing her condolences when Bentley visited her office, Rachel said, "Tell me what you have in mind, and I'll see what I can find."

"I want something out of town with a cabin on it or room for me to build one. It needs to have a few acres because I want to get a horse and possibly some other animals. I would need to have water available. I don't want to have to haul water. Although I suppose I could have a well drilled if there isn't one there already."

"How big does the cabin need to be?" Rachel asked.

"Well, there's just me and my dog, so we won't need anything huge. But two bedrooms would be nice in case anyone were to come visit," he said, thinking about Cedrick. He hated to see Ember quit her dreams of becoming a lawyer. The idea of taking Cedrick in had percolated in his mind since his latest call from Ember. "Yes, definitely two bedrooms," he said.

"I assume you will continue your work with the highway patrol," Rachel said.

He shrugged his shoulders. "Maybe for a while, but frankly, after losing my wife to a drunk driver whom I had arrested and who should never have been able to get out of jail so soon, I'm not sure I want to continue with the highway patrol."

"You will need a way to finance the property," she reminded him. "What kind of job would you look for?"

"First, I plan to pay a large cash down payment if the price isn't too outrageous," he said. "I want to try my hand at writing novels. I've written a few short stories that my high school English teacher told me showed some promise in that area. I actually have a novel started that Evie told me was good. I'll just have to see. I'm good with my hands, and I suppose I could do some handyman work too."

"It sounds like you've given this some thought," she said.

"Not much, honestly, but the idea appeals to me," he responded.

"I've got several listings here." She scrolled through some for a moment, and then suddenly she stopped and showed her phone screen to Bentley. "Take a look at this. It's log construction but has three bedrooms. Would that work if the price is right?"

"Maybe," he said even as he wondered if this was a bad idea. It was too soon to be worrying about a different place to live. His mind was simply not working like it should. He should have waited, but he was here now, and he couldn't just walk back out.

When Rachel laid a couple of pictures in front of him, he gasped involuntarily. What he was looking at was a beautiful log home with full covered decks on both the front and back, and there was a loft inside. "This is nice," he said. "Evie would have loved something like this. But I don't want to pay that much."

"I haven't even told you a price," Rachel said with a gentle smile.

"Yeah, but I can guess it would be too much."

"Let me tell you the asking price, and if it is within reason, we could go take a look at it. The loft would make a nice place for you to write your books," she said.

"Tell me the price."

"Originally it was listed at $250,000.00."

"Too much!" Bentley exclaimed.

"Hear me out," Rachel said. "This property belonged to an older couple. The husband died and his wife didn't live much longer after his death. The place fell to a daughter and son-in-law who live in New York. Money is not an issue with them, and they just want the property gone. They called me last week and told me to drop the price to $125,000.00. And they will consider an even lower offer if it will help me move it sooner. They've already sat on the place for six months with the price they'd been asking. They want it sold. They said it's a burden to them."

Bentley sat back in his chair and rubbed his aching eyes. "I wish I hadn't lost Evie. She would have loved this place. I can afford it at that kind of price, but I . . . well I just don't know what to do. I need Evie to help me decide." Tears threatened, and he blinked them back.

"Bentley, why don't you ride with me, and we'll go look at the place. At this price, it will be gone soon, and I don't have anything even close to as nice as this for such a ridiculously low price," she encouraged. "I know this is an especially bad time for you, but do you have anything else to do this afternoon? Maybe this will give you something to do to take you mind off your troubles at least for a couple hours."

Bentley felt like a traitor to Evie to be considering such a major change so soon, and maybe it would be a huge mistake, but at the same time, it wouldn't hurt to look. It beat sitting in his house brooding over the loss of someone so precious to him. Ember and Cedrick wouldn't be here for several hours according to Ember's latest call. It would keep him occupied to go look at the place.

"Sure, let's do it," he said. "I've got nothing else to do."

***

Ember and Cedrick hadn't yet left the city, and they wouldn't for a couple more hours, as she had explained to Bentley. Professor Aldrich had made some calls, and she asked them to come back in about an hour and a half later, wanting to know more about what Claude had done. Ember was anxious to go see Bentley and offer whatever comfort she could, but she also had Cedrick to think of.

After they were seated in the office again, Professor Aldrich said, "I've done as I told you I would and made some calls. First, you were right; your Uncle Claude has spent all but about a thousand dollars of your money, Cedrick. A criminal investigation has been started."

"Will he go to jail?" Cedrick asked.

"Most certainly," the professor responded. "Does that upset you?"

"I don't care if he does or not," Cedrick said. "I just want Evie back." Tears welled in his eyes, but he managed to hold them back.

Ember put a hand on Cedrick's shoulder. "Thanks for doing that, Professor. I guess I'm not as nice as my brother, but I want him to go to prison for a very long time. More than that, I want the man who killed our sister to be caught and go to prison for the rest of his life."

"Interesting you should mention him. The man's name is Silas Villard. Let me tell you what I've learned about him in the past couple hours," Professor Aldrich said. She then told them about the fires he caused, the death of his grandfather over which he was to be charged with murder, the attempted murder of two oil-field workers, and the burning of their company trucks. "The second truck was located late this morning."

"Have they caught him?" Ember asked anxiously.

Professor Aldrich shook her head. "Sadly, he is still on the run. The sheriff believes he's on foot in the mountains. They've been searching but haven't located him. They are determined to do so, though, and have called in extra law enforcement. A massive manhunt is underway."

"They have to find him," Ember said. "He'll keep hurting people if he doesn't get caught."

"And keep starting fires," the professor said. "They suspect he is a serial arsonist. He may even be responsible for some of the fires we've had around the state lately. But that's enough about Villard for now. Since you're going out to Duchesne later today, there is something I want you to do. Tell your brother-in-law that if he doesn't already have another attorney to represent him, I have someone in mind. I've spoken with the attorney who helped the three of you acquire your settlements over the death of your parents, and he will represent Bentley in this matter as well."

"I'm sure he'll need that help. I know that the insurance companies involved with my parents' wreck didn't want to pay anything. But our attorney ended up getting us quite a generous settlement," Ember said. "I'm glad you called him because I was going to."

"Have Bentley contact him. I will continue to follow up on the matter of your sticky-fingered uncle." She smiled.

"Thank you, Professor."

"I've been busy, Ember. No one wants you to leave law school. I've called each of your other professors, and they have agreed to give you work to take with you for the next three weeks so you won't fall behind. In other words, we are begging you not to drop out yet, but to give it three weeks."

Ember shook her head. "Thank you, but I don't think anything will change in three weeks."

"Let's at least explore some other options. I can give you the names of a couple of good family-law attorneys who might have some ideas. Please call them." Professor Aldrich handed a piece of paper to Ember. "Here is their contact information. They are former students of mine, and I have spoken to both of them. They know your situation and have assured me that they will help find some alternatives for the two of you."

Ember's heart was aching. She didn't want to leave school. She also didn't want to make her little brother live with someone else, and that, she was certain, was the only thing those other attorneys would be able to help her with. "I guess we'd better get going," she said after thanking Kathleen. "We need to see if there's any way we can help our brother-in-law. He is really hurting."

"That's understandable. You will give us the three weeks, won't you?" the professor asked.

"Yes."

"Watch for your assignments in your email. And keep in touch, Ember. I will be praying for you."

With that, the siblings went back to Ember's apartment to pack for their trip to Duchesne. Ember's roommate, Kamryn Baldwin, was there, which was totally unexpected. "What are you doing back already?" Ember asked.

"I broke up with Tom. He said some hurtful things, and he . . ." Kamryn looked at Cedrick. "Never mind. He's a jerk. I'll tell you more sometime. Do you have Bishop Hunter's number? I need to see if he has some time to counsel me."

"I do," Ember said. She opened her phone, found the number in her contacts, and then texted it to Kamryn. Her roommate's phone pinged. "There, that should be it."

"Thank you, Ember. What are you and your little brother doing?"

Once again, Ember tearfully explained the tragedy that had struck them. "We're going to Duchesne as soon as I pack. And just so you know, I may quit law school so I can take care of Cedrick. I have three weeks to decide."

"Oh, Ember, I'm so sorry," Kamryn said. "Is there anything I can do?"

"Not right now, but thanks. We need to get ready and leave within the next few minutes."

As Ember and Cedrick prepared to step out the door, suitcases in hand, Kamryn said, "I know I haven't been going to church very regularly lately. But with Tom out of my life, that's going to change, I promise."

"That makes me very happy, Kamryn."

"You are my best friend, Ember. You have no idea how much your example means to me."

Ember put her suitcase on the floor by the door and turned to her roommate and held out her arms. The two of them hugged. Then Kamryn said, "I promise you that I will never date another guy who is not active in the Church. I've learned a hard lesson."

"The same goes for me," Ember said.

"But you never have," Kamryn said.

"No, but I'm promising you that I won't," Ember told her with a smile.

"I'd like to come to your sister's funeral. Would that be okay?" Kamryn asked.

"I would love it if you would."

"Let me know when it is, and I'll be there," she said.

That gave Ember an idea, but she kept it to herself. She might consider mentioning it to Bentley, and she might not.

CHAPTER TWELVE

Silas Villard had seen aircraft flying low overhead. But he was staying alert, and whenever he heard approaching aircraft, he hid in thick trees. Then he would move on. He lucked out and found a cabin he was able to break into. It had an attached garage with an older-model brown Jeep in it. He knew now what he would do. No one could stop him from doing what he had planned.

He helped himself to some canned food and bottled water, then packed up more and put it in the Jeep. He couldn't find a key, but this Jeep was one he could easily hot-wire. The Jeep had a spare can of gas in the back. He pumped his fists. Maybe he could get his revenge during the coming night and burn that trooper's house—the cop who had started his streak of trouble. And if the cop was burned along with the house like his grandad was, so much the better.

Then something happened that hadn't happened in a long time; Silas felt a twinge of remorse over what he'd done to his grandad. At one time they'd been great pals. If only the old man had bailed him out of jail, then he'd still have him to consult about his troubles. There would be a funeral, but Silas would not attend, and that also sent a wave of sadness through him. He shrugged. What was done was done. If he had to do it over again, he wouldn't set that fire.

Trooper Radford, on the other hand, deserved to be punished for what he'd done, and Silas would see to it that it happened. He relished the thought of hurting the trooper.

Silas was in no hurry to leave, as he believed he had the cops fooled. In his mind, he didn't think he'd done anything wrong other than burning his grandad's house. Surely they would believe him if he told them he was sorry he'd done that. He had simply been treated unfairly, and he expected such treatment would continue. He checked around the cabin for any clues that might give him away. Even though he was innocent, and even though the cops may or may not still be looking for him, he knew he needed to be vigilant.

He looked in a mirror in the cabin's bathroom. He was too recognizable. The bushy beard and long hair had to go. Luckily, the owner of this cabin had it well stocked, and that included scissors, razors, and shaving cream. It took him quite a while, but he was finally able to remove his beard and hair. He shaved right to the skin, then looked at his reflection and grinned. He liked this new look. Nobody could possibly recognize him now.

His clothes were filthy and torn. He lucked out again, and after rummaging through a closet, he found clothes that fit him reasonably well. He even changed his boots for a pair he found in the closet. He added a clean, warm coat to his ensemble, for when the nights grew cold, and again examined himself in the mirror. This would have to do.

He was in no hurry to leave. He had the stolen pistol tucked in his pants and his rifle next to the door, and if, by some stroke of bad luck, the owner of the cabin showed up, he would deal with him. His bravery was bolstered by the beers he found. He drank a bunch, put more in the Jeep, and then settled down in the cabin for a much-needed nap.

He only slept an hour, but he guessed that was enough because he was wide awake following his nap. It was time to find his way out of this area. He was pretty much unrecognizable with his shaved head and face and new clothes. No one would have any reason to look for him in the brown Jeep. He looked at the registration and said, "Thank you, Dewey Steller, for the nice wheels and the use of your cabin." He stuck the registration back in the jockey box.

He hot-wired the generous Mr. Steller's Jeep and backed it out of the garage, not bothering to shut the big door. He then made his way out of the area. He had a long and satisfying night of revenge and entertainment ahead of him.

***

Ember was glad to see that Bentley's truck was at home when she pulled up on the street in front of his house in the late afternoon. Cedrick was asleep in the passenger side of her car. She looked at him adoringly. How, she wondered, could Uncle Claude be so cruel to such a great kid?

In addition to Bentley's pickup, his highway patrol cruiser was also in the driveway. With a sudden lump in her throat, Ember missed her sister's white Saab. Like Evie, the car was gone. She'd never see it again or ride in it again with Evie, laughing and singing like they'd always done. For five minutes she sat there in her light-blue Saab, lost in her sad thoughts. She may have sat there longer, but suddenly Cedric sat up and asked, "Are we there?"

"We are," she said, reaching over and patting his shoulder. "Should we go in and see Bentley? He's expecting us, you know."

"I'm hungry, Ember. Do you think he'll have any food since Evie isn't here anymore to cook for him?"

She smiled sadly at her little brother. "There will be food, Cedrick. I'm sure that people have brought him more than he could possibly eat, and I know he will share with you. Let's go let him know he's not completely alone," she said with a catch in her throat.

She got out, stepped up to the little gate, and waited for Cedrick to join her. They exchanged sad glances, and then Ember opened the gate. This was going to be so hard.

As the two of them approached the door to the small white house that Evie and Bentley had rented, the front door opened, and there, his face grim, stood Bentley. Ember's heart pounded, her stomach turned over, and then she forced herself to smile as she hurried toward him. Cedrick hurried faster. Bentley hugged him tightly as they both shed tears. Then Cedrick loosened his grip on Bentley, and Ember moved those last few steps toward him.

He held out his arms. "Thanks for coming, you two. I'm so lost." His voice broke.

Ember stepped into his embrace, and for a long time they stood there crying. Finally Ember pulled back, looked up at him, and said, "Bentley, I'm so very sorry. You lost the best girl a guy could have ever found."

He nodded but appeared too emotional to speak as he waved the two siblings inside and closed the door. He finally found his voice and said, "It still seems like a horrible nightmare. I don't know what I'll ever do without her. This house . . . it feels so empty."

"You'll stay here, won't you?" Ember asked.

He shook his head. "Probably not. I've been thinking about that today. This can never be just *my* home, because it was *our* home," he said. "I'm looking for someplace else."

"I think I understand," Ember told her brother-in-law.

"Hey, you guys, are you hungry? It's almost dinnertime, and I have more food in the fridge than I could eat in a month," Bentley said, forcing a smile that he clearly didn't feel.

"Funny you should mention food. Cedrick was just saying how hungry he is. And I told him I was sure people would be bringing in more than you could eat."

"You can have all you want, Cedrick. Let's go heat something up." Bentley led the way into the small kitchen with Cedrick at his side. Ember followed, watching the two of them and feeling like she'd lost most of her world. She and Evie had been as close as two twins could ever be. It was going to be so hard without her.

***

Despite the enjoyable times they had spent together in the past, Bentley had worried about how sad and awkward it would be for Ember without her beloved twin here, but it seemed okay. She, like her sister, was a thoughtful and gentle person. And Cedrick was like the little brother he'd never had. He wanted them both to feel comfortable and welcome.

He opened the fridge and swept out a hand, indicating Cedrick should look inside. "You choose, Cedrick."

"Wow!" Cedrick said. "That's a lot of food."

"There's more in our freezer in the garage," Bentley said.

"Gee, Bentley, people must really like you." Cedrick examined the offerings the fridge held.

"No, they really loved Evie. Everybody loved Evie."

"I loved Evie too. Me and Ember both loved her, huh, Ember?"

Bentley looked at Ember and saw the pain in her eyes. It was very much like his pain.

She nodded. "Yes, we did, and we still do, don't we, Cedrick? She's still our sister. She'll always be our sister. She's just gone to be with Jesus and with Mom and Dad."

"I know that," Cedrick said. "I miss Mom and Dad too."

Bentley felt a rush of affection for his young brother-in-law. He had lost so much for one so young. Cedrick turned back to the refrigerator and studied the offerings there. "I don't know. It all looks good. Ember, you pick."

She did so and popped a casserole into the microwave. Bentley pulled some milk from the fridge. Then he set the table for three. Once the casserole was heated, they sat down.

"There are a bunch of cookies and even a couple of cakes," Bentley said. "I don't know why the good people in our ward think I can eat so much, but I'm grateful for their kindness."

They visited as they ate. They talked of Evie and how much fun she'd always been, and how caring and unselfish. Then Ember said, "Do you have any idea what you will do for the funeral?"

"Bishop Green and I have talked about it a little. Since neither you guys nor I have much extended family, it will mostly be just people from our ward and the town who attend. I expect some of the cops I've worked with will come. And people Evie worked with at the hospital will want to be there, I'm sure. But I don't really know any of them."

"Do you have any idea who you want to have speak or provide music?" Ember asked.

Bentley did know who he thought should speak. He just hoped she could do it. It was silent around the little kitchen table for a moment. "I told the bishop that I thought you should speak," Bentley said at last. "No one, including myself, knew Evie as well as you did."

He thought he'd made a mistake mentioning his idea to her when she dropped her head, rubbed her eyes, and sobbed quietly.

"You can do it," Cedrick pitched in.

Ember looked up finally. "Thanks for thinking of me, Bentley. I would be honored. Who else?"

"The bishop and I wondered about a good friend in the ward. Detective Hank Parker is our elder's quorum president, and he and his wife are close friends of ours. I know he would do a good job. Then, of course, Bishop Green would speak last. I think that's enough," Bentley said.

"What about music?" Ember asked.

Bentley shrugged. "Maybe just hymns. I don't know though. I don't know anyone to suggest to the bishop."

"I do," Ember said.

"You do? Who?" he asked.

"My roommate, Kamryn Baldwin, has a beautiful voice. I got this idea when she told me that she is planning to come to the funeral. I could accompany her on the piano if that's okay. The last time she sang in our ward, I accompanied her," Ember said. "She knew Evie and liked her a lot. And Evie has heard her sing and told me what a beautiful voice she has. With Evie gone, Kamryn is my best friend." She paused and looked at Bentley uncomfortably. "If you don't like that idea, that's okay too."

"I think that would be great," Bentley said. "And I know that Bishop Green would like the idea as well. In fact, I'll call him as soon as we have some cake. You do want cake, don't you, Cedrick?"

"Yes, please," he said, like the young gentleman he was.

After dinner, the three of them cleaned up the kitchen and did the dishes. Then Bentley called Bishop Green. He mentioned Ember's idea, and the bishop readily agreed. "If you'll give me her number, I'll call and ask her. Also, did you mention to Ember that you wanted her to talk?" Bishop Green asked.

"I did, and she will. Also, like Evie, she plays the piano very well, and she can accompany Kamryn," Bentley said.

"Text me her number, and I'll call Kamryn this evening," the bishop said.

Bentley got the number from Ember and sent it to the bishop. "She will do it, won't she?" he asked Ember.

"Oh yes, she loves to sing. She's a good person. And since she has already told me that she wants to come to the funeral to support me, she would never say no."

Once the call had ended, Cedrick asked, "What are we going to do tonight?"

Bentley hadn't given it any thought. This was not a situation with which he had any experience. Evie had been the one to make guests feel welcome. Then he had a thought. "Would you two like to go for a little ride with me? There's something I'd like to show you."

"Whatever you want to do," Ember said.

"Yeah, I'd like that," Cedrick said.

"Then let's go."

CHAPTER THIRTEEN

Silas Villard was very careful to keep the stolen Jeep under the speed limit and to avoid weaving back and forth on the road. The last thing he needed was to get pulled over for speeding or to be accused of driving drunk again. He wasn't any drunker than he had been the night he was falsely arrested by Trooper Radford. He had revenge and a beautiful fire on his mind. While driving past the trooper's house, he saw both his brown pickup and his patrol car parked in the driveway. There was a small, light-blue car parked in front. That had to be his wife's car. Silas hadn't considered that the trooper could be married. This was getting better all the time. They'd both suffer from his fire tonight.

As he slipped past the house for the third time, anxious for darkness to come, he noticed the hated trooper, a pretty brunette, some young boy, and a gray dog leave the house and get in the truck. He was certain the girl was Mrs. Radford, but he had no idea who the kid was. That troubled him. He had never hurt a kid.

He wrestled with the problem as he drove and finally made a decision. If the kid had made the mistake of visiting the trooper's family tonight, that was his misfortune. He didn't like the idea, but Radford had to pay. He just wished the boy wasn't with him.

He had a moment of panic when he followed the truck and saw that it was leaving town on the highway toward Salt Lake. Surely he and the missus were not going somewhere for the night. He'd gotten lucky finding this Jeep and getting out of the hills like he did. He feared his revenge was going to have to wait yet again. Maybe at another time the boy wouldn't be there. Silas wondered if he was going to have to hide out again and wait for another night to avenge the wrongs Trooper Radford had inflicted on him. He cursed. He didn't want to wait, but he also didn't want to burn an empty house. And when it came right down to it, he didn't want to burn the boy either.

He finally decided to find a new place to hole up for a few hours. Maybe the trooper and his wife were just taking the kid to his home to drop him off and would be back later. That would solve the dilemma of the boy. Fine. He would check again at about one o'clock in the morning. If the Radfords were home, there would be a beautiful fire. If not, he'd drink more of the beer that the Jeep owner had so conveniently left for him at the cabin. He'd wait for a few hours. Then, hopefully, the Radfords would be home without the boy, and he could have his night's entertainment and sweet revenge.

***

Dewey Steller was hopping mad. The first thing he'd noticed as he and his two buddies drove up to his remote cabin was that the garage door was open and his Jeep was gone. He parked and ran inside, followed by his friends. He was a short, overweight man around fifty-five years old. This cabin had been his dream ever since his wife had left him ten years ago. He spent all the time up here that he could, and like this evening, he often brought friends with him.

The second thing he noticed was that his front door had been forced open. That was infuriating. The third thing he noticed was that his stash of beer was gone, every last can of it! He had more in his truck, but not enough for the three days he and his buddies had been planning to spend here.

His well-stocked cupboards had also been raided, and someone had slept in his bed. Infuriating anger turned to outright rage. His buddies shared his fury. "We gotta call the cops," Dewey said, glad that they hadn't yet begun drinking, because he didn't want them to find him under the influence when they came to investigate.

One of his pals told him to try his cell phone. "There's no reception up here," Dewey said. "We're going to have to drive back down to report it. Duchesne is where the sheriff's office is so we'll go there. They'll probably want to come up here and look at the damage, so I guess our night is ruined. Sorry, guys. I just hope whoever stole my Jeep doesn't wreck it. It's not new, but it runs great."

So the three Salt Lake City men piled into the truck and headed for Duchesne to report the crime to the local sheriff's office.

***

"What is this place?" Ember asked as Bentley pulled in front of the cabin and stopped the truck. "It looks nice."

"Is this yours, Bentley?" Cedrick asked, his eyes wide with wonder.

"No, but I'm thinking about buying it."

"How much property comes with it?" Ember asked.

"Forty acres," he said.

"Room enough for horses," she said. "Evie told me you guys were going to get horses. She said you were looking for a place to board them."

"I'd found a place, but since I'm alone now, I think I'd rather have my horse up here, when I get one."

"This is quite a ways out of town," Ember reminded him, "but I can see how you'd like it. I guess you can spend your days off from the highway patrol working on the yard or building sheds or whatever."

"I will do that, but I'm not sure I'm going to keep working as a trooper. Evie's death has taken the pleasure of that job right out of me."

"Oh no! What will you do?" Ember asked.

"I'll write the books I've always wanted to write," he said. "This would be the perfect place to do that."

"I didn't know you wanted to write," Ember said. "What genre?"

"Mystery and suspense," he responded. "I actually already have one book about a fourth of the way done. Evie was reading it a chapter at a time. She really liked it. She encouraged me and had faith that eventually I'd find a publisher. In the meantime, I'll live on my savings. And maybe I can get a few jobs doing handyman work. I can live cheap, so I'll be all right."

"Bentley, you have Evie's insurance money. You will use that, won't you?" Ember suggested. "It wouldn't make sense to let it go to waste."

"I guess, but I feel guilty about it. It was her money, not mine," he said.

"Bentley, as terrible as it is, she's gone now. Please use the money. I have no doubt that Evie would want that. Cedrick and I want that too, don't we, Cedrick?"

"Yes," he said. "Just don't let Uncle Claude steal it like he stole mine."

That turned the tide of the conversation. "He took all your money?" Bentley asked.

"All but about a thousand dollars, but I don't know what he did with it," the boy said. "I don't know what I'm going to do now."

"Cedrick, I will take care of you. I'll quit school and find a job and an apartment for just the two of us," Ember said.

"Evie told me that becoming a lawyer is your dream," Bentley said as they wandered through the cabin.

"When Cedrick finishes high school, I can always go back to law school," she said with determination in her voice.

Bentley felt terrible. He and Evie were seriously planning to take Cedrick into their home. But now, that wasn't possible. Or was it? He suddenly had a thought—inspiration really. "Ember, he can come live with me. You can finish law school. I'd feel better about using Evie's money if I was sharing it with Cedrick. Would you be okay with that, Cedrick?"

The boy's eyes lit up. "Would we live here in this cabin?"

"We could. That's for sure."

"And could I have a horse too?"

"Of course. Then you and I could go riding." They had arrived at the back door and stepped out onto the deck. Bentley waved his arms in a large circle. "Look at all this country out here. We could have nice long rides."

Bentley glanced at Ember. She didn't look very enthused about his idea. "Ember," he said, "don't you think that Cedrick and I could live here?"

"Of course you could," she said. "But I'm thinking about his schooling. You'd have to take him into Duchesne every day for school. That would be hard for both of you, especially in the wintertime."

"I don't need to go to school," Cedrick said. "I have a friend who is home-schooled. His mom says it's a great program. Most of it's online with real teachers helping. And Bentley could help me when I need help."

"But you will need friends," Ember countered.

"We'll go to church in Duchesne. This cabin is still part of my current ward. There are some great young men in our ward. I'll see to it that he gets to his activities," Bentley said. "And you could finish your law degree."

"Like I said, I could do that later," she reminded Bentley.

"I'm sure you could, but you also need to think about the fact that you will want to get married at some point, and that could change everything," Bentley said. "As for me, I will probably be a bachelor for life, but you mustn't tie yourself down and fail to give yourself a chance for happiness—like Evie and I had."

"I'm so sorry you lost her, but I *can* take care of Cedrick."

"Please, Ember. You can come visit me a lot, but I want to live here with Bentley. I promise I'll work hard at my studies. You know I will. And I'll be happy, and he won't be so lonely. You could even ride one of our horses sometimes. You'd like that, wouldn't you?"

"Of course. Evie and I loved to ride," she agreed. Ember looked at the two of them in the growing dusk and finally said, "But he's my brother. I'm all he has."

"In a way, he's my brother too," Bentley responded.

Ember stood up and stepped off the deck into the back yard, which was really just an open space with lots of pinion and cedar trees that covered most of the forty acres and extended into the distance beyond that. Bentley and Cedrick sat there quietly, letting her think. She stood there for at least five minutes. Bentley prayed silently, asking the Lord to help her make the right decision.

Finally, she turned and walked back to the guys. "I have three weeks before I have to be back at school . . . if I go. Can I think about it?"

"Of course, but I promise, Ember, I would take good care of him, and he's right. I wouldn't be so lonely then. I could write while he studies," Bentley said. "And if I get some handyman jobs, he could help me."

Slowly, Ember nodded her head. "It could work. But let me pray about it for a few days. Should we head back to town?"

"Sure," he said.

"Please, Ember. I want to live here with Bentley," Cedrick said as they walked back through the cabin to the front door.

Back in the truck, as they drove toward town, they talked about what Uncle Claude had done.

"Aunt Faye left him," Ember said. "But she says she'll pay back the money that Claude stole. She says she'll get a job and save part of her earnings to give to Cedrick."

"Faye is a good woman, but she's not the one who stole it. She shouldn't have to do that. I'll take care of Cedrick if you decide it's okay," Bentley said.

"Let me tell you what I've done so far about the theft of Cedrick's money." Ember told Bentley about her law professor and their conversation. Then she relayed the details about the lawyer who would help Bentley collect money from the insurance company that insured Evie's car, and the attorney could help collect from Silas Villard's insurance company as well. "Claude is going to have to pay Cedrick back, once he gets out of prison," she concluded, "because that's where he'll be going."

"We'll see," Bentley said. "But I will call that lawyer. Thanks for the idea."

"Bentley," Ember said after they'd driven for several minutes in silence. "You should buy the cabin. If you do, then I think the Lord will let me know that it's okay for Cedrick to live with you."

Bentley had a feeling that she'd been praying the past few minutes, as he had. She would make the right decision. In fact, he thought she was about there, and he was grateful.

Before he did more about the cabin or his job, he had his beloved Evie to bury. That was going to be the most difficult thing he'd ever done. How he wished he still had Evie.

CHAPTER FOURTEEN

SILAS WAS ELATED LATE THAT night when he discovered that the trooper's truck was back at the house. They probably just took the boy back to his home like he'd figured. He decided to wait until all the lights were off, maybe around two in the morning, and then do what—in his vengeful mind—he had to do. He rubbed his hands together in malicious anticipation, and then took off in the stolen Jeep. "I'll be back, Trooper!" he called softly but angrily out the window as he drove past the house.

At two o'clock, the lights were all off. It was time. He checked to make sure no lights were on in the neighboring houses before he got the can of gasoline from the Jeep. He quietly poured gas around three sides of the house before he ran out near the back. He figured that should do it, so he struck a match, tossed it, and ran out of sight where he could watch but not be easily seen.

***

Twy came running into Bentley's bedroom, barking fiercely. "What is it, Twy?" he asked as he was roused from a deep and much-needed sleep.

Twy didn't need to answer; Bentley smelled smoke and heard the crackling of flames.

He shot out of bed, grabbed his cell phone, and ran into the spare bedroom. "Ember, get up!" he shouted. "The house is on fire. I'll grab Cedrick. Hurry!"

Ember reacted immediately, jumping from the bed and rushing into the front room. Bentley had already grabbed Cedric from the sofa where he'd been sleeping and was steering him toward the back door. "Out back," he shouted to Ember. "Go fast!"

The fire was already entering the front of the house, and flames were rising high on every side. Thankfully, there wasn't a wall of flames at the back of the house. The three of them ran that way. By the time they reached the back door, flames were already licking at the door frame.

"We've gotta run!" Bentley shouted.

The three of them ran through the door and made it into the back yard. Flames had caught on Ember's nightgown. Bentley tackled her to the ground and rolled her over until the flames were extinguished. Then Ember checked the three of them for burns on their bodies while Bentley called 911.

"I think we're all okay," Ember said, her dark hair reflecting the flames.

Bentley was looking around for his dog, and he panicked when he didn't see him. "Twy!" he screamed hoarsely. "Come here! I hope he's not still in the house . . . I need to check."

"You can't do that, Bentley," Ember said desperately. "It's too dangerous. You can't go back in there."

"He saved our lives," he argued, but as he stepped closer to the back door, he knew there was no way he could go back in and live. "Twy, come here," he called again, hoarse from smoke inhalation.

Twy finally appeared from deeper in the backyard. He had something in his teeth.

"What is it, Twy?" he asked the young dog as relief washed over him.

Twy shook his head, growled, and then let Bentley take what appeared to be part of a denim shirt from his mouth. He shoved the cloth in the pocket of his pajamas and shouted, "We need to get around front to my patrol car. Whoever this cloth belongs to probably started the fire. He might still be out here somewhere."

He heard sirens as they rounded the burning house at a safe distance, although the heat was still intense. He had intended to get into the patrol car and make sure enough help was coming when he realized his keys, including the key fobs to both the truck and the patrol car were in the house. He couldn't get into either his patrol car or his truck. And he was sure Ember's keys were also inside the house. "Get down and stay here," he said to Ember and Cedrick. "I have a hose in the back. I'll try to put out some of the flames."

"Be careful, Bentley, and watch for whoever did this," Ember called after him.

Bentley sprayed the hose at the house, but the small amount of water from the hose did almost nothing to slow the flames in their deadly advance. However, cops and a fire truck showed up within minutes, so he dropped the hose. The firefighters began to spray huge streams of water at the front of the house, driving back the flames. He rejoined Ember and Cedrick beside his patrol car.

"Are you sure an arsonist really caused this?" Ember asked as neighbors ran out of their homes.

"I'm sure," he said. He was pretty confident he knew who had done it too, and the thought was terrifying. He pulled the piece of cloth Twy had brought him out of the pocket of his pajamas and looked at it closely from the lights of the fire truck. "This has blood on it. Twy attacked whoever started the fire."

***

Silas sat in his Jeep two blocks away, cursing the dog that had torn the flesh of his shoulder. He'd had to beat the dog off with his fists, but it had taken part of his shirt sleeve when it finally ran away. He hadn't dared stay too close for fear neighbors would wake up and see him. The house was burning beautifully, and it truly excited Silas.

"That's what you get for messing with Silas Villard. Enjoy your burning death," he muttered as blood continued to seep from his shoulder.

He'd watched until a bunch of cop cars and a fire truck passed right by where he was parked in the stolen Jeep. It angered him. They were spoiling his fun. But he didn't dare stay longer. So he started the Jeep and drove away, angry that he couldn't watch his beautiful fire until the last flames were extinguished.

***

The firefighters were good at what they did. They were able to save some of the back of the house, but that was about all. Bentley's neighbors were great. They helped find some clothes and shoes for Bentley, Ember, and Cedrick. So at least they had something to wear until they could get to a store. Bentley's supervisor, Sergeant Carter, came, as did Detective Parker.

Sergeant Carter told them he'd see what they could do about getting keys, or rather, key fobs for the vehicles. He and Hank Parker both asked if Bentley had any idea what had caused the fire.

"It had to be arson," Bentley said. "It was burning the worst from the out-side on three sides when my dog woke me up. He saved our lives, and he brought me this." He handed the bloody piece of denim cloth to the detective.

"This is bloody, and it's fresh," Hank said as he examined the torn cloth. "We can get DNA from this and identify who did it. I wonder how badly he's hurt."

"Not badly enough, I'm sure," Bentley said with disgust.

"We've got officers going to all your neighbors' houses to see if anyone saw anything or anyone," Hank said.

Just then a deputy ran up and asked Hank to come with him. Hank left on the run with the other officer. When he came back ten minutes later, he said, "Three different people saw a brown Jeep leave the area shortly after the firetruck and our officers showed up. We've been looking for one that was reported stolen last evening from a cabin just a few miles from where Silas left the last stolen oil-field truck he burned."

"So it's Silas again." Bentley moaned. "I had a feeling it was."

"It looks that way," Hank said. "We have everyone looking for the Jeep, but Silas seems to have a way of avoiding capture. But we'll give it our best shot."

"He wants me dead, doesn't he?" Bentley asked.

"He probably thinks you already are," Hank said.

"Unless he saw us escape from the house," Bentley countered.

"Yeah, there is that," Hank agreed. "But I think, based on where the Jeep was spotted, that he probably didn't. It would actually be best if he thinks you're dead."

Bishop Green showed up at what was left of the house a few minutes later. "Oh, Bentley, I'm so sorry. What happened here?"

"Silas Villard is what happened," Bentley said bitterly.

"What is with that man?" the bishop said.

"He's pure evil. Bishop, I'd like you to meet Ember and Cedrick Skeed, Evie's brother and sister."

"It's nice to meet you both. I just wish it didn't have to be under these circumstances," Bishop Green said before turning back to Bentley. "It looks like you lost about everything."

"My stuff doesn't matter. I lost *everything* when I lost Evie."

"I know you did, and I'm so sorry. But financially, this will be a tough thing."

"Not as bad as it could have been. Evie was not only the sweetest person I know, but she was also one of the smartest. She insisted that we buy renters' insurance. Because of her, I bought it a month before we were married. There's nothing here that I can't replace. I know the owner has insurance as well."

"You can't replace pictures and important documents," the bishop pointed out.

"All our important papers, including our marriage certificate, baptism certificates, and so on, are in a safety deposit box at the bank. Again, that was Evie's doing. Of course, my driver's license and credit cards will need to be replaced, and so will Ember's," Bentley said. He turned to Ember. "I'm sorry."

"Don't be. It's not your fault. What about your photos?" Ember asked.

"We scanned all our old photos, and of course everything from the past few years in both of our lives are stored in the cloud. I can reprint the burned pictures when needed. Even our wedding pictures are in the cloud."

"Was that Evie's idea as well?" Ember asked.

"Of course it was."

"Let's talk about what your immediate plans are," Bishop Green said. "The three of you will need a place to stay for a few days. And you'll need to get some clothes. I can help with that. Sister Green and I have plenty of room in our house, so why don't you come over in a little bit. You can park your vehicles there too. There's plenty of space."

"We have no car keys." He nodded at the still-smoldering heap that used to be a comfortable white house. "They're all in there."

"You got out with some day clothes on, I see," the bishop said.

"No, some neighbors loaned us what we have on. We came out in our pajamas. We left them at the Christiansens' house. But Ember's nightgown is not in good shape. It caught on fire coming out," he explained.

"Are you okay, Ember?" Bishop Green asked with concern.

"Bentley put me on the ground and rolled me over before the fire burned my skin. I'm fine, thanks to him," she said.

Cedrick finally spoke up after silently listening to the adults for the past few minutes. "Maybe we can stay in the cabin, Bentley."

"What cabin?" Bishop Green asked.

Bentley explained, and then said to Cedrick, "It's not mine yet."

"You are going to buy it, aren't you, so we can live there?" the boy insisted.

Ember spoke up then. She said with conviction in her voice, "Yes, he's going to buy it, and yes, you can live with him if that's what you want."

Cedrick squealed and hugged Ember. "It'll be good if you'll come visit us a lot."

"You know I will, Cedrick." She winked at him. "Especially if you let me ride your horse." She turned to Bentley and said, "I'll call Kamryn in a few hours and ask her to bring some clothes for me when she comes. Cedrick has some clothes at my apartment too, so she can also bring his. We'll have to get the rest of his things from Aunt Faye's house sometime. Also, I have a spare key fob to my car hanging in my kitchen cabinet. Kamryn can bring it. Then we'll take you to Vernal or Heber or someplace where you can buy what you need."

"It sounds like you have it figured out, Ember. You seem to be a lot like your sister," Bishop Green said.

"We were very close," she said before choking up.

"They even bought the same kind of car." Bentley paused and glanced at his sister-in-law as fresh tears ran down her cheeks.

The bishop spoke again. "Come get in my car and we'll take you to my place. My wife will have a nightgown you can wear, Ember."

"Bishop Green, it would be great if you would give Ember and Cedrick a ride to your house. I want to stay here for a while longer. I can walk over later," Bentley said. "It's not that far."

"I understand," the bishop said. "We'll stop and get your nightclothes from your neighbor. They'll be on a bed in one of the spare rooms when you get there. My wife will put a note on the door so you'll know which room."

He thanked the bishop and then watched with low spirits as Bishop Green and the others drove away. He couldn't believe how shattered he was, how utterly lost and alone he was, even with Evie's brother and sister here.

At least he'd be able to take care of Cedrick. He was grateful that Ember had agreed to that. The two of them would make a life together.

CHAPTER FIFTEEN

Deputy Tren Bobbly was one of the officers searching for the stolen brown Jeep. He spotted it driving east on Highway 40 about ten miles west of Duchesne. He called it in to the dispatcher and said, "I need backup."

His boss, Sheriff Goldman, responded to his call for aid. "Don't try to stop him yourself, Deputy. Just keep him in sight, and some of us will come."

"Okay," the deputy responded.

He followed for about a mile before the Jeep suddenly stopped and the driver jumped out with a rifle in his hands. He aimed and fired at Tren, who ducked as the windshield shattered, glass hitting him. Tren slammed on his brakes as another shot hit his pickup, causing steam to rise from the radiator. He cranked the steering wheel and slid to a stop sideways on the road. He jumped out, using his truck as a shield. Yet another bullet struck the truck.

Suddenly worried that the gas tank might blow, Bobbly ducked and ran for the side of the road, rolling into the grass as another bullet chased him, throwing chipped pavement toward him. He felt a sharp pain in his neck as another shot rang out, but he ignored it as he crawled down the shallow embankment and pulled out his pistol. He bravely, albeit foolishly, lifted his head and fired at the man from the Jeep. He heard a yelp, and the man dove back into the Jeep. Then to Tren's horror, the Jeep turned and headed straight for him.

He jumped to his feet and ran for all he was worth to some cedar and pinion trees thirty or forty feet away. The Jeep drove off the road toward him, but the deputy managed to get behind a large tree, and the Jeep swerved and drove back onto the road. Tren shot at the fleeing Jeep again and took out the back window, but the driver sped up and drove away, once again heading west.

Tren limped back toward his damaged truck, thankful that it hadn't blown up. He was out of shape and had tired too quickly. He was breathing hard, and his neck hurt really badly. He vowed right then and there that he would stick to a solid workout schedule. He was winded and bruised from when he hit the ground, and he could feel some pain on his face as well as his neck. He reached up to his face and his hand came away bloody. Blood also ran down his neck. Fragments of glass had hit him, but he didn't think it had done too much damage. However, whatever had hit his neck worried him. It could have been a chunk of pavement, or maybe a bullet had grazed him.

The door of his truck was hanging open. He reached inside, grabbed his mic, and reported his location. "My truck is shot up, and I can't drive it. The last I saw of the brown Jeep, it was headed west. I blew out the back window and maybe more windows, and I'm sure I hit the driver with at least one shot."

"Are you okay?" Sheriff Goldman asked.

"I'm bleeding. I got hit by something. It was either a bullet or chunk of pavement. But I don't think I'm hurt too badly."

Sheriff Goldman said, "Dispatch, send an ambulance." Then to his deputy, he said, "Sit down and wait for us. I'm not far away, and Hank is right ahead of me."

***

Hank Parker had been one of the first to respond to the call for help from Deputy Bobbly. To his surprise, Bentley had said, "Let me go with you."

He didn't hesitate, because Bentley was, after all, a sworn peace officer. "Okay. Get in and let's go. I have a spare pistol under the seat. I'll grab it for you so you'll be armed."

The two of them dashed for Hank's gray Ford F150 truck. Hank retrieved the spare pistol and then handed it to Bentley before he jumped behind the steering wheel. Hank put the truck in gear, and they headed west, with Sheriff Goldman not far behind them.

Hank and Bentley spotted Tren seated on the pavement beside his truck as they pulled up. A car was parked next to it, and someone was kneeling on the ground beside him. Tren's head was slumped forward.

Hank leaped from his truck with Bentley right behind him. The Good Samaritan stepped back and uttered something about the officer's neck.

Hank knelt and said, "Tren, it's Hank. Can you lift your head?"

"Something hit me in the neck," the young deputy said as he slowly lifted his head, wincing in pain.

There were three separate wounds, one much worse than the other two. Each was bleeding. There were also numerous glass cuts on his face and arms.

"Relax, Tren, help is on the way," Hank assured him.

Tren looked at Bentley, who was also on his knees. "I'm sorry about your wife and your home," the young deputy said. "It was Silas Villard. He got away, but I think I hit him with a shot from my pistol."

Sheriff Goldman had joined them, and he said, "Maybe you hurt him badly enough that he'll wreck when he gets up the road a ways."

"I hope he does," Tren mumbled.

"An ambulance is on the way," the sheriff said. "Hank, you and Bentley go west and see if you can overtake Silas. Go fast. I'll wait here with Tren." He turned to the man who had stopped to help Tren. "Thank you for your help, sir. Did you by any chance see the shooting that took place here?" When the man told him he didn't, the sheriff thanked him, wrote down his name and phone number, and told him he could get on his way.

Hank and Bentley jumped in the truck and sped up the dark highway.

"Tren is lucky to be alive," Hank said. "I think at least one of those wounds was from a bullet, and it's awfully close to his carotid artery. The other wounds are probably from chunks of pavement and glass."

"I just hope he'll be okay," Bentley said.

***

Silas realized that he needed to ditch the Jeep. But he wasn't about to head out on foot again. The cops would probably come after him with dogs. An idea popped into his head as he saw the lights of a semi up ahead. He parked the Jeep in the middle of the road and popped the hood. He pretended to be checking something under the hood.

As he had hoped, the semi stopped. "Hey, mister. Can I help you?" the driver, a small man around sixty years of age called from his window.

"Yeah, my Jeep quit on me right here in the road. I need a ride to town." Silas hated to give up the rifle, but he was out of bullets. He had a pocket full of ammunition for his pistol, which he held in his right hand out of sight of the truck driver.

"You look like you're hurt," the man called down.

"Please, I am. Give me a ride," Silas begged, or pretended to. He wasn't about to give the man a choice in the matter.

"You can't leave your car there in the middle of the road," the driver said as Silas circled around the front of the truck, keeping his pistol out of sight.

Silas managed, despite the pain, to climb up to the passenger door of the semi and open it.

"Seriously, mister," the driver protested. "We can't leave your car there. Someone could hit it."

"The lights are on. Any driver that's not asleep will see it," Silas said as he settled himself into the seat. "It's quit working, so I can't move it anyway."

"Somebody could get hurt," the driver argued.

At that point, Silas, already in a dangerous mood, produced his pistol. "That somebody will be you if you don't shut up and drive this rig. And don't be flashing lights at anyone or you'll be dead. And don't think I won't shoot you. I've killed two people already tonight and wounded another one. You can be next if you want. I can drive this thing if I need to, but I'd rather not, so get this thing moving."

***

The driver, Burke Printz, could see that the man was dangerous. "You got it," he said. And he drove the big rig forward.

About a mile later, a cop with flashing lights in the grill approached from the east. "Don't try to signal that cop or you will die, and so will the cop."

Burke glanced at the hijacker. The gun was being held on Burke with the stranger's right hand. His left hand looked pretty useless. It was bloody and hanging limply at his side. Burke did as he was told, but then the cop suddenly slowed and turned. It sped up behind the truck, the lights still going. The cop hit his siren.

"Don't stop," the hijacker said.

"I've got to. If I don't, I'm sure they'll set up a roadblock ahead somewhere and give us no choice," Burke said.

"Then I'm crawling into the sleeper. Don't you dare give me away or you and the cop will both die, and I'll take this truck," the hijacker said. "I can drive it with one arm."

"I gotta stop, but I won't give you away," Burke promised. He was terribly frightened, but he knew he had to control his emotions. His life depended on it.

"My gun is on you. One false move . . ." The threat in the man's voice convinced Burke that he did indeed need to keep the man's presence in the truck a secret.

***

Hank approached the driver of the truck and climbed up on the steps. "Something wrong, Officer?" the driver asked. "I know I wasn't speeding. What did I do?"

"You didn't do anything wrong. I just have a quick question, then I'll let you go. Did a brown Jeep pass you going west anytime in the past few minutes?"

"No, but there's one parked in the middle of the road back there two or three miles. The back window is shattered. I slowed down, hollered out the window, but got no response. There was no one around."

"Are you sure someone wasn't lying down on the seat inside?" Hank asked.

"I can see into cars pretty well from up here. Of course, it was dark, but I didn't see anyone. I think whoever was driving it must have walked away."

"Okay, thanks, you can be on your way," Hank said.

"I can't say there wasn't somebody either dead or sick in the Jeep," the driver added.

"I'll check it out. Thanks for the information."

"Is something wrong?" the driver asked.

"We needed to talk to the driver of the Jeep. He may have seen something down the road a ways where an officer was shot. Thanks again. Drive carefully," Hank said and swung down off the truck.

***

"I guess the Jeep is ahead two or three miles," Hank told Bentley once he was back in the car. "Let's go have a look."

The Jeep was right in the middle of the highway, just like the trucker had said. Hank and Bentley approached with caution, but the vehicle was unoccupied. Shining a light into its interior, Hank spotted quite a bit of blood. "It looks like Tren hit him all right, or he could be bleeding from when your dog bit him . . . or both. Where in the world has he gone now?"

"A few cars have gone by," Bentley said. "I wonder if he hitched a ride with someone."

"That's possible, I suppose." Hank was thoughtful for a moment. "The truck I stopped . . . the driver seemed okay, but I wonder if . . ." He trailed off again.

"What are you thinking?" Bentley asked.

"It's possible Silas was in the sleeper unit of the truck. But the driver seemed as cool as a cucumber. He didn't appear frightened or nervous," Hank said. "Actually, now that I think of it, he was too calm. I think we need to have a look at that truck again. Stopping him might be dangerous, both for officers and for the driver, if Silas is in it. But first we need to get this Jeep out of the road."

"I'll see if it will start," Bentley volunteered.

The Jeep wouldn't start, so the two officers pushed it to the side of the road and shut the lights off. "What now, Hank?" Bentley asked.

"Two things: we need to get a wrecker here to tow the Jeep, and we need to see if we can stop that truck up the road a ways. I'll get on the radio now. Let's head back that way."

CHAPTER SIXTEEN

SILAS VILLARD WAS NERVOUS. EVEN though the truck driver had done exactly what Silas had ordered him to do, he was worried that the cops might think he was in the truck. He had no way of knowing if the driver might have signaled something with his eyes or . . . who knew what? Silas didn't trust anyone.

If the cops attempted to stop the truck again, it would result in a shootout, and even though he knew he could take the truck driver and some cops out, they might still get him. He'd already been shot once in the same shoulder that stupid dog had bitten. He didn't need to be shot again. And the trooper had paid with his life for what he did to him. He needed to decide what to do, and it needed to be soon.

They had driven past the spot where he'd had the shootout with the deputy. There were cops there and an ambulance. The truck driver did exactly as he was told and drove right on by. But a mile down the road, Silas told the trucker to stop. Then Silas made the driver jump out of the truck and run into the trees. He shot a couple of rounds behind him to make sure he kept going. Then he put the truck in gear and drove down the road a short distance. It was hard driving with only one good arm, but he managed.

When he saw headlights coming from behind him, he pulled the truck toward the side of the road, then steered it farther and jumped out. The truck turned over as it bounced off the road. The car he'd seen coming stopped, and the driver, a woman of about thirty, stepped out of the car.

"Are you okay?" she asked him in alarm. "I saw what happened. I'll call for help."

Silas pointed his gun at her. "You are not calling anyone, woman. You are going to give me a ride. You drive. I'll keep my gun on you, and you'll take me where I tell you to. You'll live to tell your kids about it if you do what you're told."

The lady sat still when he got in her car. They headed east, in the direction she'd been driving.

"I will be ducking whenever anyone comes toward us. You will not try to attract attention."

She murmured that she understood. When they reached Duchesne, he had her turn south onto Indian Canyon Highway.

He'd wanted to get off Highway 40. He felt like he was free of danger again once they were headed south, but he was also in a lot of pain. The woman commented on his bloody arm, and he told her he was fine, to just drive where she was told.

**

The sheriff and several other officers headed back toward Duchesne. Hank led the way, driving fast and hoping to catch up with the semi, as that was the only thing they could think to do. They passed several cars going west and a couple of trucks, but Hank was interested only in the truck going east. They hadn't gone far before Bentley said, "There's a guy coming out of the trees by the side of the road."

"We better check him out. It could be Silas." Hank radioed the other officers and told them that he and Bentley were going to stop and see what the deal was with the guy that was approaching the road. The two officers pulled their pistols as the man stepped out onto the road and waved his arms frantically.

"That's not Silas," Bentley said, disappointment in his voice. They put their weapons away.

"Silas certainly wouldn't want us to stop," Hank agreed.

He pulled over, and the man rushed to the pickup. "That guy you wanted stole my truck," he shouted. "I'm lucky he didn't kill me. He was in the sleeper with a gun pointed at my head when you stopped me. I lied to you, but I didn't dare tell the truth or he would have killed me and you too. At least that's what he told me."

"Hop in," Hank said. He grabbed the mic and told the other officers what had just occurred. So they all sped past him. He asked the dispatcher to broadcast the description of the truck but to tell anyone who spotted it to follow and not attempt to stop it until there was plenty of backup.

Sheriff Goldman came on as soon as Hank stopped speaking. "You can cancel that," the sheriff told the dispatcher. "We've found the semi. It's on its side just off the highway."

No officers approached the wrecked semi until enough backup had arrived. At that point, they ordered Silas to come out, and when he didn't, Hank cautiously approached, climbed up on the side of the cab, and shone a flashlight inside. He didn't see anyone, so he lifted the door up, climbed in, and checked the sleeper unit.

"It's empty," Hank announced as he exited the cab.

Bentley dropped his head into his hands. "He got away again." He moaned. "He must have hijacked another vehicle. He could be anywhere now."

Burke Printz, the driver of the truck, said, "He's hurt pretty badly. His left arm was almost useless, and it looked to me like it had bled a lot."

Hank briefly explained what had happened to Silas.

"I knew the guy was bad," Burke said. "He reeked of beer, and . . . well, there was something about his eyes." He shook his head. "I'll stay with my truck until a semi wrecker can come. I'm sure glad I didn't have a load."

One of the highway patrolmen, who had joined the others at the spot where Bobbly engaged in the shootout, was assigned to stay and deal with the truck wreck while the others went back into town to decide what the next course of action would be. Bentley had Hank drop him off at Bishop Green's home.

Discouraged, brokenhearted, and exhausted, he trudged toward the door. To his surprise, Ember opened it.

"Finally," she said. "I couldn't sleep, so I was waiting for you. Are you okay?"

"I guess I'm as good as I will be for a long time," he said.

"Where have you been?" she asked.

Bentley shook his head and then briefly explained what he'd been doing.

***

Silas's latest chauffeur was a pretty woman of about thirty with long black hair and a small scar on her face, but she was very quiet. He liked it that way. If she didn't talk, she couldn't disturb his thoughts. But after about thirty minutes, as they reached the top of Indian Canyon, that changed.

"You probably don't care, but my name is Rosalyn Dishner," she said. "My mother is expecting me at her home in Roosevelt about now. I'm coming to visit her from California where I live. She'll be worried and will likely call me anytime now because my mother is a worrier."

"Too bad," he said, angry at her for speaking. "Let me see your phone."

"It's in my purse on the floor by your seat. You moved it when you got in," she said. "Please get it for me so I can tell her that I'm okay but will be a little late, that I've been delayed. I promise I won't tell her why I'm delayed. I won't mention you."

He picked the purse up, found the phone, rolled down his window, and tossed it out. "There. You won't have to lie to your mother because you're not all right. Do I look like a nice guy to you?" he said with a snarl.

"No, but you could try to be one," she said. "Where am I taking you?"

"Just drive and shut up. I'm thinking."

"Sorry, but I've been quiet for the past half hour. Now I would like to talk. What is your name, and why are you doing this to me?"

He looked at her in the dim interior of the car. She should be shaking with fear, but for some reason, she wasn't. It was disturbing to him. He wanted her to fear him, to know that he was in control. She wasn't cooperating like he wanted, and it infuriated him.

"I'm not doing anything to you, just letting you give me a ride, but if you don't shut up, I will do something, and you won't like it when I do," he said fiercely, waving his pistol at her.

"I'm not afraid of you," she responded flippantly. "You just like to act nasty, but you probably really aren't mean. My guess is that you are in some kind of trouble, but that's not any of my business, and frankly, I don't care."

"You're right, woman; it's not your business, but since you ask, you might be interested in knowing that so far tonight I have killed two people and injured another one. But they had it coming. People need to leave me alone," he said. He figured she'd be scared now. She should know that her life was in his hands. He had a gun, and he would not hesitate to use it if he decided he needed to.

"What did the people you killed do to you?" she asked as she slowed down, driving carefully down the winding highway on the far side of Indian Canyon. "It must have been pretty bad."

Silas was getting very angry. What was the matter with this woman? Didn't she have the good sense to fear him? "One of the people I killed this morning was a trooper, and believe me, he had it coming. His wife was just in the wrong place."

Surely now she'd be afraid. But she calmly asked, "How did you kill them? Did you shoot them?"

"I burned their house down with them in it," he said savagely. "Now shut up or I'm going to take your car, and you won't enjoy what I do to you when I do."

"You may be right, but please, at least tell me your name," she said, still seeming unperturbed.

What was with this woman? Silas wondered.

To his dismay, she started to laugh. "You really think you're bad, don't you? Frankly, I don't think you've killed anyone. I don't think you have it in you."

Now she was taunting him. He became more furious. "Listen, woman—"

"I told you my name is Rosalyn. Don't call me 'woman.' Call me by my name, mister. And if you'll tell me your name, I'll call you by it instead of mister. Sound fair?" she asked.

"You want to know my name?" he shouted. "Fine! I'm Silas Villard. That should scare you."

"Thank you, Silas," she said. "It's nice to know your name. What was your grandpa's name, the one you burned to death?"

"So you know who I am, do you? Now you know that if I decide to, I can kill you and take your car, and there ain't a thing you can do about it."

"Really," she said as she pulled off the road at the intersection of Indian Canyon Highway and Emma Park Road. "You want my car? Take it." She opened her door and stepped out. He did the same. She rounded the car and stopped when they came face-to-face.

He was holding his gun and pointing it at her pretty but infuriating face. "I'm going to shoot you for having such a smart mouth."

Silas didn't get the chance. Rosalyn moved so swiftly that he didn't even see it coming. She knocked the pistol loose from his hand, and then she proceeded to beat him severely.

"I could kill you now if I wanted to," she said, "but I don't. You'll get what you have coming to you. I'll be leaving now."

He listened as she got in the car, trying to get up but not having much luck. The car drove off, and there was nothing he could do to stop her. "I'll find you again, woman," he hissed through his bleeding mouth and lips. "And when I do, I'll make you pay for what you've done."

Then Silas Villard passed out.

***

Rosalyn Dishner was not afraid of someone like Silas, but others certainly had plenty of reason to fear him. She was a professional fighter, and she was very, very good. She turned around at that intersection so she could search for her phone and call 911. Silas needed to be arrested, because she had no doubt that he'd done what he said he had earlier that night. She knew about him because her mother had told her on the phone about the terror the man was causing in Duchesne County.

At least he didn't have his pistol anymore, because she did, and she intended to turn it over to the sheriff in Duchesne. But right now, she needed her phone.

CHAPTER SEVENTEEN

Rosalyn thought she knew about where Silas had thrown her phone out of the car, but she couldn't find it and didn't want to take too long. There was no traffic, which was disconcerting, because if she could flag someone down, maybe she could borrow a phone to alert the authorities as to where they could find this killer. She drove back to where she'd left him unconscious on the pavement, determined to wait there until someone came along who had a phone. Then she'd wait until he was taken away.

Her mother would be worried, but there was nothing she could do about that until she was able to borrow a phone. As she approached the intersection again, expecting to see him lying there, a surprise awaited her: Silas Villard had vanished.

That didn't seem possible. There had been no cars coming down the canyon; otherwise she might have thought one of them had picked him up. She stopped and got out with her lights shining on the spot where she'd left him.

Rosalyn spotted a little blood there, which was to be expected, as he'd had an injured left shoulder. The way she'd pounded him might have caused it to start bleeding again. Of course, she'd also caused his face and nose to bleed. She looked closely around the ground and spotted a tooth. She must have knocked it out.

Did he manage to walk away? She doubted it, but she guessed it was possible. Nothing else made any sense. She berated herself for not throwing him in her car and driving him either back to Duchesne or on to Price. Not that she owed the guy anything. After all, he had been about to kill her when she beat him up. She shrugged. There was nothing she could do about it now, but she did want to report it, because if her mother was right, he was wanted by the police for killing his grandfather. As to what he claimed to have done to the trooper and his wife, it might or might not be true. She hoped it wasn't.

Rosalyn decided to wait there for a while. Streaks of orange light peeked over the mountains. Daylight was not far off, so the traffic should pick up, she reasoned. Surely someone would come along soon.

After a few minutes, she saw lights coming toward her from the direction of Indian Canyon. As the lights got closer, she could tell it was a semi. She stepped out of her car and flagged it down.

When she explained what had happened to her and what she'd done to Silas, the semi driver told her, "There has been traffic on the radio discussing a semi hijacking west of Duchesne. They said he wrecked it, and they think it was intentional. I saw the semi on its side. I slowed down at that spot, but it looked like it had rolled very slowly. There was a highway patrol car there. I figured things were under control, so I drove on."

She chuckled mirthlessly, then said, "He hijacked me when I stopped to see if I could help him. That was not a wise decision on his part. You see, I'm not afraid of guys like him if I get close enough. I'm a professional fighter. I only regret now that I didn't load him in the trunk of my car after I'd beat him up so I'd know where he was while I went back up the road to find my phone. When I couldn't find it, I came back here, expecting to see him still lying here, but he's gone. Will you let me use your phone to call 911?"

"Sure. My name's Mack, like the semi I drive," he said. "I guess my folks could tell when I was born that I would be a truck driver someday. Makes sense since my father was one. Dad drove a Mack just like I do now, and I rode many a mile with him in his Mack as a kid." As he was rattling on, he'd pulled out his cell phone. "Here you go. Make however many calls you need to. Oh, I didn't catch your name."

"I'm Rosalyn," she said and then called 911 and gave them what information she had. Then she decided to call her mother. She knew she'd still be up worrying because she'd expected her to show up in the wee hours of the morning. Without giving any details, she explained that she'd been delayed. "I'll be along in another hour or so," she assured her mother.

With those calls made, she thanked Mack and headed back toward Duchesne and Roosevelt. She hoped her widowed mother was no longer worrying about her.

***

Silas woke up wondering where he was, but it didn't take long to realize he was in an emergency room somewhere; however, he had no idea how he'd gotten there. A doctor was working on his shoulder, the one that had been shot and bitten by a dog. He had to get out of here. But he waited.

The doctor told him his shoulder would be okay now that it had been disinfected, stitched up, and bandaged. He'd been given something for pain, so he felt pretty good. All he needed was time to heal.

"I'm Doctor Garver. What's your name? We didn't see any ID on you," the doctor said.

Silas wasn't about to tell him his true name, so he said, "I'm Dan, but how did I get here?"

"A young couple brought you in and left you with us. They said they found you unconscious up by Emma Park Road when they approached the intersection from the south. Even though they'd passed through Price already, they picked you up and brought you here. They didn't think they should wait for an ambulance as it might take too long, and they didn't want you to die there. They thought you were hurt worse than you are, although it looks like you did get pretty roughed up. You even lost a tooth."

"That was nice of them," Silas snarled sarcastically as he reached in his mouth and discovered that the doctor was right. He'd lost a tooth. "I wouldn't have died."

"You don't have to take that tone, Dan," Doctor Garver said sternly. "You aren't hurt too badly, but they didn't know that. They were just helping you. You ought to be grateful, especially with that bullet wound and dog bite on your shoulder."

"You would be angry too if you'd been treated the way I have been lately," Silas said.

He recalled what had happened. That girl had beaten him up. How, he had no idea, but he would make her pay. First he needed to get away from this hospital before any cops showed up, because he figured some would. That was the way his luck ran.

"What happened to you?" Dr. Garver asked. "I need it for my report. There's extra protocol involved when someone comes in with a bullet wound."

Silas tried hard to think what he should say. It only took him a minute to concoct a believable story. "My car broke down at the top of Indian Canyon. These two dudes, big guys, offered me a ride into Price. I got in with them, but then they started talking all tough and threatening me, so I asked them to let me out, told them I'd walk. They did stop, right there where that couple found me, but when I got out of their car, they did too, and they beat me up. I'm a pretty good fighter, but I didn't stand a chance against two guys that big. They had a dog with them, and it bit me. They must have robbed me, because my wallet was in my pocket, and it had several hundred dollars in it. And my cell phone and my keys." Silas forced a groan of frustration. "I wouldn't be surprised if they went back up and stole my car. So now do you see why I'm angry?"

"I certainly do, Dan. It's very understandable. However, being beat and bitten doesn't explain a bullet wound."

"They must have shot me for fun when they left me there," Silas said with a growl.

"In that case, you're lucky to be alive," the doctor said. "I'm going to have some x-rays taken to see if you have any broken bones, and it wouldn't hurt to do a brain scan and make sure you don't have a concussion. If everything checks out okay, you can call someone to come get you."

"How can I call? I told you they took my phone," Silas grumbled.

"We have phones here that you can use. And based on what has happened to you, I'm going to have a police officer come speak with you," Doctor Garver told him. "They'll look for those guys and your car. But they will need descriptions."

"No need to bother the cops. They'll never catch the guys anyway," Silas said. "I'm sure they got my car running and that it's long gone."

"I'm sorry, but I'm obligated to. But first, let me step out and arrange for someone to take you to get the x-rays and scan." With that, the doctor left the room.

Silas, though he was feeling weak and still in pain despite the drugs they'd given him, also left the room. They tried to stop him at the desk, but he said, "I'm okay now. I need to be somewhere." He left the hospital as they continued to try to call him back.

It didn't take him long to hot-wire an older-model car that was in the parking area. Then he was on his way. He needed to find a place to hide out, but first he needed to get as far from Price as possible.

***

It had been a very long and terrible night. Detective Hank Parker felt awfully bad for Bentley. The young trooper had been through more than anyone should ever have to endure. Yet Hank knew that Bentley and his sister-in-law and her little brother were truly blessed to be alive, because there was no doubt that Silas Villard had meant for them to be burned to death in the house fire. If it hadn't been for Bentley's dog waking him up, they would have been.

The sheriff had told his deputies to go home because there was nothing more they could do now, and they all needed rest. Two of them stayed out as they were scheduled to be on duty anyway, but Hank and the others headed for their homes.

Hank had just crawled into bed beside his wife when his phone rang.

"Hank, this is Sheriff Goldman. Sorry to bother you already, but we just got a call from a dispatcher in Price. They think our suspect may be in the emergency room there. I know this is asking an awful lot, but would you mind heading over the mountain?"

"Not a problem. I'd love to put that guy in cuffs—very tightly applied," Hank said.

As Hank dressed, the sheriff was explaining what he'd learned. "He forced a woman to drive him up the canyon after he stopped her on the highway near the wrecked truck. She's the one who made the first report. She's a professional mixed-martial-arts fighter, and she whipped him soundly, I guess."

The sheriff then explained to Hank what had transpired after that, summing up with, "The next call we got was from a doctor who told us that some guy with no ID was in the emergency room there. He claimed to have been beaten up and robbed by two burley men and bitten by their dog. But he had what the doctor thinks was a bullet wound in the same arm as the one with the dog bite. That fits with what Burke Printz, the truck driver, told us. The Price police are responding there now to see what they can learn from him. It may or may not be Silas, but I think it's worth checking out. Hopefully, the hospital will detain him until you can get there and see whether it's him."

Hank made good time driving over the mountain, but when he walked into the emergency room in Price, he was told the guy had left on his own before the cops from Price got there. So the cops also left. They asked Hank if he wanted to wait and talk to Dr. Garver. Hank decided that as long as he was here already, he might as well wait.

A few minutes later, a doctor entered the waiting area. "I'm Doctor Garver. Why don't you come back where we can have some privacy while we talk? You're here from Duchesne, is that right?"

Hank offered his hand. "Yes, I'm Detective Hank Parker," he said.

After the two men were seated, Dr. Garver told Hank what the man he'd treated claimed had happened. "I take it that you're here because there's more to the story than that."

"Actually, it's a much different story," Hank said. "If the man is who I think he is, then he had a busy night. The bullet wound was not from two tough guys like he told you. He shot a deputy who shot him in return. He's a very dangerous man."

"I've got a few minutes, so why don't you tell me about it?" Doctor Garver said.

So Hank told him the horrifying story of Silas Villard's succession of deadly crimes.

"I wish I'd known all of this," Dr. Garver said with a frown. "I'd have sedated the guy, and he'd still be here. Do you have any idea where he might have gone after he walked out of here?"

"No idea, but one thing I think we can count on is that someone here at the hospital is going to discover they are missing a car," Hank said as he rose to his feet. "I need to be going, but thanks for seeing me, Dr. Garver."

With that, Hank walked out of the hospital. When he reached his truck, he realized he was starving. So he got in and drove to a restaurant where he could get some breakfast.

CHAPTER EIGHTEEN

DESPITE THE LONG AND STRESSFUL night, both Bentley and his sister-in-law were awake before ten. Cedrick was still sleeping. The bishop's wife fixed them some breakfast, and before they'd finished eating, Cedrick joined them. The boy was hungry and seemed relatively unshaken after the near-death nightmare of the night before.

"I called my roommate a few minutes ago," Ember said as they ate. "She said she'll be here in three hours, by one o'clock or so. I told her to meet us here. Is that okay?"

"I don't know where else she could meet us," Bentley said. "I'm kind of without a home, but I do want to walk over to my house in a while and have a look around. Do you know if my dog is here?"

"Yes, the bishop brought him over. He's in the back yard." Ember smiled. "Twy is my hero. He saved all three of us."

"He's a pretty good dog," Bentley agreed. "I'll take him with me."

The doorbell rang, and a moment later, Sister Green ushered Sergeant Carter into the kitchen. She offered him some breakfast, but he said, "Thanks, but I'm fine. I just need to talk to my trooper."

Sergeant Carter seemed to know most of what had occurred the night before and during the early hours of the morning. He shared what he knew.

"So he got away again!" Bentley's voice shook with anger. "Who knows where he'll pop up next and who else he'll hurt. The guy is a menace. I hope to never see him again because I'm not sure what I'd do. Maybe I should be afraid of him, but I'm not."

They talked for a while, and then Sergeant Carter said, "I had keys made for your patrol car and your truck. I didn't get any for you, Miss Skeed. I'm sorry."

"That's okay," she assured him. "I didn't expect you to. My roommate is bringing my spare set to me in a little while, and she's bringing some clothes for me and Cedrick."

"Thanks for your help, Sergeant," Bentley said. "I'll clean my stuff out of my patrol car, and then you can take it. I need to go to the credit union and get new credit and debit cards and some cash. Then I'll drive to Vernal and buy some clothes and footwear. I'm in borrowed things right now, and I'm grateful, but the fit isn't great. My feet hurt." He attempted a smile but couldn't quite manage it.

"Wait, Bentley, why are you going to clean out your patrol car?" Sergeant Carter asked with a look of concern.

"I won't need it after today, Sarge," Bentley said. "My job got people killed, including my wife. I can't do this anymore. If it were just me who was in danger, I could face it, but it's not. I've learned that in the worst possible way. I'm not going to stay with the highway patrol. I'll get my resignation to you in writing when I get a chance to borrow a computer and type it up."

"Don't do this, Bentley. You're a great trooper. We need you," Sergeant Carter said in a pleading voice. "Let's give it some time for you to think it over."

"I don't need more time. My mind is made up," Bentley said. "I'm sorry to leave you short-handed, but I'm serious about this."

"What will you do?" Sergeant Carter asked. "You've got to stay busy, and you need an income."

"I have some ideas, so you don't need to worry about me. You've been great to work for, and I will always be grateful to you. Please don't take this personally," Bentley said earnestly.

Sergeant Carter appeared to be stunned, and Bentley felt bad about that, but he had no desire to get back in that patrol car again. He didn't say so to his sergeant, but his first priority now was Evie's little brother. He was determined to make a good life for the kid. He glanced at Cedrick, who seemed to understand and smiled at Bentley.

Ember rose from her seat and came around to where Bentley was standing, ready to leave. "You are a good man," she said. "My sister was lucky to have you."

She put her arms around Cedrick, and suddenly the two of them burst into tears.

"I'll be back in a little while," Bentley said, fighting to keep control of his emotions. "Sergeant Carter, I'll meet you at what's left of my house and give you back the keys after I get my personal stuff out of the patrol car."

"I'll give you a ride over and back," Sergeant Carter said.

"I'll ride over with you if my dog can too, but you don't need to hang around. I'll have my truck since you got me a spare key fob. I'm going to spend a few minutes there by myself," he said with a frown. "I need to do that."

There wasn't much in the car that belonged to Bentley. His backup .38 Chief revolver was the main thing he wanted out of the car. He felt naked without a weapon on him, fearing that Silas would come back—which he most likely would—if he found that he had failed to kill him. Other than that, there were a few papers and a jacket, which he needed. He put the jacket on, strapped the gun to his belt, and held the keys out to Sergeant Carter.

To his surprise, tears shone in Carter's eyes. He took the keys, then grabbed Bentley by the hand and shook it firmly. "You can still change your mind, you know," he said as the handshake ended. "You are one of the best officers I've ever worked with."

"Thank you, Sarge. I appreciate all you've done for me."

After Sergeant Carter drove away, Bentley walked into the front yard and stood there gazing at the blackened mess that had been his and Evie's joyful home. Oh, how he missed her. Alone now, he let the tears flow, and great sobs racked his body. Twy rubbed against his leg, and Bentley dropped to his knees and threw his arms around his dog. "It's just us now, Twy," he sobbed.

After a while, he became aware that he was no longer alone. Neighbors had gathered around. He stood up, wiped his eyes, and accepted condolences from a half dozen people. He still wanted to be alone, so after thanking them, he wandered around to his back yard, the one he had so recently worked in. The neighbors drifted back to their homes, giving him the solitude he so badly needed.

Twy seemed to sense his mood and stayed with him rather than playfully running around the way he usually did. Bentley opened the utility shed, looked in it, and then shut the door again. Nothing in there belonged to him. It was all the property of the people he'd rented from. He had nothing left here but his truck, and he decided it was time to get in it and drive to the bank. He needed cash and new credit and debit cards.

***

Silas Villard was in Salt Lake City where he'd ditched the stolen car and taken yet another one. When he got the engine running, the radio was on. He was surprised when he heard his name mentioned. The newscaster said that law enforcement officers were on the lookout for him and that he was considered armed and dangerous.

He smirked. Yes, he was dangerous, but he was not armed. He had to find a way to rectify that problem soon. The next thing he heard shocked him:

The newscaster mentioned that he had burned the home of a highway patrol trooper in Duchesne, but all three people in the house had escaped unscathed. Credit was given to the trooper's dog for alerting its master to the danger, enabling them to escape through the back door. Then the newscaster mentioned that the other two people were the trooper's sister-in-law and brother-in-law, who had gone to Duchesne to be with the trooper because of the death of Evie Radford, who had been killed by what authorities suspect was an intentional act of revenge. After all, Silas Villard had threatened the trooper and said he would soon wish he'd never arrested him. The newscaster then briefly described the accident.

Silas sat back in the stolen pickup, pumped one fist, and grinned wickedly. He hadn't known that the blonde girl who had driven in front of him had been the hated trooper's wife. Well, at least he'd gotten some revenge. And yet, in his mind, he still blamed her for the accident. How could it be an intentional act by him when she had caused it?

"You're next, Trooper Radford," he said aloud. "I'm glad your wife is dead, but you need to die too, and so does that miserable dog of yours. I can't believe he bit me, but I'll shoot him after I shoot you, Radford." No one could hear his rant, but that didn't stop him from verbally venting his anger.

He drove off in the stolen pickup truck, thinking about the fact that he hadn't seen Radford and the others come out of the house when it burned. He had not even known the kid was there. Of course, the location where he had hidden to watch the fire burn didn't give him a view of the entire house.

He was more or less sober now, and he knew he had to avoid getting arrested again. For now, until the search for him had died down, he'd travel out of state and lay low. But he was not through with Trooper Radford for causing all his troubles. He also wanted to figure out the identity of the woman who had assaulted him; he would make her pay as well. He even wanted to get back at the chubby deputy sheriff who shot him. But all that would have to wait. Trooper Radford was the one he had to get first, and he swore that he would.

***

Ember had been watching for Bentley through the front window and hurried out to meet him, followed by her little brother. "Can you wait until Kamryn gets here to go to Vernal?" Ember asked Bentley after he'd climbed from his pickup and approached the bishop's house.

"I feel so uncomfortable in these borrowed clothes, Ember. It will be two hours before Kamryn gets here. I'll come back as soon as I can though. I'm sorry."

She looked at his swollen eyes and knew he'd been crying. Her heart broke for him. She understood his need to go to Vernal now, so she said, "Be careful, Bentley, and watch out for Silas."

Bentley lifted his jacket, exposing his pistol. "I'm armed now. I'll be okay."

"Bentley," the sweet voice of his twelve-year-old brother-in-law said. "Can I come with you?"

"Sure. If it's okay with your sister," Bentley said.

Tears wet Ember's eyes. "I think that would be nice. Can Twy stay here and keep me company? I think I'll walk over to your house for a little while."

Bentley nodded. "Climb in, Cedrick. Twy, you stay with Ember." The dog looked up at him, then he looked at Ember, and the amazing animal walked over and stood beside her. "That's right, big fella. You'll take good care of her, won't you?"

Ember put a hand on the dog's head and watched as Bentley and Cedrick drove down the street. She was glad to see the two guys spending time together, since it seemed she would be able to go back to law school while Bentley took care of her precious little brother.

"Come on, Twy," she said. "Let's go for a walk."

As Ember walked around what was left of her twin sister's home, she couldn't stop the tears. Evie was such a wonderful girl and had married an amazing man. She was wounded by the heartbreak she saw Bentley going through. He didn't deserve that any more than Evie had deserved to die.

She stood in the back yard and prayed that God would bring Bentley comfort and would help her through this tragic affair as well. She also thanked the Lord for sparing their lives in that terrible fire. She even thanked Him for the wonderful dog that had been the means of waking them in time to escape the deadly flames and smoke.

To Ember's surprise, she also found her prayer turning to the man who had killed Evie and tried to kill Bentley last night. She asked God to help him find his way to a better life and asked that someday she would be able to forgive him. Finally, she prayed that Cedrick and Bentley would be able to help each other make it through the weeks, months, and years ahead. As she said amen, a feeling of peace filled her, and she thought she heard a soft voice say, "It'll be okay. I'm where I should be."

It sounded like Evie's voice, even though it had been so soft it was hard to believe it was real, but she believed it. And she felt even more comfort. "Evie, I love you, dear sister. And I will always remember you."

CHAPTER NINETEEN

SILAS VILLARD WAS NOT WITHOUT acquaintances who were his kind of people. He'd helped others commit various crimes; now he was in need of help, and he knew just who to turn to. Lonnie Defollo lived in Magna. He'd spent a few years in prison while in his twenties. He was in his thirties now, and although he still lived a life of crime, he was very careful and had managed to stay out of jail for several years.

Silas didn't know if he'd find Defollo at home, but if not, he'd wait around until he showed up. Luckily, Lonnie was at home when he pulled up in front of his house shortly after noon. He knocked on the door, and Lonnie answered. "Villard, what are you doing here?"

"Hello to you too," Silas said. "Ain't it okay to visit an old pal?"

"Sure, but first tell me, is that pickup on the street hot?" Lonnie asked.

"So what if it is?" Silas asked.

"I don't need no trouble, Villard, and right now, from what I hear on the news, you are trouble. I can't be hanging around with you. You got more cops after you than I've ever had after me. You need to move on."

"I will," Silas said meekly, "but I need a favor first."

"I got no favors for you that might get me into trouble," Lonnie warned him. "I guess I could hear you out, but it's gotta be quick, and I don't want that stolen truck sitting in front of my house."

"I'll pull it around back, if that makes you feel better."

"You do that, then come in the back door. You can have a beer while you tell me what you think I can do for you. I'll decide if it's worth the risk."

Silas was not in a position to argue, and a beer sounded great. He had worked up a mighty big thirst since his last drink.

He parked out of sight behind Defollo's house and entered by the back door. Defollo waved him into the kitchen and handed him a cold bottle of Coors. He chugged half of it down.

"Thanks, brother," Silas said, and then he burped. "That was badly needed."

"There's more, but go ahead and tell me what you think I can do for you before you get another one. And I want you gone before my buddies come," Lonnie Defollo said bluntly. "So out with it; what have you come begging for?"

"I need a pistol and ammo for personal protection and some cash so I can get out of state for a while," Silas said.

Lonnie leaned his hardback kitchen chair back on two legs and studied Silas for a moment. "If I give you what you want, what do I get in return?" he asked.

"I got cash in my house in Myton, and I got several twelve packs of beer."

"You got any guns there?" Defollo asked.

"Of course I do, but I got 'em hidden under the floor," Silas said. "You never know when the cops are gonna go snooping around. The cash is with the guns. I've learned to be very careful."

"Not careful enough, it seems to me. How much cash you got stashed there?"

"Close to a couple grand. If you'll give me a thousand today and a decent pistol and some ammo, you can have it all," Silas said generously.

"Anybody else know about your guns and cash?" Defollo asked.

"Nope, nary a soul," Silas said. "It's your secret now."

"Somebody bailed you out on that DUI mess you got yourself into," Lonnie noted. "You owe him too, don't you?"

"Not really; he owed me," Silas said. He'd promised to pay the guy back, but he had no intention of doing that.

"I see," Lonnie said.

"I ain't guilty of that DUI. That hotshot trooper made a bogus arrest on me."

"Maybe, maybe not," Defollo said with a grin. "I hear your old grandad wouldn't bail you out. You could have told him about the cash, and he probably would have done it, don't you think?"

Silas shook his head. "I thought he'd help me, but when he refused, I had to get a friend to bail me out. I didn't mean for him to die, Lonnie."

"The friend you say owed you, does he know about your stash?" Lonnie asked, looking at Silas with suspicion.

"Nope, just me and you. That other guy and me are even now."

"I suppose the trooper had it coming, so you killed his wife and tried to kill him by burning his house down last night." It was not a question. Lonnie had obviously heard the news.

Silas squirmed uncomfortably. "I didn't know the blond gal was his wife, and anyway, it was her fault, not mine. She drove right in front of me. There was no way I could miss her. It was an accident, pure and simple."

"The cops don't believe that," Lonnie said. "Now, back to business, 'cause I gotta get you on your way. You have cash and guns at your house. Why don't you just go get your stash?"

"Hey, Lonnie, you know better than to ask that. The cops will be watching my place."

"So you want me to go get it?" Lonnie said, cocking an eyebrow.

"Only after things cool down," Silas told him.

Lonnie nodded, but his eyes were cold. "I'm inclined to help you, but if I do, if I go to your house and the goods ain't there, you know what will happen to you, don't you, Silas?" Lonnie gave him a dangerous look. "You may be able to outrun the cops, but if me and my buddies come after you, we will find you. And when we do . . ." Lonnie pulled a finger across his throat.

Silas swallowed. Maybe coming to this guy hadn't been such a good idea after all, but he was desperate. "It will be there," Silas assured him.

"Okay, you get a thousand from me, one pistol, and a box of ammo. Then I get whatever I find at your house after the heat is off you. Is that a deal?" Lonnie asked.

"You got it."

Lonnie handed Silas another cold beer. "Stay put. I'll be right back."

He was gone for about five minutes, and when he returned, good to his word, he had a pistol—a 9mm Ruger. He placed it on the table in front of Silas, and then he put a box of bullets there, and finally, a wad of cash. Silas picked up the cash and started to count it. "No need to count it, Silas. If you don't trust me, you can get out of here right now and leave the gun and the money."

Silas swallowed hard, and then said, "I trust you, Lonnie."

"Good, then take what I'm lending you and get out of here. The pistol works, and it's untraceable. And remember, what's in your house is mine to get when I feel the time is right."

"You got it. Thanks, Lonnie." Silas chugged the last of the beer, stuffed the money in a pocket along with the box of ammo. Then he shoved the gun inside his belt. "One of these bullets has Trooper Radford's name on it."

Lonnie shook his head. "I got a bit of advice for you, Silas. Forget about the cop. You already got your revenge with the death of his wife and burning his house, so leave the state and don't come back. You need to put this behind you. So go. I don't want to ever see you again."

"Sounds like good advice," Silas said, not meaning a word of it. A minute later he was back in the stolen truck and pulling onto the street. He'd like to have had a third beer, but Lonnie was in a mood, and he didn't want to press his luck. For now, he'd go to California where he could hide out among the masses until the heat was off him in Utah, and then he'd be back. Trooper Radford wasn't going to get off so easy.

He stopped at a gas station and fueled up the stolen truck. It cost him forty bucks. He had no ID, so he couldn't buy booze. That made him angry, but he'd steal some after a while. He was good at that. He'd stolen plenty but had never been caught.

Back in his truck, Silas took time to count the money. He fumed when he discovered that Lonnie had shorted him a couple hundred bucks. He thought about going back and making Lonnie pay for lying to him, but he realized that could be a bad mistake. So he drove onto the roadway, but he was not a happy crook, to say the least. He hated being double-crossed. Maybe someday, he'd find a safe way to make Lonnie pay for cheating him.

***

It had cost Bentley a pretty penny, but he had some nice dress boots, a pair of sturdy work boots, several shirts and pants, and all the accessories he would need for a while. He bought Cedrick a new set of clothes as well, right down to the cowboy boots and felt hat like the one he'd bought for himself. The two of them had formed a bond as they traveled.

Bentley was going to enjoy having Cedrick around. He was a tremendous young man. Despite how badly his Uncle Claude had treated him, he did not say one bad thing about him on their entire trip. He was a lot like Evie. They'd had good parents who'd raised them right. Bentley wished he could have known them.

Bentley committed himself to keeping the boy safe and happy and making sure he got a good education.

When they pulled up in front of Bishop Green's house, Cedrick bounded out of the truck and met his sister as she was coming out of the door, a very attractive young woman walking beside her.

Bentley took his time getting out of the truck, but he heard Cedrick say, "Look at what Bentley got me. He says he's going to make a cowboy out of me."

Ember smiled and looked him up and down. "He's sure got you looking the part, little brother. Hey, you've met Kamryn before, Cedrick. She'll be here until after the funeral. She brought a bunch of clothes for us, and we can drive my car again." She showed Cedrick the key fob.

By then, Bentley had joined them. Ember introduced Bentley and Kamryn to each other.

"I'm so sorry for your loss," Kamryn said, and to his surprise, she reached out and gave him a brief hug.

When she stepped back, he said, "Thanks for agreeing to sing at Evie's funeral. Ember tells me you have a wonderful voice."

Kamryn beamed. "Thank you both. I'm glad I can do this for you and for Evie."

"Sister Green is holding lunch for us," Ember said. "Are you guys hungry?"

Cedrick scowled. "Of course we're hungry, Ember. Aren't we, Bentley?"

"You got that right, little brother," Bentley said fondly.

"You know what's awful?" Cedrick said, looking at Kamryn. "There was a whole bunch of good food in Bentley's fridge that got burned up."

Bentley couldn't help but chuckle, and so did the young ladies. "I hadn't even thought about all that food being destroyed, but now how am I going to get people's pans and casserole dishes back to them? I don't even have the list of who gave me what. I was so careful about writing that because I knew Evie would want me to be."

They had approached the house, and Bentley knocked softly on the door.

"You don't need to do that," Ember said. "Sister Green told us to just come and go as we need, to make ourselves at home."

So he opened the door and held it as the others filed in ahead of him.

"It's good to have you back," Sister Green said with a kindly smile. "Lunch is ready, so wash up and come into the kitchen while I set it on the table."

Bentley, despite himself, enjoyed the two young ladies' constant chatter. They weren't Evie, but they were sweet. He found himself relaxing as the lunch proceeded. He had just finished eating when his phone rang. He pulled it out of the pocket of his new western shirt and looked at the screen.

"It's Rachel Delaney," he said as he accepted the call. As he said, "Hello, Mrs. Delaney," Ember held a finger up, signaling that she had something to say. "Just a second," he said.

"Please tell her you are buying the property," Ember said with a gentle smile.

He nodded an acknowledgment and then spoke into his phone. "I was going to call you in a few minutes."

"Bentley, I know about the fire. I'm sorry, and I'm glad you and your in-laws got out safely. I understand you have your dog to thank for that."

"Yes, Twy is our hero," he said, glancing at the others.

"As well he should be. Now, to business. If you want the cabin, it's yours, and you can move in right away. I spoke to the owners, and they said to tell you that under the circumstances, you can have it for a hundred thousand and live in it while we're waiting to close on it. You can swing that, can't you?"

"Yes, I can. That's an amazing price. Thank you so much."

"If you can come to my office this afternoon, we'll get the paperwork started."

"I can come right now if it's okay with you."

"That's perfect," Rachel said.

Bentley ended the call. "I guess I need to go see Rachel. Despite everything, the Lord is blessing me. Well, he's blessing me and my buddy Cedrick."

"I know I shouldn't ask, but how much are you getting it for?" Ember asked.

He told her, and her mouth dropped open. "You're kidding. That place is worth five times that, at least."

"Like I said, Ember, I'm blessed, and Cedrick and I can move in later today. It's a big cabin, all furnished with bedding and everything we need. You guys will stay with us, won't you? There's plenty of room."

"Of course," Ember and Kamryn said in unison.

"Great. Now I'd better get over to my realtor's office."

"Just one thing, Bentley," Ember said, raising a finger again.

"What's that?" he asked.

"Evie would want you to use the insurance money. So please, tell me you will and that you'll pay cash for the property."

"I suppose she would want that, especially since it's also for Cedrick."

Bentley managed to control the tears, but it was very hard. Making this move without Evie and so soon after her death made him feel guilty, but he shrugged it off. He had a feeling she'd approve.

CHAPTER TWENTY

Silas had fumed and stewed and drunk a lot of stolen beer after reaching California. He was restless. He decided he couldn't wait any longer to get rid of Trooper Radford, so in one stolen car after another, he made his way back to Utah. He had attempted to change his looks again by dying his hair—which was growing out a little—a light blond. He also dyed the short beard so that it was the same color as his hair. His shoulder was healing fairly well, and he could use his arm again without too much pain. He was anxious to get to Duchesne, where he would do what had to be done, and then return to California where no would ever find him.

**

The cabin was large enough to accommodate four people quite comfortably. Kamryn gushed over how pretty it was, and then she said, "I could live in a place like this. It's great."

The ladies fixed some dinner while Bentley and Cedrick explored the outdoors. Bentley could envision a few nice sheds for animals and another to keep hay in, which he would have to buy.

"We can build some sturdy corrals and tight sheds right here fairly close to the cabin," he told Cedrick, "so in cold weather we can easily slip out and feed our animals."

"Will we have more than just horses?" Cedrick asked with shining eyes.

"I think we might," he said thoughtfully.

"Like what?"

"Oh, I was thinking about a milk cow or two. And we'd have to have a bull before too long as well. But I don't want a mean one."

"Wouldn't one cow give more milk than you and I could drink?" Cedrick asked.

"I'm hoping so," Bentley replied.

"Then why would we need two?" Cedrick asked.

"Because a cow can't be milked the month or two before she calves. So we'd need to have one to alternate. Does that make sense to you?"

"I guess so, but what would we do with so much milk?" Cedrick asked, his brow scrunched in confusion.

"When I was growing up, my mother made cheese. I think we could try doing that. I don't remember exactly how she did it, but I'm sure we could find instructions on the Internet."

Cedrick grinned. "I like cheese. But what else?"

"We can churn our own butter from the cream," Bentley said, and he explained how that process worked.

"Cool, and would that use all the milk?"

"Probably not. So I was thinking that we could build a pen for a pig or two and we could use the extra milk to help feed them."

"Would we eat the pigs?" Cedrick asked, wrinkling his nose.

"You like bacon and ham and sausage, don't you?"

"Well, yeah, of course. And that's where bacon and sausage come from."

"You're right, and also ham and pork chops."

"Wow!" Cedrick's eyes got big. "So, I guess it would be good if we had pigs," he said, then his countenance fell, and he rubbed his eyes. "Evie would have loved it here, don't you think? She loved animals. I wish it was going to be me and you and her."

Bentley put an arm around the boy's shoulders and said quietly, "So do I, buddy. So do I."

***

The day of the funeral arrived, and they all dressed and went to town, just as they had the night before for a viewing. That had been rough. Evie, who had been dressed in her temple clothing by Ember and Kamryn, had looked like an angel in the coffin, and despite himself, Bentley had broken down and cried like a baby. He did it again at the second viewing an hour before the funeral. The comforting arms of two young ladies with tears in their eyes encircled him. Cedrick was standing at the casket, looking sadly at the beautiful, peaceful face of his sister. It was all very difficult. And it still didn't seem like it was real.

Bentley wished Evie would suddenly sit up and climb out of the casket and hug him.

The funeral itself was a beautiful tribute to Evie and to the Savior. Ember's talk was wonderful. He was glad he'd asked her. When Ember and Kamryn went up to perform the musical number, Cedrick grabbed hold of Bentley's arm. As Kamryn began to sing, Bentley got chills. He didn't ever remember hearing someone sing so beautifully. He hoped that Evie's spirit was here listening. She had loved good music, and like Ember, Evie was an accomplished pianist.

When the song ended, it was totally quiet in the chapel. Kamryn's glorious voice had brought the Spirit to the meeting so strongly that the entire congregation was weeping. It was another fitting tribute to Evie, a young woman whose life had been exemplary and who was loved by all who knew her.

After Evie's grave was dedicated in the cemetery at the mouth of Indian Canyon, there was a meal at the ward meetinghouse for friends and family. Aunt Faye had come to the funeral and had joined them at the church for the meal. There was no sign of Uncle Claude, for which Bentley was grateful. He would have only brought a bad spirit with him, and they didn't need that. Aunt Faye was very sweet as she spoke tenderly with young Cedrick.

"I'd like to still have you live with me, but I have a new job that will make it hard to be there for you when you need me," Faye said.

"That's okay," Cedrick said. "I'll be living with Bentley now."

"How will you manage that, Bentley?" she asked with obvious concern as she wrinkled her brows. "As a trooper, you never know when you might be called out, and that would leave him alone."

Cedrick shook his head and glanced at Bentley and then back at Faye. "He isn't a trooper anymore, Aunt Faye. He's going to write books, and we have already found a great homeschool program for me."

"I won't let his education suffer," Bentley said as he entered the conversation. He then explained how it was all going to work.

"I'm glad to hear that," Faye said. "I plan to save money from my new job. I will soon have part of my income to give to you to make up for what Claude stole from you. You'll need it for your mission fund and for college."

"You don't need to do that; you didn't take it," Cedrick said sincerely.

Before Faye could respond to that comment, Ember asked, "What did Claude use the money for? That was a lot of money."

"My attorney, the one I hired for our divorce, learned that he'd been going to Wendover to gamble. That's how he used it. Actually," she amended, "that's how he *lost* it."

"Cedrick's right, Faye," Bentley said. "It's not your responsibility to pay it back. Don't worry about it. I'll take good care of Cedrick and help him save money. You need to take care of yourself."

Ember spoke up in agreement, but she looked at Bentley, who shook his head ever so slightly. Bentley was pretty sure she knew what he was thinking. Sure enough, she said nothing about the steps she'd taken to hopefully bring Claude to justice. They had discussed it earlier and thought it was best to keep it quiet, because at this point, nothing was certain. Faye didn't need to have that added worry on her plate.

After the meal, Bentley, Cedrick, Ember, and Kamryn returned to the cemetery where the grave had now been closed and flowers placed on top of the mound of dirt. As they stood there and talked quietly among themselves, they paid no attention to the occasional car or truck that passed the cemetery on the adjacent highway. Evie's grave was close to the highway, but their minds were focused on Evie and how much she was missed. They didn't even notice one older-model car that had once been blue but was now mostly rusted as it slowed down and then stopped on the shoulder of the road.

"I need to be on my way, guys," Kamryn said. Her car was parked behind Bentley's pickup on the side of the highway. "Ember, you should stay here as long as you feel like it. When do you think you might return to the apartment?"

"I think I'll stay another day or two and help Bentley and Cedrick get the cabin set up nicely. I want them to be comfortable," Ember said. "Aunt Faye has agreed to stay at the cabin a day or two also."

"That's good of her. I'll be going then." Kamryn stepped around Bentley with arms outstretched for a hug when a shot rang out. She screamed as she fell forward into Bentley's arms.

Bentley laid her on the ground and pulled out his pistol, looking for the shooter, whose shot had, he was certain, been meant for him. "Help her, Ember," he cried out as he saw the rusty old blue car with a blond-haired man leaning over it, a pistol in his hand.

Bentley dropped to the ground and rolled away from the others as another shot rang out, hitting the ground about a foot behind him. He rolled onto his knees and fired a quick round at the shooter. The gun flew from the man's hand, but he dove to the ground and picked it up. Then he piled into the rusty car and sped off toward Duchesne.

Bentley had no doubt that it was Silas Villard again, his looks altered so he would not be easily recognized. Had Kamryn not been hit, he would have rushed to his truck and taken chase. "Cedrick, call 911," he said as he threw his phone to his brother-in-law. "We need an ambulance and the police."

Then he dropped to his knees beside Ember, who was applying pressure to a wound in Kamryn's back. It was bleeding badly. Kamryn was moaning. It looked bad, really bad.

Bentley helped Ember and Faye, who had joined her on the ground. "You'll be okay," he said to Kamryn, even as he doubted his own words. He could not believe this was happening.

Kamryn lay on her stomach with her face turned to the side.

"Let me and Aunt Faye put pressure on the wound while you give her a blessing," Ember said.

Ember and Faye took over again, and Bentley silently prayed that he would be inspired to say the words the Lord would have him say. He felt the Spirit strongly as he promised her she would recover from the injury. It was a short, heartfelt blessing. After he lifted his hands from her head, she murmured, "Thank you, Bentley." Then she took a deep breath and faded into unconsciousness.

Cedrick handed the phone back to Bentley. "Help is coming."

***

Silas was cursing up a storm as he drove east. His shooting hand was bleeding where the trooper's bullet had creased it. At least he'd been able to recover the gun he'd gotten from Lonnie. But he had missed the trooper. That stupid girl, whoever she was, had stepped in front of the trooper just as he fired. He didn't know who she was, and he didn't care. He hoped she'd die. What angered him was that his next shot had missed as the cowardly trooper dove to the ground and rolled away instead of facing him like a man. The fact that Silas got hit in the hand was nothing but a lucky shot or, for him, an unlucky one.

Once more, he'd been foiled. But he would be back. He would get the trooper the next time. In the meantime, he had to get away. He turned off Highway 40 just moments before a cop screamed past with wailing siren and flashing lights. He briefly saw the cop in his rearview mirror, but the cop didn't seem to pay any attention to him. Thankfully, Silas knew the backroads of this county. They couldn't catch him now. He knew where he had to go.

***

Bentley was the only one who saw Silas and the car, but it wasn't much more than a glimpse. He knew the guy had blond hair and a blond beard, both short. The car was old, rusty, and bluish colored. He gave Hank those descriptions without much hope that Silas would be captured. The guy was slippery as an eel.

Kamryn was still unconscious when the EMTs loaded her into an ambulance and headed to the hospital in Roosevelt. Once they left the cemetery, Bentley took Ember, Faye, and Cedrick with him and drove toward the hospital.

"I'm so glad you gave her that blessing," Ember said at one point on the ride over. "At least we know she won't die."

Bentley looked at her. "Giving blessings is a hard thing, Ember. I try to listen to the Spirit, but I wonder if what I said to Kamryn was what I wanted rather than what the Lord wanted."

Ember's eyes grew wide. "You mean you think she might die?"

"I hope not, but after what I've been through the last few days, my faith is kind of weak. We've just got to pray and ask the Lord to sanction the blessing. But of course, whether He does or not is something we can't force. God does what He knows, in the big picture, is best."

Faye spoke up from where she was sitting with Cedrick in the back seat. "I believe your blessing was inspired."

Ember sobbed. "We've got to have faith that Kamryn won't die too. Like Aunt Faye, I believe in your blessing. I know you were inspired. She's a magnificent girl, Bentley."

"I told her this earlier, but her song at the funeral was beyond beautiful. She sang like an angel," Bentley said.

From the back seat they heard Cedrick's voice. "Maybe she's gonna be an angel like Evie is."

That innocent statement sent chills through Bentley. He glanced at Ember again and could see that she had reacted the same way. She had goose bumps on her arms and was furiously rubbing them. When she spoke, it was to Cedrick. "Kamryn will live, Cedrick. We've got to believe it. I trust the blessing that Bentley gave her."

"Then I do too," the boy said with an earnestness that raised more goose bumps.

CHAPTER TWENTY-ONE

As they approached the hospital, a Life Flight helicopter was rising from the helipad behind it. "That's probably taking Kamryn to a larger hospital. She must be hurt worse than the doctors here can handle. Take me back to my car, and I'll drive to wherever they're taking her," Ember said.

"We need to find out where that is first," Bentley said. "We'll go inside and find out. But I'm going out too, and where I go, Cedrick goes."

"I guess we do need to find that out," Ember agreed. "All of us should go."

It took a few minutes, but they finally learned that Kamryn Baldwin was indeed on the Life Flight, and she was on her way to the University Hospital in Salt Lake City. "At least that's close to where Kamryn and I live," Ember said as they rushed back to the pickup.

"We'll go to the cabin and pack, and then we can head for Salt Lake," Bentley said firmly.

"You guys can stay at my place," Ember offered. Bentley didn't comment on the offer. Her apartment was small, not roomy like the cabin.

Faye made a similar offer but admitted that she was also living in a very small apartment, and it was not close to the hospital. When Bentley thanked her and declined, she said, "Maybe sometime I can come out and stay with you guys in your cabin. I was looking forward to it tonight, but I guess I'll just head home as soon as I'm back in my car."

It was dark by the time Bentley, Ember, and Cedrick reached the hospital. The three of them rushed inside only to learn that Kamryn was in surgery and would be for a while. So they sat down to wait, each filled with sad and worried thoughts.

The hours dragged by, and still no word was forthcoming on how Kamryn was doing. Bentley silently pleaded with the Lord on Kamryn's behalf, and he could tell that both Ember and Cedrick were praying as well.

***

It was a very dark night, just right for what Silas Villard had in mind. He'd driven the rusty stolen car around on backroads for hours before finally hiding it about a mile from his house in Myton. He needed money, and he needed weapons. He hoped that Lonnie Defollo hadn't already been there and found his stash. He didn't care about the threat Lonnie had made. He'd been able to avoid the cops for the past week, and he had no doubt that he could keep Lonnie from finding him, if the guy even tried. Anyway, he wasn't afraid of Lonnie. He wasn't afraid of anyone.

Silas was glad for the darkness of the night. He had a flashlight in his pocket, but he preferred not to use it, even though he didn't honestly believe anyone would see the light if he used it before he came into the residential area of town. He stumbled several times, hurting the hand the trooper had shot and the shoulder the deputy and the trooper's dog had injured. It was pure bad luck that now both hands were hard to use, but he could still do what he had to. He'd wrapped his hand with a rag from the stolen car, but he was pretty sure it was bleeding again. He hoped his shoulder wasn't bleeding too, but he didn't think it was. The doctor had done a good job sewing and bandaging the wounds.

Thinking about what had happened when he'd tried to take the trooper out with his pistol stoked his hatred for the guy. He would not give up until Radford was as dead as his wife.

It was slow going in the darkness, but Silas was in no hurry. He was especially watchful as he entered the town of Myton, mostly concerned about the cops. For all he knew, they might be watching his house, although he really didn't think they would expect him to go there. They were all stupid. They would think he was driving as far away as he could, as fast as he could. That was the reason he dared to make the attempt. Also, it was the middle of the night, and if a cop had been stationed to watch his house, he'd probably be asleep. He smiled at that thought.

Silas did not go directly to the house. Instead, he circled around the neighborhood looking for cop cars. He saw none. The only things that bothered him were the occasional barking dogs. But whenever he heard one, he changed direction so if the owners came out to see what was disturbing their dog, they wouldn't be able to see him. Due to the lateness of the hour, he didn't think anyone was likely to bother looking outside anyway. After all, dogs barked a lot. Silas had his 9mm pistol if he needed it, but he'd have to shoot left-handed, because he didn't think he could use his shooting hand at this point.

After a while, when he was confident that no cops were watching for him, he entered his house through the back door, which was unlocked. That was good, because he'd lost his keys.

He kept the lights off so that he wouldn't attract unwanted attention. But he did use the flashlight. It was clear the cops had searched his house, because it was a mess—a worse mess than usual.

The secret hole in the floor was beneath a rug in one of the two bedrooms, the one he slept in. He moved the rug, opened the hatch, and shone his light into the hole. To his immense relief, his stash was still there. The cops hadn't found it, and Lonnie Defollo hadn't been there yet.

He retrieved all the money and stuffed it in his pockets. Then he pulled out his AR15 and twelve-gauge shotgun. He also had a .357-magnum pistol in a holster. He took that out and strapped it on. When his right hand seared with pain again, he cursed the trooper.

Now that he was here, he wasn't leaving his most important belongings. Other than the cash and the guns, there were only a few other things that were important enough to take.

It didn't take him long to realize that, because of his injuries, he would not be able to carry much back to where he'd hidden the car. He knew it was risky, but he could see no alternative to driving the car to the house, quickly loading anything he thought he could use, and then heading for the backroads again. After one more attempt to get the trooper, he'd disappear into the great melting pot of Los Angeles, California.

He wore his pistol and a jacket he'd pulled from his coat closet. Lonnie's 9mm and the bullets for it were in a bag now, which he would carry with him back to his car. He strapped the rifle on his back and headed out, making it back to the car without incident. Feeling a little apprehensive, he started it and drove back to his house, turning the lights off when he hit the outskirts of town. He parked behind his house and began to load the car. He took a few of his clothes, the shotgun, all of his ammunition, all of his beer, and the fifth of whiskey he had bought just before he started the fire that burned his grandad's house down.

He also took some canned goods. He loaded all of his knives and some pots, pans, bowls, plates, and silverware. He took his coats, his sleeping bag, a couple of pillows, and some blankets. Even though there might be other things he could use, he worried he was already taking too long. So he hurried and got into the car and crept out of town. Once on the backroads, he sped up. He planned to get as far away as he could before daylight. Then he would find a secluded place to camp and hide out while he waited to make his next attack on the detested trooper.

He'd been having a good summer starting wildfires and watching them burn. That was his passion, but because of the trooper, he didn't dare do that now.

His hatred and anger boiled.

***

Kamryn finally came out of surgery. They were told that the damage from the bullet had been quite extensive but had not hit any critical organs or her spine. The doctor they spoke to was confident that she was patched up in the best way possible; now it would take time for her body to heal. The good news was that she was out of danger of losing her life and that she would, in time, make a full recovery. When Ember asked if they could see her, they were told she would be in a medically induced coma for a few hours, and it would be best to come back in the morning.

As Ember, Bentley, and Cedrick walked toward the parking garage, Ember said, "See, Bentley, you listened to the Spirit. You shouldn't doubt yourself."

"I felt like I was listening, but it's so hard to be sure. I just hope she doesn't have any long-term effects from her injuries," he responded.

"It sounded to me like the surgeon doesn't think she will," Ember responded.

They talked until they reached their vehicles, then Ember said, "You will stay at my place, won't you?"

"I don't think so," he responded. "I appreciate the invitation, but I would feel really uncomfortable being in Kamryn's space after she was hurt so badly because of me."

Ember put her hands on her hips. "Listen, mister. You can't blame yourself for what happened to her."

"The bullet she took was meant for me. So I do feel at fault."

"The fault is Silas Villard's and no one else's," she said sternly.

"We think it was Silas, but how can we be sure? The guy was blond, and his hair and beard were way shorter than Silas's. We don't even have enough evidence to have him charged with shooting Kamryn unless both he and the pistol he was shooting can be found. Now you go get some rest, Ember, and I'll find a hotel for Cedrick and me. We'll try to rest as well. Call later when you're ready to see Kamryn, and we'll meet you at the hospital."

Ember's company had been comforting, but he didn't want to spend more time with her than was necessary. "I'm sorry for all I've put you through," he said.

"None of it was your fault," she said with a touch of temper. "You've got to quit blaming yourself."

After they left Ember, Bentley and Cedrick found a hotel room and settled down to get some badly needed rest. They had only been asleep for around five hours when Bentley's phone rang. He assumed it was Ember. But when he looked at the screen, he was wrong. "Hello, Hank."

"Bentley, are you in Salt Lake?" Hank asked.

"I am," he said.

"How is Ember's roommate?"

"We were told a few hours ago that she'll live. But she was injured pretty badly. They are keeping her in a coma for a while. They promised to call Ember when it was possible to visit her. Cedrick and I are just waiting for Ember to call us so we can go to the hospital."

"Listen," Hank said. "I called to update you on what we've learned. I decided to go to the house where Silas was living in Myton. We've checked there from time to time, but I'm kicking myself for not keeping an eye on the place last night."

"I take it he must have been there at some point or you wouldn't be kicking yourself."

"That's right."

"How do you know he'd been there? Did someone see him?"

"No, but there is no question about it," Hank said. "The blond guy with the rusty blue car was Silas. A lot of his personal items were taken from his house. There was a hole in the floor of a bedroom. It was obviously a hiding place for something. It had a trap door that had been concealed beneath a rug. The rug was folded back, the hole was left open, and the space under the floor was empty."

"What do you think was in there?" Bentley asked.

"It's hard to be sure, but I would bet on firearms, ammunition, and maybe even some money. It wasn't meant to be seen by anyone searching the house. When we came in earlier, we missed it. I put the trap door back in place, and it blended so well with the floor that it would have been hard to find even if we'd moved the rug, which I don't believe any of the deputies did," Hank explained. "By the way, that was a beautiful and fitting funeral. Ember's talk was great, and her roommate has a beautiful voice. I'm not usually a crying man, but it did make my eyes get a little wet. I sure hope she'll be okay."

"Yeah, me too," Bentley agreed. "She didn't deserve what happened to her. The bullet she took was meant for me. And, Hank, I told you this before, but your talk was perfect. Thanks so much for doing that for me and for Evie."

"I was honored to be asked. Listen, Bentley, when are you going to be back at work?"

"You didn't hear?" he asked. "I'm not coming back. I resigned."

Hank's eyes widened. "You can't do that! You're a great trooper."

"I already have," he said.

"I'm sad to hear that, Bentley. So what are you going to do, and where will you live?"

"I'm going to do something I've always wanted to do. I'm going to write a novel, and if that works out, I'll write more. I've always loved to write. Evie had been encouraging me to try it since we first got engaged, and I have a novel started that she told me was really good."

"I hope it works out for you, but believe me, law enforcement will miss you," Hank said.

"I suppose I'll miss it, but what happened to Evie drove the desire to be a cop right out of me."

"If you change your mind at some point, I'm sure there would be a job for you in the area."

"Maybe, but I don't think I will."

"It's the public's loss, Bentley. You were doing a lot of good. But I guess I sort of understand where you're coming from."

"Thanks for saying that. And I'll be doing more than writing. I'm going to take care of Evie's little brother."

"Wow! That's great, Bentley. I'll bet he likes that. Where will you live?"

"I'm buying a cabin in the hills west of town that sits on forty acres," he said, and then he explained what his plans were for both him and Cedrick.

"You will be missed in the ward," Hank said.

"Actually, the cabin is in the area of the Third Ward, so Cedrick and I will still see you every Sunday." Bentley then explained where the cabin was located.

"Yep, that's in our ward. I'm glad for you, but I sure hate to see you leave law enforcement," Hank reiterated.

"I just can't do it anymore. Oh, another call is coming in. It's Ember," Bentley said. "I'd better take it."

"Let me know how Kamryn does after all the surgery and recovery," Hank said and ended the call.

CHAPTER TWENTY-TWO

"She's awake and wants to see us," Ember said with excitement in her voice. "Let's visit her and have lunch afterward."

"In that case, we'll meet you at the hospital in about twenty minutes. Is that okay?"

Bentley and Cedrick got there at about the same time as Ember, and they entered the hospital together.

Kamryn looked pretty rough, but she managed a weak smile. "What happened to me? The doctor says I got shot. How could I have gotten shot?"

"You took a bullet that was meant for me," Bentley said. "I'm so sorry, Kamryn."

"How did I do that?" she asked, raising an eyebrow.

Ember then explained what had happened.

"Was it Silas? Did he get away again?" Kamryn asked.

"I'm afraid so, and yes, Silas Villard got away again. I guess I'm a marked man, but I wish he'd got me instead of you." Bentley was grateful to this young woman who had honored his late wife with such beautiful music, and he hated that she'd been injured so badly. "You don't deserve this, Kamryn."

"Neither do you, any of the three of you. Silas must be one wicked man. Do you think he'll come after you again?" Kamryn asked, shuddering.

"I'm afraid it's only a matter of time. Cedrick and I talked this morning as we were driving up here, and we agreed that we need to do something to increase the security at the cabin."

"We're going to get another dog, a well-trained one that will hurt people who try to hurt us," Cedrick said proudly.

"You already have one," Ember reminded them. "Twy saved our lives, and he hurt Silas."

"Yes, he did, but we want a trained guard dog to help Twy, probably a German shepherd. But that's not all we plan to do. I'm going to set up a security system at the cabin and around our property with cameras and sensors," Bentley explained. "But that's enough of that. Kamryn, please tell us how you're feeling."

She smiled a weak smile. "They have me so doped up that I'm not feeling much of anything. But the doctor told me this morning that it could have been a lot worse and that I will heal up just fine. I'm grateful for that. I'm glad he got me instead of you."

"I'm not, but thanks for saying that," Bentley said. He was blown away by her words. After all, she barely knew him.

"I mean it," she said softly.

The four of them visited a few more minutes, and then Bentley said, "You need to rest so you can heal. Cedrick and I are going to head home, but we'll be back to check on you in a few days."

"Thanks for coming," she said, her eyes meeting his and lingering for a moment. Then she looked at her roommate. "You too, Ember. I'm lucky to have you in my life. You are an amazing friend."

"The guys and I are going to have lunch together, and then I'll come back and sit here with you for a few hours if it's okay," Ember said. "But I won't stop you from resting."

"Thank you. That would be nice."

"Do your parents know what happened to you?" Ember asked.

"Yes, I called them just a few minutes ago on the phone here in the room. They're catching a flight from Oakland as soon as they can get one," she said.

"That's great," Bentley said. "They'll be a big support for you. We'll see you later. Get well soon, and again, I'm so sorry."

"Not your fault," she said with a forced and very weak grin. "I'm glad I could help." The grin became slightly stronger.

Bentley shook his head in amazement. She really meant what she said.

After lunch, Ember went back to be with Kamryn. Bentley and Cedrick got back in the truck.

"Where will we get a guard dog, Bentley?" Cedrick asked.

"I don't know yet, but we'll figure it out soon. Before we leave Salt Lake today, we need to check out some security systems. Hopefully we can buy something and set it up when we get back to the cabin if we get there before dark."

It took a while to find what they needed, and it was late when they got back to the cabin that night. So they got up early the next morning and spent much of the day setting the system up. When they had finished, Bentley said,

"At least we'll know when anyone comes around. We'll hear the alarms and be able to see who it is on the cameras. Tomorrow we'll see what it's going to take to get another dog." He patted Twy's head fondly as he spoke. "No offense to you, Twy. You did your job and saved us. But we need to get you a pal as reinforcement."

Twy wriggled his back end and tried to wag his stub of a tail.

***

Claude returned to his house to find a realtor's *For Sale* sign on the front lawn. It made him furious. He went inside and grew even angrier when he saw that the house had been largely cleaned out. He screamed at the walls, "This is your fault, you little brat!" Of course he was referring to Cedrick, not the walls, although Cedrick was as innocent as the walls. But Claude had become a selfish and bitter man. "I don't know where you are now, but I'll figure it out, and I'll make you wish you'd behaved yourself."

Claude was not an honest man, and dishonest people never accept blame for their own failings. He also went about the house ranting at his wife, who, like Cedrick, wasn't there to hear him. In his mind, she had no right to do this. What he failed to remember was that this house was hers. She'd bought it before they were married, and he had agreed in a prenuptial agreement that it would always be just hers. It had bothered him at the time, but he'd gone along with it. Legally, she could do what she wanted with it.

Despite that, he vowed to stop her from selling it. In a rage, he began to break windows and kick holes in the walls. He then grabbed some of his clothes and left, laughing that no one would want the place now that he'd damaged it.

***

Claude was not the only angry man, nor the only one in a destructive mood. Lonnie Defollo was in an absolute rage. He was tearing Silas's house to pieces, destroying everything he could get his hands on. He even busted most of the windows and doors. He'd found the hidden compartment beneath the floor, but it was *empty*. Silas had broken the agreement they'd made. That was a stupid thing for him to do. Lonnie was determined to make him pay for his deceit. He had lots of friends, loyal friends . . . or as loyal as one could get in his business. Anyway, he made up his mind that he would enlist the help of some guys and gals to find Silas. When they did, Silas wouldn't need this house anymore.

That thought gave Lonnie an idea, one that brought a smile through his rage. He knew that Silas had a thing about fires. Well, he'd give him one. As he drove away a few minutes later, he could see the flames and smoke rising from Silas's house. He laughed and slapped his hands on the steering wheel. This is how he repaid someone who betrayed his trust. Or at least, it was a start, but there was more to come for Silas Villard.

***

Bentley and Cedrick spent time over the next few weeks locating a German shepherd that was suitable for their needs. The dog was young and expensive but extremely well trained, and he soon bonded with Bentley, Cedrick, and Twy. His name was Bolt, and indeed, he was a very fast dog, both physically and mentally. Bentley couldn't have been more pleased. Cedrick fell in love with Bolt and showered him with affection. The two became almost as inseparable as Twy and Bentley. To Bentley, that was gratifying, because it made his young companion much safer.

Bentley purchased a used John Deere tractor that was large enough to clear the snow when it came. He wanted to be prepared. He also continued to mourn the loss of his loving wife. Each time he and Cedrick went to town for supplies or church meetings, they would visit Evie's grave. How Bentley wished she could be here to enjoy this new home with him and Cedrick, but of course, that was not to be. So he tried to minimize his mourning with hard work.

They also made several visits to Kamryn at the hospital in Salt Lake City. She was recovering nicely, and she glowed whenever Bentley stepped into her room. He could see the glow about her, and it made him both happy and a bit concerned. He was afraid she was coming to like him too much in ways that he was not interested in. They also visited Ember, and Bentley was happy to learn that she was doing well in her legal courses.

Cedrick was also excelling in his schooling. Bentley made sure he spent a few hours each day with his online classes, and Cedrick never once complained. Bentley worked on his novel. Even though it was slow going as he got back into writing it, he felt good about the progress he was making. He just wished Evie were there to critique it.

He and Cedrick also spent time building a couple of nice, tight sheds and sturdy corrals. As he and the boy were admiring the work they'd done early one evening in mid-September, Bentley said, "We need something to put in the sheds. I know we want horses, but with winter coming on, I think we should wait. Is that okay with you, Cedrick?"

"Sure, as long as we have some by next summer," he replied with a sly smile. "So if we wait on the horses, what should we buy now?"

"I was thinking about the milk cow we talked about a few weeks ago," Bentley said. "The first one, anyway. We could then begin to make our own butter and cheese as well as have some to share with . . ." He paused, deep in thought.

"With what, the dogs?" Cedrick asked.

"They could have some, I suppose. No, I was thinking about a pig. Remember? We talked about that. We'd need to build another pen, but we could do that soon."

They made their plans, and within another month, they had a fine young Jersey cow and a new calf, as well as a feeder pig. They had a large shed filled with enough hay and grain to last well into the next summer and a tight but fairly roomy shed for the cow and calf. The two of them settled in for the approaching winter, content with what they had accomplished so far.

As the weeks passed, they both progressed in their computer work: Bentley with his writing and Cedrick with his schooling. They even managed to get away from time to time to visit both Ember and Kamryn. The visits were mostly for Cedrick's sake. Bentley would have been content to stay home, but Ember was Cedrick's sister, and he needed her.

Kamryn was out of the hospital and back in the apartment with Ember. They had good visits, but short ones. The calf would take care of Bossy's milk while they were gone, but they didn't want to be gone too long, because the calf could be getting too much milk, and Bentley didn't want to make it sick. Even though Bentley had given the pig rolled corn and barley in the two-hole pig feeder he'd purchased, he also knew the critter would run out of food if he was away too long.

On one of their trips to Salt Lake, Bentley and Cedrick surprised the ladies with some homemade cheese and home-churned butter.

"Wow, you guys are amazing." Kamryn said. "I love cheese." She and Ember both looked at Bentley with admiration.

Bentley enjoyed his visits with them, but he also felt a bit uncomfortable with the way they sometimes looked at him—especially Kamryn. So he made sure the visits were short for that reason, as well as his concern for the animals. Not once did Cedrick complain about the length of their visits.

Autumn turned to winter early in December, but the two guys were enjoying the cabin and the sheds and corrals they'd built. The tractor came in handy as Bentley had to plow snow several times to enable them to get to town for church on Sunday and for Cedrick's Young Men activities during the week.

It was on the days that Cedrick was at his Young Men activities that Bentley did his grocery shopping, not just for their immediate needs but for the purpose of having plenty of supplies stored for the future. What little bit Bentley and Evie had managed to store during their short marriage had been consumed by the fire. But she had been insistent that they work on their food storage. He kept up his efforts in that regard for both practical reasons and because he felt it was a way he could pay tribute to Evie's memory.

CHAPTER TWENTY-THREE

SILAS VILLARD RECKLESSLY SPENT HIS money until he was broke once again. To rectify the problem, he resorted to holding up a couple of convenience stores in the LA area. He netted a generous amount of cash in each robbery, but when he saw his face on the news one evening in the dump of a motel he was staying at, he realized he had been caught on a surveillance camera at the latest robbery. It was being shown to the public in LA and beyond. It made him terribly angry, and he blamed the need to rob and steal on none other than Trooper Bentley Radford. He would never be satisfied until his desire for revenge against the young officer was fulfilled. After all, if it weren't for his bogus arrest, Silas wouldn't be in this mess.

He decided he needed to get away from LA for a while to let things cool down, which he knew they would, because many other crimes diverted the police's attention away from him. But he was an arsonist, and he had no desire to change that. So on his last day in California, he started a fire in some dry brush and grass that soon turned into a raging forest inferno.

Watching with fascination as the wild and out-of-control flames gobbled up huge swaths of forest and even consumed several homes, Silas felt elated and ready to resume his quest for revenge against the trooper. He hated to leave while his fire was still wrecking so much havoc, but he knew the time had come to get away from LA for a while. The last thing he needed was a confrontation with the police.

He stole two different cars as he made his way back to Utah. He never felt comfortable driving any one car for too long. Each time he abandoned one car in order to steal another, he had to fight the urge to set it on fire. But he was becoming more cautious as time passed. Nothing—not even his beloved fires— could be allowed to stop him from getting back at Trooper Radford.

He took his time driving to Utah and took a lot of backroads through Nevada and Utah. During that time, he was busy devising a plan. He had to find a way to get the trooper's attention. If that meant he had to take drastic measures, that's what he'd do. He finally decided on a course of action. It was daring, but it was one he felt good about. He had a surefire plan that would lure the trooper out of wherever he was living and allow him to get his revenge.

***

One wintery day shortly before Christmas, Detective Hank Parker made a surprise visit to Bentley's cabin. The roads were newly plowed and both Bentley and Cedrick were hard at work when the security system warned of a visitor. Bentley quickly checked the cameras on his phone, and when he recognized the sheriff's gray Ford F150 he turned off the alarm and waited at the door with Cedrick and the two dogs. When Bolt sounded a warning growl, young Cedrick placed a hand on the big dog's head and said, "Friend." That was a word Bolt understood well, and he immediately calmed down and started wagging his tail.

When Hank was invited in a minute later, both dogs and both guys welcomed him warmly. "So is this the fierce dog you've been telling me about at church lately? He seems pretty calm to me," Hank said with a friendly smile. "Can I pet him and not get bitten?"

Cedrick said to Bolt, "Friend," as a reminder, and then he looked up at the detective with a grin on his face and said, "Now you can pet him."

After the dog and the detective were comfortably acquainted, Bentley said, "I suppose there is a reason for your visit."

"There is, and I hope you will respond to it in a positive way. The sheriff, the chief deputy, and I have been talking, and we need your help."

"Really? What do you need me for?" Bentley asked, not sure he really wanted to know.

"We actually have a proposal for you. I suppose you could use a little extra money," Hank said.

"We're doing okay," Bentley responded. "By the way, have you figured out who burned Silas's house down? Was it him or someone else?"

"We don't believe it was him," Hank said. "But that question leads me to what we want to propose to you."

"I'm listening, but frankly Hank, we're doing okay financially. I feel optimistic about the novel I've nearly finished writing, and Cedrick is doing really well with his online schooling. With milk from our cow, we're able to make our own butter and cheese, using the excess to help fatten our pig. Even our calf is growing nicely. We'll be looking for a young bull and another milk cow soon, too. And come spring, we'll buy a couple of horses."

"That's great. It sounds like you guys have things well in hand. I admire the work you've done on your little homestead." He paused and looked around the room. Bentley said nothing, just waited to hear what Hank had to say. Hank finally went on. "We think you should consider becoming a private investigator."

"Say what?" Bentley asked in surprise.

"You heard me," Hank said with a grin. "Let me explain what we have in mind before you respond."

"Okay, but I don't know that I'm interested."

"Hear me out, please. It's like this, Bentley. We aren't thinking you'd be out trailing cheating spouses or that kind of thing. No, what we want is someone who can help us pursue some criminal matters. The other detectives and I are frankly overloaded, and the sheriff can't afford another full-time deputy right now, but he could pay you to help us from time to time. You would be paid on an hourly basis for your work. A lot of what we would be asking you to do could be done right here in your home on the computer. And I have a feeling that Cedrick might be able to help some."

Hank turned to Cedrick and asked, "Are you pretty good with computers?"

"Yes, I am," the boy said with a grin on his face. "Let's do it, Bentley. Please?"

"For the most part it would be on your own time, at your own pace, and if you wanted to take other cases, that would be okay too," Hank said. "I'm not speaking about a lot of hours or even consistent work."

Even though he was hesitant, Bentley could feel himself warming to the idea. There were times when he actually missed law enforcement and this might help fulfill that yearning. "You know, it might give me ideas for my stories," he said, not mentioning anything about how he missed being a trooper more than he thought he would.

Cedrick pumped his fists. "Yeah, let's do it."

He was so enthusiastic that Bentley asked, "How soon do you need an answer, and how long would it take to get me licensed?"

"It won't take long at all. We've looked into it. And the sooner you can agree to do it, the sooner I can put you to work on the case of Silas's burned house," Hank said.

"I'm not sure I see how I can be of help with that," Bentley said. "I don't feel sorry for the guy. It's karma, seems to me."

"I agree with that. He probably got what he had coming, but Silas is not the only victim. There's a bank that lent Silas money to buy the place, and an insurance company that doesn't want to pay out because they think he did it himself. They want us to find Silas so they can deal with him rather than the bank. And of course, they haven't been able to find Silas, so they are leaning on the sheriff to do that, since there are so many outstanding warrants on him anyway. That's no surprise, but the insurance company can't close the case until he is found, unless they want to pay the bank, and that seems to be something they don't want to do. I really don't know about what can and can't be done in that regard. Anyway, the insurance company and the bank are getting antsy. So here's the thing, guys," Hank went on, winking at Cedrick, who was all smiles, and without giving Bentley a chance to respond. "Somewhere, sometime, Silas has made somebody extremely angry."

"I'd guess he's made a lot of people angry," Bentley said with a frown. "That includes me. I know I need to forgive him, but so far I haven't been able to do that. But even though I despise the man, I didn't burn his house down."

Hank chuckled. "That's right. Anyway, we'd like you to look into possible associates of his. Even though he and the bank owned that old house in Myton, I've learned that he spent a lot of time in the Salt Lake area. What I haven't learned is who he spent time with and what kinds of things he was involved in. I doubt very much that he was gainfully employed, at least not in a legal way."

Hank had definitely aroused Bentley's interest, and he finally spoke up. "What the heck, Hank, I don't need more time to think about it. I'd like to try it. It's not like I have to keep it up if it doesn't suit Cedrick and me that well."

"Yes!" Cedrick said with more fist pumping. He was grinning broadly. "I'll help all I can."

Before leaving, Hank provided Bentley with the information he needed to start the process of getting licensed. "However, you can start doing research on Silas and his associates anytime, as long as you do it here in your home since you won't be licensed yet. It would be kind of unofficial. Oh, and keep a log of the time you spend."

The first thought Bentley had after Detective Parker left was how much he'd like to have told Evie about his new plans. He had always loved telling her about things he wanted to do, and she was always receptive to hearing whatever he was enthused about. And he *was* enthused about this, despite the misgivings he'd had when Hank first brought it up.

"We need to call Ember and tell her," Cedrick said enthusiastically.

"You can call her, if you like," Bentley said. His thoughts were on his late wife, whom he missed as much today as at any time over the last several months.

Cedrick made the call, and when he was finished, he said, "Ember says she wishes you, and me too, the best. She says she's excited about it for us."

It took a few days, but Bentley became a licensed private investigator. However, as Hank had suggested, he had already started to look into Silas's background. He was able to find a whole lot more than what his criminal record showed. It appeared that there were some seriously bad characters he'd interacted with. Very little was mentioned about one of them, but for some reason, Bentley got an itch in his brain when he read the man's name.

Lonnie Defollo had spent time in prison but had apparently stayed out of trouble since his parole. At least he hadn't done anything the police could tie him to. Bentley dug deeper. Eventually, on social media, he found a post from a woman who was identified as Queen Wise. Cedrick, who was watching over Bentley's shoulder, asked the very thing that Bentley was wondering. "Do you think that's really her name?"

"I don't know. Sounds fishy, doesn't it? We'll check it out further, but right now let's see what she has to say in this post," Bentley said.

What she had to say sparked a sharp rise in Bentley's interest level. Among a few other things that meant nothing to Bentley, she mentioned a guy by the name of Silas. She claimed she didn't know his last name, but she did write that the guy had borrowed money and a gun from a friend of hers, Lonnie Defollo, with a promise to make it up to him. She was vague on how that was to happen but made reference to Silas's house. She also said that she believed Silas's house was old and not in good shape. It was located in the town of Myton. There was nothing mentioned about it having burned down, but when he looked closely, he realized the post was an old one and had been made before the fire.

Bentley and his young brother-in-law exchanged significant glances. "That's got to mean Silas Villard, even though she says she doesn't know his last name," Bentley said. "Let's see what else we can find out. I think we should start with some research into whether or not Queen Wise is a real or a fictitious name."

"I think it's made up," Cedrick said. "Who would name a baby girl Queen? That's just silly."

"My thoughts exactly," Bentley said, grinning at Cedrick. "We think alike, you know that? I think you and I are going to make a great team."

Cedrick beamed at Bentley's words. "I think so too," he said.

Bentley got a catch in his throat. There were so many things about Cedrick that reminded him of Evie. It's too bad the two of them hadn't been able to take him in together the way they'd planned. It would have been wonderful.

He smiled at Cedrick and went back to work. Further research revealed that Queen Wise had surprisingly been given that bizarre name at birth. Furthermore, she had a criminal record and had spent the better part of four years in prison. The pictures of Queen that he found were not particularly flattering. She was statuesque, had unruly hair, and her face bore traces of the hard life she had lived

Commenting on her looks, Cedrick said, "She could at least try to make her hair look nice, and she could smile."

"Point taken," Bentley said. "But we shouldn't be critical of how she looks. Maybe she doesn't have a lot to smile about. Let's see what else we can find about her friend Lonnie Defollo."

Another fifteen minutes of research produced nothing more. Bentley was disappointed, but he was also determined to dig deeper later on. Turning to Cedrick, he said, "I think what we've found is important, don't you?"

His enthusiastic young assistant agreed and said, "Should we call Detective Parker and tell him what we've discovered?"

"I think we should," Bentley agreed and made the call.

After completing the call, which was enthusiastically received by Hank, Bentley looked at his watch and said. "We better go milk Bossy, don't you think? We've spent longer on this than I'd planned."

It was snowing lightly as they stepped out the back door and made their way to the sturdy, tight shed they had built for the cow and calf. Bentley was proud of the progress they'd made on the corrals and sheds. With the weather turning colder and stormier, there wasn't much else he could do until spring, even though there was a lot more he wanted to do. What he had done was sufficient for now.

Once they had milked the cow and finished the other chores, they went back inside. Cedrick went to work on his studies and Bentley sat down at his computer and began to write. His novel was coming along nicely. He'd back-tracked a lot, so it was taking more time than he'd thought it would at first. But he wanted it to be the best he could make it. A few more chapters and he'd have a first draft completed. He typed for a while, then leaned back with a sigh. Other than the constant ache in his heart over losing Evie, he was fairly content with his life.

CHAPTER TWENTY-FOUR

IT WAS ALMOST NOON WHEN Bentley reached a good temporary stopping point on his novel. He went into the small kitchen and heated some soup and made sandwiches for lunch. He had just pulled the bowl of soup from the microwave and put it on the table when the alarm from the gate on his lane began to blare. Company was unusual this far from town and especially during a snow storm, one that was now putting down a fair amount of snow. He wasn't expecting any visitors, and there hadn't been any since Hank had been there.

Cedrick came running into the kitchen, his eyes wide. "Who's at the gate?" he asked with worry in his voice, echoing Bentley's thoughts and feelings.

"I don't know, but I better check." The gate had a combination lock on it and only a few people had the number. "Let's take a look."

He shut off the alarm and then accessed the video feed on his phone. He and Cedrick looked at it closely. There was someone standing at the gate, but he couldn't see a vehicle on the lane. The two of them watched as the individual, who was not dressed appropriately for the cold weather, walked through the snow into the trees and around the gate and back onto the lane. After a moment, the figure started walking toward the cabin, head bent against the falling snow. It wasn't a large person and he or she stumbled every few feet. It seemed to Bentley like whomever it was had to be very exhausted as well as cold and wet.

The dogs began to growl, sensing the approaching presence of possible danger. Bolt, the highly trained guard dog, approached the front door with a rumble coming from deep in his chest. The big German shepherd looked back at Bentley as if to say, "Let me out there. I'll take care of the problem."

"Stay out of sight, Cedrick," Bentley cautioned as he laid a hand on Bolt's head. Twy had also approached, growling a warning of his own.

"Are you going to let Bolt outside?"

"It might be someone who is no danger to us, and I don't want him hurting an innocent person." Bentley strapped on his pistol and continued to watch even as he wondered who would be coming to see them, and on foot, no less! It was very unlikely that it was an innocent person unless someone was lost. Again he thought about the weather as he watched the trespasser. Whoever it was had long dark hair and wore a light jacket and no head gear of any kind, not nearly enough clothing for such a cold, snowy day. The person had on ripped jeans, which was the style, but couldn't be very warm. He wondered as he watched if it could be female, but that made no sense at all. And yet it looked like it could be.

The intruder moved from the view of the gate camera into one that was on the front of the cabin. He waited, expecting that whoever it was would come to the door. But what the intruder did, after staring at the front door for a moment, was slowly duck around the side of the house and into the view of the next camera. The cameras confirmed his suspicions. The intruder was female, and it looked like she was young. Bentley went to the back door and watched the intruder as she walked past the house and entered the cowshed. That was certainly strange. Why didn't she just come to the house?

He had parked his truck out back in the big feed shed by the tractor, so he wondered if whoever it was thought there was no one home since there didn't appear to be any vehicles. Next to the cabin, the cowshed was the best shelter on the property.

"Okay, Bolt. Go check it out," Bentley said as he opened the back door. "Stay hid, Cedrick. It's a young woman, and she doesn't appear to be armed, but we can't be too careful," he called to his young brother-in-law and stepped out onto the back deck, locking the door behind him.

Bolt picked up the intruder's scent and quickly entered the cowshed through the door that the intruder had left open after passing through. He barked and there was a scream of fright. Bentley rushed to the shed and entered. Bolt had not attacked, but he was keeping the intruder at bay against a small stack of hay at the back of the shed. He was acting exactly like he had been trained to do. Bossy was restless and moving around in her stall. The calf in the next small pen also seemed nervous as it paced around the confined space.

Bentley flipped on the lights and moved toward the intruder and Bolt. The girl was shivering from a combination of cold and fright. "Don't let him hurt me," she begged. "I'm sorry. I'm in trouble. I need help. I couldn't see a car so I didn't think there was anyone home. I'm so cold."

Bentley holstered his pistol. He'd come out without taking time to grab a coat and was shivering, but not nearly as hard as the girl was. He could only imagine how cold she was. He said, "Stand down, Bolt." The dog did as ordered and stepped back beside Bentley.

"Who are you?" Bentley asked as he moved toward the girl, "and how did you find your way here?"

"I'm Piper. I got away from a guy who kidnapped me. Please, help me. He's coming after me. He'll hurt me if he catches me again."

Bentley stepped close to her and put an arm around her as he thought about what she'd said. He was certain she was telling the truth. She was slender and appeared to be a few inches over five feet. He could see that she was just a teenager, maybe sixteen or so. She was trembling badly. His heart ached for her. "Come on, let's get you into the house and warm you up."

"Thank you." Her voice shook. "Please don't let that awful man find me."

"I'll keep you safe," Bentley promised as he kept an arm around her and led her out of the shed and toward the house, shutting the door to the shed behind him. Bolt followed them. At the back porch, he said, "Bolt, on guard."

The big dog's ears stood up, he looked at Bentley, and then ran around the house. If anyone else approached, Bolt would know it. Grateful for the dog as well as his alarm system, Bentley opened the door and ushered Piper into the warm cabin. He had a fire going in the fireplace, and he led her to it. "Cedrick, come help us," he called out.

Cedrick appeared and said, "Who is this?"

"Her name is Piper, and she's nearly frozen. Will you make her a cup of hot chocolate?" Bentley asked.

Bentley wrapped a blanket around Piper's shoulders, and then pulled up a chair next to her. "What is your last name, Piper?" he asked.

"Boyle," she said.

"How old are you?"

"I'm sixteen."

"Where are you from?" he asked.

"I'm from Los Angeles," she said. "My mother doesn't know where I am."

"You said you were kidnapped?" Bentley asked.

"Yes. I was at a grocery store getting some things for my mom. This guy grabbed me as I was getting into our car. He made me drop my keys and the sacks of groceries. I tried to scream for help but he put a hand over my mouth." Piper began to sob.

Bentley put an arm around her shoulders and said, "It's okay, Piper. You are safe here. Tell me about the person who kidnapped you."

Piper described the guy in some detail, leaving no doubt in Bentley's mind who the kidnapper was. She had described Silas Villard. Granted, his hair color was different and so was his lack of a beard, but the girl had told him enough for him to know that Silas had kidnapped her.

"Did he mention his name at any point?" Bentley asked.

"Yes. His name is Silas."

Confirmation!

"Did he hurt you, Piper?" Bentley asked as she accepted a cup of hot chocolate from Cedrick with a murmur of thanks.

She took a sip of the chocolate. "A little. I know I'm too feisty and I should have just done what he asked. But that's not how I am. I kicked and scratched him. I soon learned that he only hurt me worse when I did that. He is a very scary man," Piper said with a shiver.

"Yes he is!" Bentley said darkly.

"You know him?" she asked, her eyes wide with surprise.

"Only too well," he said, attempting to keep the bitterness from his voice.

Piper studied his face for a moment. Then she said, "He was looking for a cop he claimed ruined his life. He didn't say the cop's name but I think he said he was a trooper. Do you know who he was talking about?"

"I'm afraid so, Piper. He was referring to me. I was a trooper with the Utah Highway Patrol, and I arrested him for drunk driving. He's a terrible man and after he got out of jail he did some horrible things," Bentley said.

Cedrick had been listening without speaking, but he finally spoke up. "He killed my sister, Bentley's wife," he said. The boy was unable to mask the bitterness in his voice. Like Bentley, he was also having a hard time forgiving the man for what he'd done to Evie.

"Oh! I'm so sorry," Piper said, her eyes growing wider. She took another sip of her drink. "He was looking for you. He said you lived in the hills, but he didn't know where. He was driving all around, looking. He said he'd know your truck when he saw it. But I didn't see a truck."

"It's in a shed beyond the one you went in. I don't know how he figured out even approximately where we live," Bentley said. "I thought he'd left the area."

"He had," she confirmed. "I'm from Los Angeles. But when he kidnapped me, he said he was going back to Utah to get revenge against the trooper he hated. You, I guess. He was going to make you go with him and promised he'd let me go if you did that. That's why he kidnapped me. He said he was going to trade me for you."

"I'm so sorry you are involved in this, Piper. Where was Silas the last time you saw him? I mean, you know, how far did you walk and how did you get away from him?" Bentley asked.

"I don't know how far I walked, but I just kept going. I made several turns, and I guess I got lucky, because I found you. But he will find you too."

"It wasn't luck, Piper. God was looking out for you. Tell us how you managed to get away from Silas." Bentley said as he pulled out his cell phone. He handed it to Cedrick. "Please call Detective Parker. When you get him on the phone, hand it back to me."

As Cedrick was making the call, Piper said, "The more we drove around without seeing your truck, the madder he got. He cursed the snowy roads and blamed them on you! How could he do that? He wasn't making sense. Anyway, he was drinking beer and throwing the cans out the window. He got really drunk. We were sitting at some place where the road split. He said he was trying to decide which way to go. He was saying awful things. He was angry that he hadn't found you yet. He kept drinking. Then he passed out. I was able to find the keys to the handcuffs he had fastened on my wrists, and I took them off."

"You're smart and very brave," Bentley said.

"I was desperate. I got out of the car and started to run," she said. "I was afraid he'd wake up and follow my tracks in the snow. But I guess it's good it's snowing because it covered my tracks."

"Bentley, here's Hank," Cedrick broke in and handed the phone to him.

"What's going on?" Hank asked with urgency in his voice. "Are you guys okay?"

"We are. But Silas is in the area. Let me put my phone on speaker so you can hear Piper. She's a teenager who was kidnapped by Silas in California, and he was going to make me give myself up to him in exchange for her."

"This isn't good. Is she hurt?"

"She says she has some bruises but nothing serious. She's just cold and scared," Bentley responded as he put his phone on speaker. "Piper, the man on the phone is a police officer, a detective and a good friend of ours. Tell him what the car was like that Silas was driving."

For the next few minutes, Piper told Hank as much as she could. Silas had stolen two cars before the one he was driving when she got away from him. At Hank's urging, she described the guns he had, what he was wearing, and how he looked. Finally, Hank said, "I'll get every cop we can call out looking for that car. I'm coming to your place, Bentley. Keep a sharp lookout for Silas. He must be close if Piper was able to walk to your cabin in the storm."

"She was, and it was lucky she found our place. It's also a blessing that the snow covered her tracks. Still, if he comes here, Bolt will take care of him," Bentley said confidently. Even as he said that, he prayed that Silas would not be able to shoot the big dog.

As soon as the call ended, Bentley said. "I'll fix you something to eat, Piper. What would you like?"

"Anything, please. I'm starved. Silas didn't let me eat much."

"I'll scramble some eggs, fry some bacon, and make some toast. Will that be okay?"

"Yes, thank you. And thank you for being so good to me," the girl said with a trembling voice.

"I'm sorry you had to go through what you've been through, Piper. Cedrick will stay with you while I work in the kitchen," Bentley said.

"I'll come in there with you if that's okay with you guys," she said. "I'm warmer now. And I'll keep the blanket around me. I feel safe when I'm near you."

As he fixed some eggs and toast, Bentley had a chance to look more closely at the girl. She was a pretty, slender girl with long brown hair and brown eyes. Her cheeks were still red from the cold. He guessed she was around five-six. She talked more about her ordeal while she waited at the table. She had finished the hot chocolate, so Cedrick handed her a glass of milk.

"I saw your cow. I didn't think anyone was home and I was going to just keep walking. But I saw the shed and thought it might be warmer in there and that maybe I could stay there for a while. Is the milk from the cow?" she asked.

"It is," Cedrick told her.

"I've never had milk that was from a cow before. I've only had milk that was from the store," she said. "This is good."

Bentley chuckled. "The milk in the stores is all from cows, from big dairies. It's had the cream removed and is pasteurized."

"I don't know what that means, but this tastes better than any milk I've ever had," she said.

"I'm glad you like it," Bentley said.

Suddenly, Piper set the glass on the table and said, "I need to call my mom. She must be terribly worried. I'm worried about her too. Can I use your phone, Bentley?"

"Of course," he responded. But before she could make the call, his phone rang.

It was Hank and he said, "I found the car. It ran off the road just a short distance from the highway. It's on the road to your place. Silas isn't in it! So I have no idea where he could be now."

CHAPTER TWENTY-FIVE

SILAS WAS IN THE CAB of a semi—*again*. The driver had stopped when Silas stumbled onto the road and aimed his rifle at him. He told the driver that he'd had a wreck and had pointed in the general direction of where he'd left the car, stuck in the snow off the side of the road. He'd said, "I need a ride to the next town."

The driver had angrily agreed, telling Silas that he didn't appear to have a choice. But now, they were already past Duchesne, and Silas was still in the truck. He had threatened to shoot the driver if he attempted to stop any place other than where he told him to. "If you don't do as I say, I'll shoot you, put your body in the sleeper, and I'll drive your truck."

The driver did as he was told and they passed several cop cars that were heading west. Silas chuckled. "Cops are stupid," he said. "They'll never catch me." To himself he thought, *Trucks are a good way to keep out of sight of the cops.*

The driver chose not to enter into a conversation, so the miles passed in silence as Silas once again grew angry at his foiled attempt to get his revenge on the trooper. He was also very, very angry at Piper and told himself he'd make her pay someday for deserting him before he'd accomplished what he had nabbed her to do. He hadn't planned to hurt her worse than he already had and wondered why she couldn't see that. She didn't know the trooper, so it shouldn't have mattered to her that she was going to be traded for him. *Foolish girl.*

Silas promised himself that he'd soon try again to get his revenge against the trooper, and this time, he would not fail. He didn't know for sure how Piper had gotten away from him, but he cursed to himself at the thought of her. He knew that Trooper Radford would have given himself up for the girl, because that was the kind of fool he was.

***

Piper's mother, Rhea, a widow of about forty, reacted with joy when she heard her daughter's voice on the phone. "Where are you, Piper?" she asked. "Why did you run away?"

"I didn't run away, Mom. I was kidnapped. I'm near a place called Duchesne in Utah. I'm okay, Mom, so please don't cry," Piper said.

"Don't cry? I was afraid you were dead. But now that I hear your voice and learn that you were kidnapped, I can't help but cry."

Piper gave her mother a moment to get her emotions under control, and then she said, "Mom, I want to come home as soon as I can."

"Of course you do, my dear. Where did you leave our car?" Rhea asked.

"It's in the parking lot of the store where I was kidnapped. The car is there unless someone stole it," Piper said. "I'm sorry, but I dropped the keys when the guy grabbed me so someone could have stolen it." Then she proceeded to tell her mother the ordeal she had been through.

After a few minutes, Rhea said, "You say you are with a cop in his home?"

"He used to be a cop but he's not anymore. Mom, he's a great guy."

"Let me talk to him, please."

***

Piper handed the phone to Bentley as an alarm went off. She explained that her mother wanted to talk to him. He had only spoken to Piper's mother for a moment when another call came in. It was Hank. "Mrs. Boyle, I'll call you right back. A detective is calling me. Your daughter is okay and she is safe here with me. She's an amazing, brave girl."

"Bentley," Hank said as soon as the call ended, "I'm at the gate. Bolt is here with me. I'm sure glad he knows me. I just wanted you to know that I'm coming through."

"Okay, thanks. I heard the alarm but I was on the phone. I'll see you in a minute," Bentley said.

He waited to call Rhea back until Hank had been introduced to Piper. Hank was getting all the information from Piper that he could. Bentley listened as more details of the girl's ordeal unfolded. The anger and bitterness he felt toward Silas increased. What an atrocious man he was, entirely devoid of conscience, and Bentley honestly didn't know how he could ever forgive the man for the many unspeakable crimes he'd committed. And yet Bentley silently thanked the Lord that the girl was okay and had, by some miracle, found her way to his secluded cabin.

He called Mrs. Boyle back. "Rhea, Piper is talking to my detective friend right now. He will call Child Protective Services in a moment. What we need to figure out is how to get her home to you. We will follow whatever is suggested by Child Protective Services and make the appropriate arrangements."

"I'm sorry, but I don't have enough money to drive clear to Utah, and there is no way I could ever afford a plane ticket to come up there, and then purchase tickets to get Piper and me home," Rhea said. "Also, I don't even have my car."

"I can help with the money," Bentley said. "I can buy her a bus ticket back to California if that's okay, and CPS will no doubt provide her with a safe traveling companion."

"Oh, Trooper, would you really do that for me? Can you afford it? I'll find a way to pay you back, but it will take a little time," the woman said as she softly began to sob.

"I can do this for you and your daughter, and I don't want to be paid back," Bentley said. "I'll get her an inexpensive phone too so you two can keep in touch as she travels."

"I can't thank you enough," Rhea said. "You can't imagine how worried I've been. Piper is a good girl, and I was sure she'd never run away. The police here have been looking for her. I'm surprised they didn't find my car at the store where she says she left it. Of course, I didn't know which store she was going to, so I wasn't much help to them. Maybe it was stolen like she said. I'll need to call my insurance company if we can't find it."

Bentley smiled at the constant stream of chatter from Rhea. It was an indication of how relieved the woman was. He talked to her for a couple more minutes, and then he handed the phone to Piper as Hank finished his interview with her. While Piper and her mother talked, Bentley and Hank spoke about contacting CPS and arranging for Piper's safe return to her mother. Then their conversation turned back to Silas. "There are no guns in the car he wrecked, but there are a few cans of beer—no empty ones."

"Piper says he was throwing them out the window. So you figure he took the guns with him?" Bentley asked.

"It's the only thing that makes sense. Knowing what we do about Silas, I would have to assume that he used the guns to hijack a ride. He's getting a lot of experience doing that. He could be anywhere by now," Hank said.

"I can't believe the man's luck. We should have had him this time."

"I've already taken some action. I've ordered roadblocks be set up both east and west of here to see if he can be intercepted," Hank said. "Of course, whoever he hijacked will be in danger, so it's going to be very tricky."

Bentley didn't have a lot of hope that Silas would be intercepted, but for right now, he was focused on taking care of Silas's latest victim. Piper was amazingly strong, but as the day slowly passed, Bentley could see that she had been struggling with the emotional trauma of being kidnapped by an out-of-control maniac. She eventually began to cry, and Bentley comforted her the best he could. Twice more he let her call her mother, and those talks, which he and Cedrick let her have in private, helped to cheer Piper up.

Finally, he used his phone to figure out the bus schedule. "If you'd like to stay with us tonight you may," Bentley told her. "Then I can get you on a bus tomorrow with someone from CPS. Will that be okay with you?"

"I don't want to be a burden," Piper said, rubbing her eyes.

Bentley smiled at her and said, "You are not a burden, Piper. Anyway, Cedrick and I get kind of lonely out here all by ourselves. We'd love to have your company."

"Yeah, you can help us milk the cow and feed the calf and the pig. We're getting baby chicks in a few months. I wish we had chickens now so you could help gather the eggs," Cedrick said with youthful enthusiasm. "We're also going to get another cow and a bull and some horses. Tonight we can watch movies or play games or whatever you want to do."

"I guess it would be okay if I stay here," she said. "You guys are so nice. And you have such a wonderful life. It sounds like lots of fun living here."

"It really is fun," Cedrick said, grinning at Piper. She smiled back at him.

Hank called late in the afternoon. "It seems that Silas got away again. I'm sorry, Bentley, because I'd really like to have locked this guy up."

Bentley was not surprised that Silas couldn't be found. He said, "We'll just keep our defenses up here in case Silas tries something else, even though I can't imagine that he's dumb enough to still be anywhere near here now."

Later on, Piper asked Bentley and Cedrick if they would tell her more about Silas and what he had done to them. "Not just to us, but to a lot of others," Bentley said. "He appears to be an arsonist. You know, that's a person who likes to start fires and watch them burn."

They told her briefly about the fires he had started, at least those they knew of. And they told her about other crimes they knew he had committed. Their story brought tears to Piper's eyes. Finally, she said, "I'm sorry for what you guys have gone through. What happened to me was terrible, but you guys have had it worse."

"We're getting through it," Bentley said. "But it's been hard. It's a miracle that you found us like you did. I don't know if you believe in God and angels, but I do, and I'm telling you, He helped you find us. I believe angels were watching out for you and guiding every step you took."

"I do believe in God. I prayed the whole time I was with that horrible man. I know that God helped me get through it." She stopped and stared down at her hands for a moment. "Maybe there were angels helping me. Anyway, I can't thank you guys enough for being here for me," Piper said.

She stood and walked toward the fireplace. She pointed to a picture of Evie that Bentley had displayed on the hearth. "Is this Evie?" she asked.

"Yes, that's her," Bentley said softly,

"She's beautiful," Piper said. "I'm so sorry about what happened to her." Tears welled in the girl's eyes as she spoke. "I wish I could have known her."

They had a good evening. Piper enjoyed helping with the chores and even tried to get a little milk from the cow. "How do you do that?" she asked in frustration, frowning at Cedrick. "I can't get anything to come out."

"I couldn't at first either," Cedrick said with a grin.

Piper had fun feeding the calf from a bucket with a nipple on it, and then she stayed in the pen with it and petted it lovingly. Bentley was pleased to see her face shining so brightly and to hear her laughter. "I'd love to live here," she said longingly when she finally left the calf's pen. She helped fork hay to the cow and calf. She laughed at the way the pig ate. "I can see why people are called pigs when they shove their food down."

They played games and watched movies for several hours that evening. When they finally decided they all needed to get some sleep, Piper said, "I didn't think I'd ever be able to sleep again, but I think I will be okay now. I feel safe here with you guys and your incredible dogs. Thanks for letting me help with the animals. I love this place. I love you guys."

"And we love you too, Piper," Bentley said. "Despite how you came to be with us, I've enjoyed your company."

"So have I," Cedrick said with a sleepy grin.

The next morning, after they had finished doing the chores, they ate a hearty breakfast, which Piper helped prepare. Once they had finished eating and had cleaned up the kitchen, they all piled into Bentley's truck and drove to town.

Hank had been busy, not just doing his detective work, but finding clothes and a phone for Piper, and working with CPS to find a safe and suitable chaperone for the bus trip back to Los Angeles. He had them come to his house where his wife helped Piper choose some of the clothes neighbors had donated.

Hank didn't say where he got the phone he gave to Piper, but it saved Bentley a trip to Roosevelt.

When it came time for Piper and her chaperone to catch the bus, she shed tears and hugged both Bentley and Cedrick. "You guys are amazing," she said. "I hope I can see you again sometime. I'd love to bring my mom and spend some time on your homestead with you."

"We'd like that as well, wouldn't we, Cedrick?" Bentley said. Of course the boy agreed.

A few minutes later, Piper was safely on a bus and on her way home, her ordeal nothing but a horrible memory, one she would not soon be able to forget. However, the time she'd spent with Bentley and Cedrick was an experience she would cherish for the rest of her life.

***

Silas was on his way too, but not home, as he no longer had one. He'd abandoned the truck driver and the truck in Vernal, where he'd tied up the driver and left him in the sleeper unit of the truck. He was getting pretty adept at stealing cars and it took him only a few minutes to snatch one and take off. About the same time that Piper was on her way home, Silas was on his way back to LA.

When he arrived in LA, he merged unobtrusively into the large city. He stole some more money by holding up a convenience store while wearing a mask. Later, he started another fire, this one in a warehouse. He was constantly on the lookout for cops, altering his appearance from time to time. He felt invincible.

The fire he lit turned into a huge inferno. He spent several hours mingling with the crowd that was attracted by the flames and watched his handiwork with gleeful fascination. No one paid any attention to him. He felt invisible, and wondered how he could stay that way when he made his next attempt to punish Trooper Radford. He didn't plan to do that right away, because he knew the cops in the Duchesne area would be watching for him. He needed to let things cool down there as they had in LA. There was no longer anything about him on the TV or the Internet. After a while, he'd figure out another way to find Radford and make him pay. He swore he would not fail again. His obsession with revenge was beyond belief and out of control.

***

Not many days after Piper's rescue, Bentley received a threat in the mail. There was no return address, and the threat had been typed. Hank found no fingerprints on either the letter or the envelope, and there was no signature. It had been mailed from a small town in Nevada. As Bentley and Hank studied the threat, Bentley made an observation while shaking his head. "This is not from Silas Villard. Whoever sent this knows how to spell and uses proper grammar and punctuation. Silas is an uneducated fool."

The threat read: *Bentley Radford, your payday is coming. Because of you and your actions, my life has been ruined. I won't let you get away with it. I won't tell you what I plan to do, because I want it to be a surprise. And what a surprise it will be! I'll be in touch again.*

"Any idea who might have sent this?" Detective Parker asked.

"I think so," Bentley said.

Before Bentley could say who he suspected, Cedrick, who had listened as the note was read, said, "It's from Uncle Claude. I know it is."

"That's what I was thinking, but what makes you so sure?" Bentley asked, furrowing his brow.

"It's easy, Bentley. Whenever Uncle Claude got mad at me, which he did a lot, he'd always say, 'Your *payday* is coming, boy.' He never let Aunt Faye hear him say that. He was sneaky about the way he treated me because she likes me and he hates me."

Hank and Bentley looked at each other. Both were nodding. After a moment, Bentley said, "I'm getting fairly good at using the computer to find people. I'll go to work on this and see if I can track Claude down. It looks like he has become another danger to me and Cedrick, and he's got to be stopped. I'll call Cedrick's Aunt Faye; she may have heard from him. And who knows, maybe she's been threatened as well."

"We need to warn Ember too," Cedrick said.

CHAPTER TWENTY-SIX

OVER THE PAST FEW MONTHS, Lonnie Defollo had tried every way he could think of to locate Silas Villard. He'd called in favors from friends all over the Salt Lake Valley and even some from out of state without success. He wasn't anxious to get into trouble and go back to prison, but he also did not like the feeling that he'd been double-crossed. The more time that passed, the angrier he grew. He was determined to find Silas and make him pay for his treachery. Burning his house to the ground had not assuaged his anger. Silas needed to feel pain—lots of pain.

One day in March, Lonnie and a group of friends were having a party at his home, during which they were discussing the treachery of Silas Villard. Queen Wise had been sitting quietly, sipping on a beer as the others talked. Finally she said, "You guys probably saw that there's a big fire that started at a warehouse in LA."

"What does that have to do with Silas?" Lonnie asked, annoyed at Queen's interruption.

"Think about it, Lonnie," she said defensively. "They say it was started intentionally, that it was arson." She stared at Lonnie. "Who do you know who likes to start fires and watch them burn?"

Lonnie slapped his knee emphatically. "That sounds like something Silas would do, that's for sure. Good thinking, Queen."

"I may be wrong, but I'm pretty sure Silas isn't around here anymore. He wouldn't dare stay too close. He's stupid, but then maybe he's smart enough to figure out that you would have people looking for him," Queen said with a smirk on her face.

Lonnie stood up and looked around the room. "Anybody want to go to LA? I know a guy I served time with who's from there. He's part of a gang down there, a pretty big gang. I'll bet he and his friends would help us find Silas—if he's down there."

"I'll go with you, Lonnie," Queen said.

"Good. Anyone else?"

There were several volunteers, and the following morning, Lonnie, Queen, and the others were on their way to LA. At first they had no idea how they would go about finding Silas other than enlisting the aid of Lonnie's friend and his gang. They talked about it as they were taking a break at a convenience store in St. George. Lonnie asked the others if any of them had any ideas about how they might find Silas. "LA is huge with millions of people. But someone will know where he is."

Queen had a sly smile on her face. "I know what we can do. Let's pretend he's a moth."

"Now what good would that do?" Lonnie asked, scowling.

"Moths are attracted to flames." She paused and looked at the others in the group.

After thinking for a moment about what Queen had said, Lonnie exclaimed, "Queen, you're a genius." "We need to start a fire that's so spectacular it will draw him to it. He can't resist a good fire. Does anyone disagree? We could scatter out around the fire and watch for him to show up. I'll be surprised if he's not in the LA area. I've heard him talk about how that would be a good place to hide in plain sight since there are so many people."

"So, when we get to LA we need to find a good place to start a fire, one that will be spectacular. And if people get hurt, so be it," Queen said, shrugging her shoulders. "We don't care, as long as we entice Silas to the fire."

The rest of the group enthusiastically approved the plan, and Lonnie was feeling quite cheerful as they continued on their way. If Silas was in LA, they had a good chance of catching him and settling the score for his treachery, without even having to enlist the aid of Lonnie's former prison mate's gang.

***

Silas spent much of his time, of which he had plenty, thinking about what he could do to get even with Trooper Radford without once again failing in his effort. He recalled the day of the trooper's wife's funeral, and he thought about the two pretty women he'd seen with the trooper at the cemetery. Sitting in a slummy motel room nursing a beer, he began to consider those two in more detail. Who were they? He needed to figure that out. He wondered if one of them was the woman who had escaped the trooper's house fire with him and some kid.

Silas didn't have a computer, but he had bought a cell phone with the proceeds from a recent lucrative robbery. He wasn't great with it, but he had enough knowledge to get on social media and see if he could find out who the two young ladies were. One of them had made him really angry when she stepped in front of Radford just as he fired the shot that was meant to finish the guy off.

He was pretty sure she'd survived. From the news he'd watched in a motel room a day or two after that foiled attempt, he caught the tail end of a story about a girl who took a bullet for Trooper Radford and who had been flown to the University Hospital in Salt Lake City. He wished now that he'd paid more attention, because he didn't even remember the girl's name. But if she was a friend of Radford's, he should be able to figure it out.

He worked his phone for several minutes that evening and finally found what he was looking for. He already knew that the woman who had caused him to wreck his truck was Radford's wife, Evie. However, the new information he found was most interesting. Evie had a twin sister, Ember, a little brother, Cedrick, and a roommate named Kamryn Baldwin. He soon figured out that the Baldwin woman was the one he'd shot. She had stolen his perfect chance for revenge. She'd had no right to do that.

He laughed after taking another swallow of beer. He would figure out where the two of them lived. Either one would do as a hostage to get Radford to surrender to him and let him do with him as he pleased. But frankly, if he had a choice, he'd take the injured girl. She had messed up his attempt at revenge, so he had a perfectly good reason to punish her and even the score.

Silas was quite certain he could find the women. It was March now, so there wouldn't be snow to hinder him as he did what he felt he should do. This might be a good time, he thought. He didn't want to snatch both of them, because that would be too much trouble. Piper, all by herself, had proven to be too much trouble. He smiled again. Sometime, maybe he'd even the score with her too. He hadn't intended to hurt her, only to exchange her for Radford.

He thought about Lonnie Defollo. He was almost certain he was the one who had burned down his house. Nothing else made sense. Yes, he'd sort of double-crossed Lonnie, but he justified his actions with the thought that Lonnie should have just given him what he needed for friendship's sake and that he'd shorted him two hundred dollars. But no, Lonnie wanted something in return. Friendship should have been enough. He had to avenge himself for what Lonnie had done.

Silas had an ever-growing list of people who had caused him trouble, and he'd eventually get even with some—if not all—of them. In the meantime, he'd keep robbing places to keep himself with plenty of money, beer . . . oh yeah, and matches and accelerants. He thrived on causing and watching fires. He'd even been to see a few that he hadn't started here in the LA area.

Silas didn't realize how most of society despised men like him. He just went on believing that he was invincible and that the law didn't apply to him. In his mind, he was perfectly normal.

It was time to get even with Radford. So he packed up and drove out of LA in yet another stolen car.

***

The winter weeks had passed with a lot of snow that had kept Bentley busy clearing his road. But he'd been able to keep the road open, and not once did he and Cedrick miss church on Sunday. And he'd been able to take Cedrick to all his Young Men activities. He and Cedrick had also made regular visits to the three families they'd been asked to minister to by the elder's quorum president, Hank Parker.

Bentley had finished the first draft of his novel and he'd immediately begun to go through it from the beginning, making several minor changes and polishing it up. He'd finally sent query letters to several agents, and after receiving numerous rejection letters, he eventually secured a contract with a woman from New York. She told him it was a promising story and that she was optimistic about finding a publisher for the book. He felt great about that.

In the meantime, he kept himself busy and began writing a second novel. Cedrick was doing exceptionally well with his online studies. He worked hard, and whenever he was stumped over something, he would turn to Bentley for help. The two of them had become very close over the months. They were like brothers.

Spring had arrived early, and the lane became muddy, but again, with the use of his tractor and blade, Bentley had kept it passable. They had very few visitors, but he didn't want anyone who did come to get stuck in the mud.

On a sunny day in the middle of March, the alarm on the gate sounded. It took only a moment for Bentley to determine that the person at the gate was not a threat. He and Cedrick and the dogs walked down the lane and unlocked the gate. Kamryn Baldwin, completely healed from the gunshot wound she had received, greeted Bentley with a huge smile and a hug.

"I hope you don't mind me just dropping in like this, but you haven't been to Salt Lake for a few weeks and I've missed seeing you," she said.

Bentley liked Kamryn, but he wasn't comfortable with what he perceived were her intentions. She was a beautiful and talented woman, but he was not ready to see anyone romantically, and it was fairly clear she had that in mind. Evie was still on his mind all the time. He missed her desperately. And yet he had to admit that it wouldn't hurt him to spend a little time with Kamryn.

So he welcomed her to his humble homestead, and he and Cedrick walked back up the lane with the dogs as she drove her car to the cabin. It was nearing lunchtime, so he offered to make lunch for her. "Cedrick and I are getting to be pretty good cooks, aren't we, Cedrick?" he said, grinning at the boy.

"I'm not too bad myself, so if you don't mind I'd like to help," Kamryn said. It was obvious that Kamryn knew her way around a kitchen and excelled in the preparation of food. She pitched right in, and Bentley had to admit that the lunch was a lot better than it would have been without her help.

They spent the afternoon showing Kamryn around the property. "I love it here," she said. "It's so rugged, beautiful, and most of all, it's peaceful."

"We like it," Bentley said, even as he thought about the threats, three of them now, which he had received in the mail. He was quite certain Cedrick was right when he insisted they were from his Uncle Claude.

It was Kamryn, just before she was ready to leave for her return trip to Salt Lake, who brought up the topic of threatening letters. They were still outside by the corrals. "There is something I need to show you two. Ember sent me with copies of three letters she has received over the winter. She is very disturbed by them."

Bentley felt a knot form in his stomach. And the look on Cedrick's face told him that he was upset by the very thought of disturbing letters being sent to his sister. "I have them in my purse. She wasn't going to tell you guys about them, but she finally agreed to let me bring them and show you. She's scared but doesn't like to admit it."

They returned to the cabin, and Kamryn retrieved her purse from the kitchen counter. She opened it, and then said, "You guys might want to sit down before you read these." Bentley didn't like the look of fear that crossed her face when she spoke.

The three of them sat around the kitchen table and Kamryn handed the three copies to Bentley. "This was the first one she received," she said, tapping a finger on one. "This is the second one." She tapped another one. "This one came just two days ago."

Bentley, with Cedrick watching closely at his side, unfolded the first one. Before he read it he looked across the table at Kamryn and asked, "Why didn't Ember want to tell me about these before now? She and Cedrick talk on the phone all the time, and I've spoken to her a few times."

"She didn't want to worry you," Kamryn responded, shaking her head. "You know how Ember is. She's not that different from Evie. She is kind and loving and thinks about others before herself. She was thinking about bringing them to you herself after getting the last one, but her schedule is really tight right now." She grinned. "She has a boyfriend, and he takes up some of her time. He's a fellow law student. I think she really likes him."

"I'm happy for her," Bentley said. He was surprised that Ember hadn't mentioned the boyfriend to him or Cedrick.

Kamryn said, "So am I. She agreed to let me bring the letters when I told her I was thinking about visiting you guys."

"Thanks for bringing these for her. Now let's see what they're all about," Bentley said as he picked up the first paper.

CHAPTER TWENTY-SEVEN

THERE WAS NO QUESTION WHO had written the first letter, or the *first threat* to put it more accurately. It was almost identical to the first one Bentley had received a few months earlier. It read: *Ember, your payday is coming. Because of you and your actions, my life has been ruined. I won't let you get away with it. I won't tell you what I plan to do, because I want it to be a surprise. And what a surprise it will be. I'll be in touch again.*

"Uncle Claude," Cedrick said in a frightened whisper.

"That's what Ember thought. Read the next one," Kamryn urged.

Again, it was very closely worded to the second one Bentley had received. The third one was unlike any of the ones Claude had sent to Bentley. In this one, even though Claude did not give a return address, he did not attempt to hide the fact that it was from him. It was signed with his name. The threats were very explicit. "That's why Ember got scared and allowed me to bring the notes to you," Kamryn said.

A lawsuit had been served on him late one night when he'd broken into Faye's house a second time. The cops had been watching the house. He'd spent a few weeks in jail for the previous break-in and vandalism to the house as well as the theft of Cedrick's money. Unfortunately, a soft-on-crime, liberal district court judge, over the objections of the prosecutor, released him on his own recognizance. Claude did not appear for his next hearing date. He hadn't been seen since then, but the latest threats to both Ember and Bentley had been delivered recently, so it was many weeks after he was served with the lawsuit that he ramped up his threats.

Where he was, however, no one seemed to know. But wherever he was, he appeared to be a significant threat to Ember as well as to Bentley, and for that matter, to Cedrick as well. Bentley was a duly licensed private investigator, and he'd gained some experience over the winter. He was licensed under a pseudonym.

For his work as a PI, he was known as Booker Tilman. The sheriff had suggested it as a way to insulate himself from enemies who knew him as Bentley Radford. He had created a profile for himself under that name on social media where he also listed a false address and phone number for a cell phone he used only for his PI work. He did not put a photo of himself on the social media profile. It was time to put his experience to work and see if he could locate Claude.

Kamryn, as if reading his thoughts, said, "Ember and I are hoping that as a private investigator you'll be able to figure out where he is and even do something to stop him from hurting anyone."

"I'll do my best," Bentley said, even as he wondered what his best would be. So far, despite a lot of effort, he had not made any progress. His first consideration was Cedrick. He'd been entrusted with the boy's care, and he intended to make sure that no harm came to him.

"Oh, and, Bentley, Ember is also worried about her Aunt Faye. She hired someone to fix the damages that Claude made to her house. She's pretty sure he was planning to damage it again when he was arrested."

That gave Bentley an idea. He said, "Cedrick, would you like to make a visit to your Aunt Faye's house and help me set up some cameras and alarms there?"

"But nobody would be there if he comes again," Cedrick said.

"You and I will know and we can call the police. I'll set them to alert my cell phone and my computer," Bentley said. "Then, if we see him, we can call the police."

"Oh, that's a good idea. Could we also have them alert my phone and my computer?" Cedrick asked.

"That's also a good idea, Cedrick. We'll do that." Bentley turned to Kamryn, who was standing near the front door. "We'll get right on it, Kamryn. I'll redouble my efforts to locate the guy. Tell Ember to be very careful."

"I will, and she is being watchful all the time. I am too," Kamryn said. "We both live in fear every day." She trembled as she spoke. It made Bentley angrier than ever at Silas. "Thanks for your help, you guys." She gave Cedrick a hug, and then she turned to face Bentley. "You are a good man, Bentley. Thanks for all you do." With that, he also got a hug. He had to admit that it didn't feel too bad, even though it lasted a bit longer than he was comfortable with.

After she was gone, Bentley said to his brother-in-law, "We'll go to Salt Lake as soon as we get our chores done in the morning." He looked at the young man with concern and had a thought. "You know what Cedrick; I think it's time I teach you to shoot a pistol and a rifle. We have plenty of room to set up a firing range. I could use more practice too."

Cedrick pumped his fists and said, "Yes!"

"I don't expect that you'll ever need to use any of my guns, but I'd feel better if I knew you were proficient with them," Bentley told him.

"Ember and Kamryn need to be able to protect themselves," he said. "And so does Aunt Faye."

"I guess we need to suggest that they carry Mace. A little spray of Mace will stop the toughest of men," Bentley said.

Cedrick stated the obvious when he remarked, "You and me, we need to watch out for Claude and Silas."

That was a sobering thought. Right now, his greatest concern was for Evie's twin sister, Ember. Cedrick was with him most of the time. He was never alone even at his Young Men's activities. Ember was on her own. He pulled out his phone and drafted a text to her, suggesting that she and Kamryn needed to carry Mace. He would have called her, but he didn't want to disturb her if she was in class. Before he sent the text, he thought about Kamryn and her short visit. She was a very sweet lady, and he worried about her as well.

He reworded the text and then sent it to both women. When that was done, he also wrote a text to Faye. He told her of the threats Claude had been making and warned her to be careful and to carry Mace in her purse. He sent that text as well and then explained to Cedrick what he had just done.

The two of them sat down at their computers. Cedrick worked on an assignment for one of his online classes, and Bentley renewed his search for Claude, knowing it might be fruitless. But he had to try again. The man had become a very serious threat.

**

Ember was in class when she got Bentley's text. She waited until after class to call him. "I already have Mace in my purse," she said. "And I know how to spray it if I ever need to. Is Cedrick okay?"

"I'm relieved, but you can't be too careful, Ember," Bentley warned her. "I'll continue in my effort to find Claude, but I admit that it won't be easy. And about Cedrick, he's doing great."

"I worry about him, too," Ember said.

"That makes two of us," Bentley agreed. Then he told her of his plans to teach him to shoot guns safely and proficiently. He also mentioned that he was coming to Salt Lake the following day, and that he planned to put cameras and alarms in and around Faye's empty house. Then he asked, "Do you know where she's living now?"

"I don't. She says she's keeping it secret so Claude won't be able to find her," Ember responded. "I'm pretty sure she's somewhere here on the Wasatch Front."

"I don't blame her for keeping her address to herself. I think I should call her though. I know she doesn't have the same phone number because I've tried it. Do you have a current cell phone number for her?"

"I do, and I'll text it to you," Ember said. "Bentley, how will the cameras and alarms at her house be monitored?"

He explained, and then she said, "Can you include my phone too? I'd like to be notified if anyone attempts to get into her old house. I know she'd hoped to sell it by now, but it hasn't happened yet."

"If you want me to include you, I will," Bentley responded.

"I do, and when you guys come to Salt Lake, I'd like to take you to lunch," she said.

"Do you have time?" he asked. "I mean with your studies and boyfriend and all."

Ember laughed. "I thought Kamryn would mention him. I'll make time for you guys. You are two of the most important people in my life. I wish I could spend more time with you," she said, and she really meant it. "I think I'll invite Kamryn to have lunch with us too."

Ember felt bad that she hadn't had time to go with Kamryn to see Bentley and Cedrick that morning, but she was honestly too busy. She was no fool, either. She knew that Kamryn had developed a strong attraction to Bentley. She always glowed whenever his name was brought up, and Ember had no problem with that. She didn't know if Bentley would ever open his heart to anyone after losing Evie. But if he did, she hoped it would be to Kamryn.

She headed back to her apartment at seven that evening after spending several hours studying at the library with her boyfriend, Brad Jensen. She was mentally exhausted. Law school was not a snap, far from it, but she enjoyed it, especially when she was studying criminal law. That was where her heart was. She wanted to someday help put evil people behind bars, people like Claude and Silas.

As she drove, she was constantly on the lookout for Claude. She prayed that he wouldn't confront her, but she feared after that latest threat that unless he could be found first it was almost inevitable at some point. Brad shared her concerns and had become very protective of her. She prayed that Bentley would finally have success in his search in finding where Claude was living and have the police arrest him.

Her phone rang, interrupting her thoughts. She saw on the screen that it was her Aunt Faye calling. She accepted the call and was glad she had Bluetooth so she could keep both hands on the wheel as she drove.

"Hello, Aunt Faye," Ember said cheerfully. She loved Faye, even though she wondered how she'd ever found anything to love about Claude. She supposed, though, that he must have changed for the worse over the years. However, he'd always given her the creeps and she had never liked being around him.

"Hi my dear girl," Faye said. "I hesitated to call you because I know how busy you are with your schooling. But I thought you needed to know that you may be in danger."

"Yes, I know that," Ember said. "I'm being as careful as I can."

"I just spoke with Bentley. He says that you carry Mace. I hope you never have to use it, but if Claude tries to harm you in any way, don't hesitate to spray it in his face. He has become evil in a way I would never have suspected could possibly happen," Faye said. "He was a good man once. But he's not anymore. I'm sorry that his wickedness is affecting you and your brother and Evie's husband."

"Did Bentley tell you what he plans to do tomorrow?" Ember asked.

"He did, and I'm grateful to him, but I don't think Claude will come back to the house unless he is enticed there in some way."

Ember felt a sudden queasiness in her stomach. She hoped that Faye wasn't planning to do something that would put her in grave danger. She voiced her concern to her aunt. Faye then said, "I can't do *nothing*, Ember. I have to take some kind of action. His threats can't go on. He has to be stopped before he hurts one or more of us. Bentley told me about the threatening letters you received. He got them too."

"He did?" she said in surprise. "I didn't know that. He should have told me. That means my little brother is in danger!" She felt prickles on her skin and rubbed the arm that was holding the steering wheel.

"He didn't want to worry you, Ember. But he did tell Kamryn today, and she's planning to tell you about it as soon as she gets home."

"This is horrible!" Ember exclaimed as she looked at the cars behind her. She saw nothing to further alarm her, but she knew that didn't mean there wasn't danger back there somewhere. Her chills intensified.

"Yes, it is, and as you can imagine, he found a way to send threats to me. He figured out that I have a job, because the threats were sent to my employer who gave them to me."

"Oh, Aunt Faye, I'm so sorry. Why can't he just leave you alone?"

"He's become a very vengeful man, Ember. And it's gotten worse over the past few years. Ember, I have to do something, and Bentley and I have worked out a tentative plan," Faye revealed.

Ember's stomach was doing somersaults now. She wasn't sure she wanted to know what the plan was, but she had to know, because if she didn't, she'd worry even more. Finally, as she pulled into the parking area of her apartment building, she said, "I guess you'd better tell me. But I hope it doesn't in some way put Cedrick in danger."

"It won't, I promise you," Faye said. "Bentley and I both think there is a good chance that it will work. If it does, then Claude will be back in jail, and I've been assured he will not get out on his own recognizance again. In fact, there will hopefully be a very high bail set, one he can't possibly make."

Ember pulled into her parking spot and shut off her car before saying, "Okay, tell me what the plan is."

CHAPTER TWENTY-EIGHT

FAYE EXPLAINED TO EMBER WHAT she and Bentley were going to do in an attempt to entice Claude back to the house they had lived in as husband and wife and where they'd raised their family. Ember wasn't convinced that it would work, but she guessed it might be worth a try. However, she was not enthusiastic about it. The part of the plan she didn't like was Bentley putting himself in danger. She thought about calling him and telling him it was too dangerous, but she chose not to do that. She had to trust that Bentley would be wise and that God would keep him safe.

She thought about Cedrick and wondered what he would do and where he would be while Bentley was on the risky mission he and Faye had planned. She started worrying about him so much that she finally called Faye back. "Where will Cedrick be while Bentley is waiting for Claude to walk into the trap you guys are setting at your old house?"

"He'll be safe," Faye assured her. "Detective Parker and his wife and family will take care of him."

"Will he stay at the detective's house?" Ember asked.

"Yes, except for when the cow has to be milked and the dogs and other animals fed. Then Detective Parker will take Cedrick to Bentley's cabin with him. They'll do the chores, check everything out, then go back to the Parkers' place," Faye explained.

That eased Ember's mind as she entered her apartment. She had met both the detective and his wife at Evie's funeral, and she felt quite certain that Cedrick would be safe with them. "How long will this take?" Ember asked.

"That's what we don't know, but Bentley is determined to spend however much time he needs to in order to catch Claude," Faye said. "I still can't believe my husband, my ex-husband now, has stooped so low. It was bad enough that he stole Cedrick's money, but this is just appalling. He's got to be stopped and locked up before someone gets hurt."

"Or worse," Ember added softly as a shiver ran up her spine.

"Yes, or worse," Faye agreed, her voice dark and troubled.

Feeling better about Cedrick's safety, Ember checked the time. It was eight o'clock. Kamryn should have been home before Ember got back from the law school. She knew that Kamryn could take care of herself and that she didn't need to tell Ember every move she made. But there was danger facing both of them, and that made things vastly different.

She picked up her phone again and called Kamryn's number. It went to voice mail. Ember tried not to let that worry her. She could be on the phone with her parents. Or maybe someone else had called her and she was talking to that person. She decided to wait a few minutes and try again, hoping Kamryn would suddenly walk in and explain why she was late, and it would make perfect sense to Ember.

She waited five minutes and tried again. The call again went to voice mail. For the next half hour, as her anxiety grew, she continued to call Kamryn's number every five minutes. Finally, feeling panicked, she called Bentley.

"Hi Ember, what's up?" Bentley asked.

"I'm worried, and I probably shouldn't be. What time did Kamryn leave your place, or is she still there?" she asked, pretty sure that Kamryn had not planned to stay very late.

"She left hours ago," Bentley said. "Why do you ask?"

"She isn't home yet and I've tried her phone a whole bunch of times and all I get is her voice mail," she responded, trying to keep her voice calm and normal. She didn't think she was doing very well, because anxiety was eating her alive.

"Ember, you sound super stressed. Is it unusual for Kamryn to be late coming home from wherever she might have gone?" Bentley asked.

"Well, no, but we've never had threats hanging over us like we do now. She knows I'm scared, and I think she would have come straight back here from your place."

"Okay, try not to worry. She hasn't been directly threatened like you have."

"We're best friends and roommates. Any threat to me is a threat to her. We've talked about that and she understands it," Ember said.

"Give it another half hour and if she isn't back by then, call me again," Bentley suggested.

"Thanks Bentley. I'll do that. Hey, are you sure you want to put yourself in danger so you can catch Claude? Maybe he's bluffing," she said.

"Ember, we have to believe he means to do more than frighten us. Faye is convinced that he's planning something. We can't let our guard down for a second. He has to be stopped before he does whatever it is he's thinking of doing. I'll be okay. If he shows up at the house like we're hoping he will, I'll be prepared to take him down. I can take care of myself. You don't need to worry about me."

She sighed. "I'm mostly worried about my roommate."

"She's probably fine, just got busy somewhere and let her phone's battery die," he said.

"You're probably right. How is Cedrick handling the threats?" she asked.

"He's okay, Ember. Living with a man who hated him like Claude does can't be easy, but it's made him tough. Call me in thirty minutes if Kamryn hasn't gotten there yet. Call me anyway if she gets home before that."

She agreed, and the call ended. She kept thinking of what Bentley must have gone through while he was waiting for Evie to come home the night she was killed. Compared to her present situation, she couldn't even imagine the torture Bentley must have gone through. Thinking of Evie's accident made her wonder if Kamryn had been in a bad accident. She knew that was possible and would explain why her phone went to voice mail. She prayed that Kamryn had not been injured.

Ember looked at the time every minute or two. Kamryn still didn't appear. Her phone rang. She glanced at the screen and gave a sigh of relief. It was Kamryn calling. She answered.

"*I've got your roommate,*" a voice she didn't recognize said before she could even say hello. It sounded like the caller was talking through a cloth or something. She began to tremble.

"Who are you?" she asked.

"No questions," the caller said with a voice that sounded more evil than anything she'd ever heard. "Just follow my instructions or this woman dies. Contact your brother-in-law. Have him call this phone. I'll trade this woman for him. That's the only way she lives. When he calls, I'll arrange for the trade. Don't call the police or she dies."

Just like that the call ended. Ember was shaking so badly she had to sit down. She was numb with fear. She fumbled with her phone and dropped it on the floor. It took her a moment to calm down enough to pick it up. She had to call Bentley and willed her shaking hands to cooperate.

***

Bentley looked at the screen on his phone. It hadn't been quite a half hour since he'd talked to her, but Ember was calling him again. He hoped that meant that Kamryn was home and Ember could relax a little. "Hi, so she's home?" he asked as soon as he answered.

"She's not." The very tone of Ember's voice told him that something terrible had happened. She was having a hard time talking, but she managed to tell him, "Someone has kidnapped Kamryn. I got a phone call."

His gut twisted painfully. Silas! It had to be him. He asked, "Is it Silas that called?"

"I don't know, but probably. The voice was muffled." For a moment she said nothing, and Bentley waited in anguish. Finally, she spoke again. "He will kill her unless . . ." Her voice faded into unintelligible garble. Then she cried.

"Ember, try to get hold of yourself. I'll find her." He hoped. But he didn't know how he'd do it. Poor sweet Kamryn. First she was shot, and now she's been kidnapped. "Try to talk to me, Ember."

She made a valiant effort. "Call Kamryn's phone," she managed to say. "Then call me back."

The call ended with the sound of Ember's sobs. She was terrified, and his heart ached for her. It had to be Silas behind this. Or could it be Claude? It was one or the other. He'd figure it out as soon as he made the call. He had Kamryn's number in his contacts, so he called her phone, dread filling him. He was quite certain she wouldn't be answering the phone herself. "Radford, your number is up. I have Kamryn. You can save her by giving yourself up. And that is the only way." It was a muffled voice, as Ember had told him. It was either Silas or Claude, and Bentley was leaning toward Silas.

"Silas, I know it's you," he said, taking a chance. "You're in way over your head."

"You ruined my life! The only way to get it back is for you and me to meet face-to-face. Of course, you will have to die, but you deserve to. If you call the cops or don't follow my instructions, this girl will die and it will be your fault."

"No one else needs to die," Bentley said as he realized the caller had not denied it when he'd called him Silas. Right now, Silas had the advantage. Bentley could not let Kamryn die. If it cost him his life to save her, so be it. At least he would be with Evie again. But that would leave Cedrick alone and probably cause Ember to give up her dream of becoming an attorney. He could not just roll over and give in to Silas without a fight. He would do anything to spare sweet Kamryn further pain.

He was not to call the police. Well then, he'd call his elders quorum president, who just happened to be a cop, but he needed Hank's advice. He called Hank just as Cedrick wandered into the room. He wished he could save Cedrick from worry, but there was no way. "What's wrong, Bentley?" the boy asked.

He waved the hand with the phone in it. "Just a second, Cedrick."

Hank answered. "What's up, Bentley?"

"I have a problem. Kamryn, Ember's roommate whom you met, has been kidnapped," he said.

"The girl that was shot?" Hank asked.

"Yes, her," he agreed.

"How do you know this?"

"I just talked to the kidnapper on Kamryn's phone."

"Okay, so tell me what you know." Hank sounded calm, something that Bentley certainly didn't feel.

Bentley told him everything he knew about the situation, and he put his arm around Cedrick as he spoke. The boy was trembling, as was to be expected. "I'm coming out to your place," Hank said after Bentley completed telling him about Kamryn's abduction.

"I wasn't supposed to involve the cops, so I called my elder's quorum president," Bentley said. "I knew you could advise me. But we can't involve other police."

"I'll be discreet and can give you some advice. Give me Kamryn's cell phone number and I'll get someone working on locating her phone. Let's hope Silas is stupid enough to not think about the fact that we can find him that way," Hank said. "While I do that, I'll be driving as fast as I can to your cabin. You call Ember and let her know we're working on finding Kamryn. Are you sure it's Silas?"

"Pretty sure," Bentley said. "

"Okay, then we'll assume that it's Silas," Hank responded. "What about the uncle who sent the threatening letters, Bentley. Could it be him?"

"When I called the person I talked to by Silas's name, he didn't deny it, so I'm pretty sure it's him."

"That's to be expected. But if it was Claude, he would probably let you assume that just to throw you off track," Hank reasoned.

"You're right. I guess it could be either one of them. Okay, I'll call Ember. And I'll see you in a few minutes," Bentley said and ended the call.

"You've gotta find her, but you can't let him hurt her," Cedrick said, trying hard to be brave.

"We will, Cedrick. I need to call Ember now."

CHAPTER TWENTY-NINE

A HUGE FIRE WAS RAGING near LA, and Lonnie, Queen, and the men who had come with them from Utah had been spread out for the past hour watching the inferno along with other curious folks while they waited for Silas. They believed he couldn't resist coming to watch the fire, if he was in the area. The news of the fire was on all the news channels, and Silas should surely hear about it. They believed he was in the area, because Silas, or someone who might have been him had been spotted just a couple of days earlier right here in LA. They were sure he would hear about the fire and show up to watch it burn.

So far, however, there was no sign of Silas. The location, a large industrial complex, was surrounded by firefighters and cops. It had been a good plan, but so far, it had not worked out the way Lonnie had thought it would. Lonnie gave it a little more time, but Silas still didn't appear. Lonnie called his gang on the walkie-talkies he'd provided for them and told them to meet him at their cars and they would plan what to do next. As far as he was concerned, there were two options: they could continue to watch for Silas, or move on to another area and set another blaze the next day.

They had parked their cars a block or so away from the area where they'd set the fires, because they had ignited several different spots around the complex. They'd used gasoline as an accelerant, and they'd carried the empty gas cans back to the vehicles and then proceeded to watch for Silas while the fire grew in intensity. They all gathered around the cars and were deep in a discussion when lights suddenly blazed around them and cops appeared from every side. From a bullhorn they were told to put their hands in the air and step away from the cars.

Surrendering was not in Lonnie's DNA. He was not going back to prison. He angrily dropped to the ground, pulled his 9mm handgun and began to shoot at the cops. His friends foolishly followed his example. The exchange of gunfire went on for over a minute. It only stopped when a couple of Lonnie's group raised their arms in surrender from where they lay on the searing hot, smelly pavement.

The police cautiously advanced, clearly prepared to fire again at anyone who raised a gun. No one made that mistake. Some couldn't, because they were either dead or too severely wounded to do so; the rest apparently knew they were beat. Of the eight people who had come to LA to try to capture Silas, two were dead, three were severely wounded, and the other three had minor wounds. One of the dead was Lonnie Defollo. The least wounded was Queen Wise, who had been the first to raise her arms in surrender.

In one way, Lonnie got his wish. He would not be going back to prison.

***

Kamryn was scared, but not so badly that she would go down without a fight. She was also very, very angry. She knew the identity of the man who had forced her to stop by pulling directly in front of her, then viciously jerking her from her car just a couple blocks from her apartment building. He'd abandoned his stolen car right in the middle of the street, forced her back into her car at gunpoint, hopped into the driver's seat, and driven away. She was certain this was the despicable man who had mistakenly shot her while he was trying to shoot Bentley. It was Silas Villard!

He had stopped at one point and put a pair of handcuffs on her, the exact thing that Bentley had told her had happened to the teenage girl from California. If that teenage girl could get away from Silas, then surely she could. She just wasn't sure how. The only thing she could think of was to wait and see if an opportunity presented itself. So far, she had not been hurt badly. She'd bruised a shin and bumped her head when he was trying to force her back into her car after compelling her to stop. That was nothing compared to what he'd done to her before, nearly killing her with the bullet that was meant for Bentley.

Right now they were just driving around the city, mostly sticking to residential areas. She was seated behind him with her handcuffed hands on her lap. He'd fastened a seat belt around her, but she had some freedom of movement. She'd heard him talking to Bentley on her phone. She wasn't sure Silas even had one of his own. If he did, she hadn't seen it.

Silas had provided the incentive for her to find a way to get away from him when he'd told Bentley that he would free her when he turned himself over to him, but that Bentley was going to have to die for the trouble he'd caused.

Kamryn knew Bentley well enough to know that he'd sacrifice himself to save her. She couldn't allow that to happen. That meant she had to get away from Silas. There was no other way that she could think of to save Bentley, a man for whom she had developed tender feelings.

She kept her mind active, considering her options as they drove randomly around the city. So far, no promising ideas had occurred to her. She assumed Silas was killing time while he tried to figure out where he wanted to meet Bentley. She knew enough about Silas to know he was not a very clever person. In fact, he was rather dumb in a lot of ways. Kamryn, however, was highly intelligent. She knew, for example, that she had been very low on gas when she was driving toward her apartment. That gave her an idea.

Kamryn had thought about stopping to fill the gas tank but had decided that could wait until morning. She'd planned to gas up before she drove very far from her apartment. She knew she had a glaring weakness—Kamryn was a procrastinator. She'd put things off when she probably shouldn't, but it had never caused her any serious problems, only the occasional inconvenience. So, she'd failed to change, working on other weaknesses, which she felt were more significant.

Right now, Kamryn was hoping that her habit of procrastinating would prove to be an advantage to her in the next few minutes. Either Silas would have to stop at a service station for gas, or he would run out, having no choice but to stop at that point. Either way, she would try to get out of her car and flee. With that in mind, she very carefully and quietly turned in an attempt to reach the latch on the seatbelt and press down on it. It took a while because the seatbelt was quite tight and she was barely able to reach the latch, but she finally succeeded. Once free of the seatbelt, she could open the door when he stopped, jump out, and run to the nearest house as fast as she possibly could.

She prayed that the gasoline problem would soon give her a chance to escape. She took heart in the fact that Silas was doing the very same stupid thing that had helped Piper, the girl Silas had kidnapped in California, escape. He was apparently one of those people who did not learn from past mistakes.

The guy had a severe drinking problem and he was guzzling one beer after another from a twelve-pack that he'd thrown on the front seat of her car before getting in himself. The drunker he got before he ran out of gas or finally noticed that the car was running on fumes and was about to stop, the better her chance of getting away from him would be.

He apparently had not bothered to look at the gas gauge, because he passed several gas stations. Kamryn knew the car would run out of gas soon.

She took hold of the door handle with her handcuffed hands. She was ready to leap out. The car began to sputter, and then, with Silas cursing, it stopped. He was on a street lined with homes and had not even managed to pull to the side of the road. The car was still rolling slowly when Kamryn opened the door and jumped out. She stumbled and went down hard on the pavement, but she managed to get up and start running, dodging back and forth, despite pain in her right knee and both her handcuffed hands.

They were in a neighborhood with lots of houses. She headed for the nearest one, a two-story red brick house with thick, flowering bushes beside the steps that led onto a large porch. She had almost reached the door when she heard Silas cursing at her and telling her to stop or he'd kill her. She screamed for help and knocked once before she both heard and felt a bullet. It had hit her hip, causing her to fall hard onto the porch.

Kamryn expected another bullet, but only seconds after she was shot, the door opened and a man stepped out onto the porch. She heard Silas curse again, but then by turning her head she saw him running down the street, the pistol still in his hands. The man who had stepped out of the house dropped to his knees beside her. "You're shot," he said, stating the obvious. "Sue, call 911; this girl has been shot. I'm Grady Hilton. I'm off duty, but I'm a paramedic. I can begin treating you right now."

Grady wasted no time in pulling out a pocket knife and cutting her pants to expose the wound in her hip. As he worked he said to his wife, who had made the call to 911, "Get my bag."

She didn't ask what bag, and Kamryn, in her pain, hoped it was something like an advanced first-aid kit. It was. He worked at stopping the bleeding. Again, to Sue, he said, "Did you see the guy who shot her?"

Sue was obviously very sharp, because she said, "I did, and I described him to the 911 operator after requesting an ambulance and the police."

Even though she was in a great deal of pain, Kamryn was able to speak. "His name is Silas Villard. He is wanted for murder. He kidnapped me. That's my car in the street."

She heard the wail of sirens and closed her eyes, gritting her teeth. The pain was dreadful, but she was pretty sure she wasn't hurt as seriously as the first time Silas had shot her. She prayed that the cops would find and arrest Silas. If they didn't, he would try this same thing again. He didn't seem to have fresh ideas or he wouldn't have done the same thing with her as he had with Piper.

The ambulance arrived, along with several police cars. Sue Hilton described Silas to the officers, and they told Kamryn that there were other officers looking for him. They told her that since he was on foot he surely couldn't get far before they found and arrested him. As the officer spoke to her, one of them removed the handcuffs from her bleeding hands. She'd hit the pavement pretty hard and had scraped her hands badly.

Despite the pain, and it was getting worse as the paramedics worked on her wounds, she kept from crying out.

Grady said, "We'll get you on a stretcher in a moment."

She thought about Bentley as the pain surged and said, "He's going to kill my friend Bentley Radford. His number is in my phone."

"Where is your phone?" Grady asked.

"Oh, I guess Silas has it unless he dropped it when I jumped out of the car," she said.

She was on a stretcher by the time one of the officers came up to her and showed her a phone and asked if it was hers. "Yes. Call Bentley Radford and my roommate, Ember Skeed."

Grady had the phone in his hand and he asked, "What's your PIN?" She told him and he opened the phone. Silas had made the same request when he'd first grabbed her, but he hadn't asked nicely like Grady did. He'd demanded it with the threat of death if she refused.

A couple of minutes later, she was in the ambulance. Grady had joined the other paramedics. They didn't question his decision to stay with Kamryn since he was one of them. She closed her eyes and prayed for Bentley.

***

Silas cursed his bad luck. He'd run out of gas, and it was that stupid girl's fault. She should have kept her tank full. Not once did he blame himself for failing to notice that it was nearly out of gas. As was his habit, he blamed someone else— Kamryn in this case.

He should have shot the guy who came out of the house, but he'd panicked and run. He could have shot the guy before he ran. But he justified himself in doing what he'd done by thinking that the guy may have been armed. He cursed the man for being home and answering the door when Kamryn screamed. Just more bad luck. He was smart enough to know the cops would be hot on his trail. He had to get away. The only way to do that was what he always did: steal another car.

A yellow Volkswagen was coming up the street after he'd run for a couple of blocks. He lifted his gun and ordered the young lady driver from the car. Seconds later, he was driving away. They wouldn't catch him now.

CHAPTER THIRTY

BENTLEY'S PHONE RANG. HE LOOKED at the screen, expecting it to be Silas on Kamryn's phone. It was Kamryn's phone, but the voice that spoke to him wasn't Silas's voice, nor was it disguised in any way.

"I'm Grady Hilton, a paramedic in Salt Lake. I am in an ambulance with a young lady who is very concerned about you," the voice on the phone said to him.

"Is it Kamryn?" Bentley asked as he felt a chill come over him. He didn't wait for an answer before asking, "Is she hurt badly? What happened to her?"

"She is hurt, but it's not life threatening. She has a bullet wound in her hip. We are on our way to the University Hospital. She wanted you to know."

"I'll get there as soon as I can, but it will be a while since I live a long way from Salt Lake. But please let her know I'm coming," Bentley said as he thought about how truly evil Silas Villard was. Why couldn't anyone catch him? It was so maddening.

That call had no sooner ended than his phone rang again. This time it was Ember's phone and it was Ember who spoke. "Bentley, have you heard anything? I haven't. Oh, wait, my phone is ringing. I'll call you back."

Bentley was sure it was the paramedic, Grady, who had just talked to him and who was now calling Ember. Sure enough, she called him back a couple of minutes later and said, "I just got a call from a paramedic. Kamryn has been shot by Silas again!" She was clearly upset, but it was as much with anger at Silas as it was with grief over her roommate.

"Go to the hospital as soon as you can. I'll head that way shortly. She'll be okay, Ember. She is one courageous woman, I can tell you that. Hopefully this time someone will catch Silas," Bentley said, while actually fearing that the scoundrel would get away again.

When Hank showed up, his wife was behind him in her personal vehicle. Hank said, "She will take care of Cedrick. You go do what you need to do to help Kamryn."

"Thanks," Bentley said.

Before he could explain about the call from Grady, Hank went on, "We are working on tracing Kamryn's cell phone."

"You don't need to do that. It's been found and so has Kamryn. She's going to be okay, or so I'm told, but Silas shot her again and got away. She was treated by a paramedic whose house she'd miraculously run to for help."

Hank looked stunned. "How in the world did that happen?"

"I don't know the details. The paramedic, whose name is Grady, called me on Kamryn's phone to tell me. I have his contact information and will give it to you. But I need to get to Salt Lake," Bentley said. "I've got to see for myself that Kamryn is going to live."

"You go then. My wife and I will take care of both Cedrick and your animals until you get back," Hank said. "I'll also call the Salt Lake City police and see if I can get an update on the search for Silas."

Bentley grabbed the overnight bag he'd packed while waiting for Hank. Then he headed for the door, telling Cedrick not to worry about him. Cedrick was an amazing young man and he said, "I'll pray for you and for Kamryn."

***

Ember found Kamryn in the emergency room awaiting surgery. She was in pain, but not too severely since she was on a heavy dose of pain meds. She spoke easily to Ember. "I can't believe Silas shot me again." Kamryn said. "He's a despicable person."

"I'll say he is," Ember agreed. "Tell me what happened. I was terribly worried about you when you didn't come home when I thought you would. I kept calling your phone, and each time it went to voice mail. I knew something was wrong."

"I'm sorry you worried, but this is what happened." Kamryn went on to tell Ember how Silas had carjacked her and what occurred after that.

"I can't believe how brave you were," Ember said with admiration. "You actually jumped out of the car when it ran out of gas and ran screaming to the nearest house?"

"I had no choice. Bentley would have sacrificed himself for me. He would for either one of us. You and I both know that. I'm lucky Silas didn't kill me when I jumped out. I think he would have, had it not been for the paramedic that lived in the house I ran to," Kamryn said. She winced as a spasm of pain hit her.

"They've got to get you to surgery, and I hope they do it soon," Ember said.

"I do too." Kamryn grinned painfully. "It'll be good to go to sleep. Thanks for coming, Ember. I hope I'm not in the hospital long this time."

"I'm sure you won't be, but I'll be with you as much as I can. And Bentley is on his way."

"I knew he would be. He's such a great guy. Is Cedrick okay?"

"Hank Parker, the detective who spoke at Evie's funeral and his wife will take care of Cedrick."

"Ember, I'm worried about Bentley. Unless Silas is arrested this time, he'll go after Bentley again. He's like a bad penny; he just keeps coming back. He is full of hate for Bentley. He's the most evil man I've ever seen."

"Yes, Kamryn, he is,' Ember agreed.

"Is Bentley still planning to try to trick your uncle and catch him?" Kamryn asked after a pause in which her face grimaced with pain.

"He is, and I hope it works," Ember replied. "I worry so much about Bentley."

"So do I," Kamryn said. "I know this sounds crazy, but I care deeply for him."

Just then a nurse came in and announced that they were ready to take Kamryn into surgery. "I'll be waiting for you when you get out," Ember said. "And I'll be here for you until you're released from the hospital."

"Don't let your studies suffer because of me," Kamryn said.

"Don't worry, I'll be okay. I'll be praying for you."

"Please pray for Bentley too," Kamryn said.

Ember was certainly doing that. Moments later, Kamryn was wheeled away.

Kamryn had just revealed what Ember had suspected. She cared for Bentley. That was okay with her. At some point Bentley needed to move on, and perhaps he would come to see in Kamryn what Ember saw in her.

***

Hank called Bentley just as he reached Heber City. "They found a yellow VW that Silas stole after shooting Kamryn. They have no idea where he is now," Hank reported.

"Why am I not surprised?" Bentley said bitterly.

"The guy is one lucky crook," Hank said. "But his luck will run out. We've just got to keep looking for him."

They spoke for a minute more, then the call ended and Bentley called Ember. "I'm not surprised," was her reaction when he gave her the update on Silas. "Bentley, you have to be extra careful. It's pretty clear that he intends to keep attempting to get you. You can't let that happen."

"I'll be careful, but I'm more worried about you and Kamryn than I am about myself. I wish all four of us could stay together out at my cabin until Silas is caught. But I know that's not possible."

"I wish it was," Ember said. "I know Kamryn would like that."

"Listen, I'll be at the hospital before long. Tell me how Kamryn is doing."

"She's in surgery, Bentley. I can't believe this has happened to her again. It's so unfair."

"I guess life isn't fair, is it?" Bentley said as he thought of Evie's untimely and tragic death.

"Bentley, are you sure you want to try to lure Claude the way you're planning? It scares me," Ember said in a sudden change of topic.

"If he comes to Faye's house like we're hoping, I'll be hidden. I'll have the advantage of knowing that he's coming while he'll have no idea I'm waiting for him," Bentley said. "I'll be fine."

"You better be," Ember said with a fierceness he'd never heard in her voice before.

"I'll let you know when we get it set up," Bentley said as his dead wife's twin sobbed. He told her goodbye and ended the call.

Bentley had never expected this to happen, but he was developing feelings for Kamryn. What would Evie think if she knew? There settled over him a calmness he hadn't felt since losing Evie. And to his mind came the distinct impression that Evie would be okay with it. He tried to shake the feeling off, but it stubbornly stayed there, as did the calmness in his heart.

He looked at his watch and thought about his impending visit with Kamryn at the hospital, hoping she would be doing okay. He found himself longing to see her. As recently as her visit that morning, he hadn't realized how much he'd come to care for her.

When his phone rang, he saw that it was Faye calling. He answered, asked her how she was holding up, and then listened to what she had to say. "I'm going to the house tonight to put a few finishing touches on the repairs. I know you're going to the hospital to see Kamryn. But I was wondering if you could meet me there around seven or eight."

"Let's say eight," Bentley said.

"That works for me. I'll see you then. And remember to be careful, Bentley. You don't deserve to have any enemies, but you have two, don't you?"

"I'm afraid so, but I am being very watchful."

"Give my regards to Kamryn. She's a special lady. When she's up to it, give her a hug for me," she said. "You probably don't realize this, but Ember tells me that Kamryn has come to care for you. And I'm so glad that Ember has found someone. Brad is a perfect fit for her, in my opinion."

Bentley didn't respond to what Faye had said. He was keeping his heart protected. The loss of Evie was too recent. With time, perhaps he would see what would happen with Kamryn, if anything. But he didn't so much as hint at that to Faye. He did hope he'd get to meet Brad soon, because he wanted to know that Ember had found someone worthy of her.

When he walked into the hospital, a deep sadness settled over him. He was sad for Kamryn, but mostly he was sad that he'd lost Evie. Amazingly, the sadness lifted when he stepped into the room where Kamryn was now recuperating from her surgery. She was doped up on pain meds but managed a smile. Ember, who was sitting beside her friend's bed, surged to her feet and threw her arms around Bentley. She released him, and Bentley stepped over to Kamryn and placed a hand on hers. He felt a welcome peace settle over him. Kamryn looked right into his eyes and smiled a little brighter.

He stayed there for an hour. Kamryn became fairly alert and talked to Ember and Bentley about the horror of being taken by Silas, but also about how she was blessed to escape from him and live to talk about it.

As he rose to leave, Kamryn spoke softly. She said, "Thanks for coming Bentley. I knew you would." Then she turned to Ember. "If it's okay with Brad, you should go with Bentley to your aunt's place," she insisted.

"I should stay with you," Ember said.

"It's okay. Call Brad. Maybe he would want to go too and it would give Bentley a chance to meet him," Kamryn said.

Bentley approached her bedside, leaned down and gently kissed her forehead. "Thank you, Kamryn. I'm sorry that Silas hurt you again. You rest now and get well. If it's okay, I'll wait here instead of going to get something to eat. I don't have to be at Faye's until eight."

Ember had stepped into the hallway, so Bentley and Kamryn were alone. Kamryn smiled up at him. He liked her smile a lot. The awkwardness he'd felt that morning when she came to visit him at the cabin was gone.

"I'd like that very much," Kamryn said.

He drew his eyes away from Kamryn as Ember stepped back into the room. "Brad is coming with us to Faye's. He's worried about me. Not that he doesn't trust you, but he worries about me. He wants to be with me when we go to Aunt Faye's," she said as her face reddened.

"You can both ride with me, and when we're finished, I'll bring you back here. Then I'll check on Kamryn again."

A look passed between the two girls, and Ember grinned and nodded. "It's a plan, then. Are you going to be here for a while, Bentley?"

"I'll be here until it's time to go to Faye's," he said. "Can you and your guy meet me here?"

"We can. Oh, and Kamryn, I just spoke with your boss. He said he'll bring in a temp to cover for you until you get well, like he did the last time. He did say that no other secretary is as good as you, but he'll make the sacrifice. He chuckled when he said that."

"He's a good boss. He treats me well," Kamryn said.

In a few minutes, Ember left Kamryn's room, and Bentley sat down next to her bed and put a hand on one of hers again. A day ago this would have felt awkward, but now it felt right. It didn't keep him from thinking about Evie, but he didn't feel guilty. He would always love Evie, but it had been months since she'd died, and he had to admit that he was lonely, despite Cedrick's companionship.

Most of the time until Ember returned with Brad, Bentley sat beside Kamryn. She was tired and eventually fell asleep. When she did, he quietly stepped out and went down to the cafeteria for a bite to eat. Kamryn was still asleep when he returned. She awoke a few minutes later when Brad and Ember stepped into the room. "Brad, this is my brother-in-law, Bentley Radford. Bentley, this is Brad Jensen."

The two men shook hands and visited while Ember turned her attention to Kamryn. Finally, Ember said, "We should go now."

Bentley stepped over to Kamryn's bedside again and once more he kissed her forehead. "I'll be back," he said. She smiled up at him. He definitely liked that smile.

Bentley liked Brad. He seemed like just the kind of man that Ember deserved. He was glad for her. They looked good together. Evie would be happy for her.

CHAPTER THIRTY-ONE

FAYE WAS AT HER HOUSE, making sure things were in place there, hoping that when she'd advertised the fact that she'd fixed the house up and put some new furnishings in it, Claude would take the bait and come again. She was almost positive that he'd want to destroy things once more so the house would again be unsellable. If it hadn't been for insurance, it would still be in the mess he'd made of it, because she would not have been able to afford to have it fixed.

She looked around when she was finished. It looked pretty good, even though the *new* furniture had all come from yard sales and Deseret Industries. The windows and doors had been replaced, and she'd had the mess cleaned up by a company that specialized in such things. It didn't look half bad, she told herself, although she had no desire to ever live in this house again, even if and when Claude was arrested and sent to prison.

She was expecting Bentley at any moment. He'd called her just minutes ago to tell her he would be there soon. She wasn't surprised when she heard a knock at the door. She opened it to welcome Bentley. *It wasn't Bentley*!

"Finally, I caught you here! You have ruined my life," Claude growled as he violently shoved Faye to the floor. She hit her head, and fear of the man she'd once loved caused her to shake uncontrollably. She tried to get up, but he pushed her down again with his foot. "I came for the deed to the house," he said. "Tell me where it is and this will go easier on you."

"It's not in the house," she said with a whimper as she once again attempted to stand. He shoved her angrily back to the floor again.

"Where is it?" he demanded as he towered above her, his face so full of hatred and evil she felt like she didn't even know him anymore.

She didn't respond to him for a moment, trying to get her emotions under control while hiding her fear. He continued to glare down at her. When she managed to find her voice, she said, "It's in a safety deposit box. But this house is mine, Claude, and you know it. It's in our prenuptial."

"You can forget that. It's mine if I say so, and I say so. Get up, woman, and take me to the bank and open the box and get the deed out. You will sign this house over to me."

She struggled to her feet and said, "Please, Claude, I need to sell this house so I can live. You left me bankrupt."

"You need to give me the deed so you can live," he threatened. He laughed as if he'd just said something hilarious.

Faye's head hurt from colliding with the wood floor. She had to clear her mind and ignore the pain. She tried to think of a way out of this situation, but she realized there probably was none. But Faye wasn't going to give up. Anger flared and she said, "I'd consider letting you have half the money for the sale of the house, even though you tried to ruin it. But only on the condition that you give the money to Cedrick to replace what you stole from him."

"That kid was trouble from day one. I earned every dollar he had just by letting him live here. He gets nothing back. Anyway, I need every dollar the house will bring," he said, still snarling like a rabid dog.

Faye argued a little more before giving up. Claude was not going to listen to reason. The house wasn't worth her life, and she feared that if she didn't give him what he wanted, he would destroy her. If she did that though, he would get away again and she and Bentley wouldn't be able to set the trap she'd hoped would result in his capture.

"Let's go," he said to her. "You will ride with me. Once I have the deed and it's signed over to me, I *may* let you go."

That didn't sound good. But she didn't see that she had a choice. But then she realized she did have one and she said, "Claude, look at what time it is. The bank is closed. It wouldn't do any good to go there. Anyway, I'm not going to give you the deed. Get out of my house!"

***

"Someone's here besides Faye," Bentley said when he saw a beat-up, older-model Ford pickup parked behind Faye's car in the driveway. "Do you recognize that truck?"

Ember said, "No. I wonder who it could be."

Bentley parked behind the old Ford. "Faye's front door's open," Ember said. "Bentley, I think that's Claude standing just inside the door! I can't see Faye. What if he's already done something to her?"

Bentley had the same thought, and he sprang into action. "Call the police. I'm going to see what he's up to. You two stay here. He better not have hurt Faye." With that, he bolted for the door.

Faye was on the floor moaning and holding a hand to her face. Claude was leaning over her, shaking his fists. "You will do as I say or you will not leave this house alive. If we can't get to the bank until morning, then you and I are going to stay right here in this house until then. I'll tie you up and gag you if I have to."

Bentley had heard and seen enough. He grabbed Claude and spun him around. Then he planted a fist in the middle of his face with all the strength he had. Claude fell with a thud just as Ember and Brad came running in. "The cops are coming," Ember said.

She saw Faye on the floor, screamed in anguish, and knelt beside her. "Aunt Faye, it's Ember. Bentley and Brad and I are here. We'll help you."

Seeing that Faye was being attended to, Bentley knelt beside Claude. "I'll kill you for this," the older man breathed out angrily as blood poured from his nose.

"You're going to jail, Claude, and no one is going to get you out this time," Bentley countered fiercely.

Claude spat at him, and two bloody teeth came out of his mouth. He clapped a hand to his bloodied face. Bentley had no sympathy. "Now you know how Faye feels," he said as calmly as he could manage. "You shouldn't have hit her and you shouldn't have threatened her."

Claude struggled to sit up, but Bentley angrily shoved him back down, with more force than was needed, but he couldn't help himself. Claude deserved it. Claude's head bounced on the wooden floor, and when he opened his mouth to shout at Bentley again, only more blood and an additional tooth came out. He struggled to get up again, but he failed and finally lay quivering on the floor with Bentley's foot planted firmly on his chest.

"How is Faye?" Bentley asked as he glanced across to where Ember and Brad were helping her sit up.

"I'll be okay, Bentley." Faye answered for Ember. "He was going to make me sign the deed to my house over to him. But there's no way!" She forced a smile, but it was obviously a painful one.

They could hear sirens, and a minute later several cops and paramedics rushed into the house.

***

An hour had passed since the encounter at Faye's house. She had been whisked off to a hospital. "As soon as we finish with the police, we'll meet you there," Ember had promised her aunt.

Bentley, Brad, and Ember stayed at the house with the police. Finally, they stood Claude on his feet and put handcuffs on him. He sputtered and cursed, threatening both Bentley and Ember. His face was a bloody mess, but no one seemed to care. However, a paramedic attended to him and cleaned him up, then signaled that he was good to go. Two officers escorted Claude from the house. His next stop was the jail.

The other officers stayed longer and were finally satisfied that they had all the evidence and information they needed to make sure Claude would be convicted.

Ember shook her head sadly. "He can't hurt us now, Bentley. Thank you for stopping him."

Bentley's throat closed up and he couldn't respond, so he opened his arms and took her into them for a brotherly hug. Finally, he found his voice and said, "We'd better go see Faye."

"And then you need to go see Kamryn again," Ember said. "She cares for you, Bentley. She told me the other day that you are the best man she's ever known. I hope Evie doesn't mind me telling you this about Kamryn, but it's true."

"She doesn't mind, Ember. I can feel it." He touched his chest, right over his heart as he spoke.

Brad put an arm around Ember. "I'm glad Faye isn't hurt worse. You throw a mean punch, Bentley."

"I was angry," Bentley admitted. "I probably hit him harder than I needed to, but I don't feel bad about it."

Ember picked up Faye's purse. She checked in it and found that Faye's keys were there.

"Let's lock up here and get to the hospital. The paramedics said they were taking her to IMC in Murray," Ember said.

When they stepped out of the house, Bentley instinctively looked around, making sure Silas wasn't there. He didn't expect him to be, but he couldn't be too cautious. The man had stolen Evie from him; Bentley would do anything he could to see to it that he didn't also take Kamryn, which he almost had—twice.

Brad was holding Ember's hand as they approached the hospital from the parking lot. It was very late, and all three of them were exhausted. The doctor and nurses had finished taking care of Faye's injuries. She was released to them right from the emergency room. They talked of what had happened with Claude as they drove Faye to her apartment, which was many miles from her home.

"At least we don't have to set a trap for Claude," Faye said soberly. "I just pray that a liberal judge won't release him without bail."

"I don't think we need to worry about that," Bentley said. "He's not going to get out again."

Ember had been worrying about that very same thing. It was a relief to have Claude in custody again, but she feared that if he got out, he would be more dangerous than ever. She kept that thought to herself, but said instead, "I wonder if Silas has left the area or if he's hanging around."

"He's probably gone, but he'll be back. It worries me what he might try next time," Bentley responded.

They reached Faye's apartment, which was clear up in Ogden. By then it was the wee hours of the morning." Faye said, "Thanks for showing up in time to save me from Claude."

***

Silas had no idea how many cars and pickups he'd stolen over the past few months, but it made him chuckle to think about how easy it was. Most people didn't seem to worry about their cars being stolen or they would do something to make it harder for guys like him. It was fine by him. It had almost become as big a thrill as lighting fires and watching them burn. Well, he decided, not quite. Fires were the greatest.

The vehicle he was driving toward Denver was the latest-model car he'd stolen so far. It only had around a thousand miles on the odometer. It wasn't a big car or a fast one, but it was comfortable. He'd stolen it from a house not more than a mile from where he'd left the yellow Volkswagen. He'd hidden for several hours in a shed behind a house with a realtor sign on the lawn before venturing out to look for a set of wheels.

He'd watched a young lady park the Nissan on the street in front of a house just a block from where he'd been hidden. She'd turned the car off, but had left her purse with the key fob in the passenger seat of the car. It had been too easy. He drove hurriedly out of the city, going north and then west before he got to Ogden. He figured he should have dumped this car already, but it was such a nice one that he decided to take his chances. After all, he was invincible.

If a cop pulled him over it would be too bad for the cop. He smiled to himself as he worked the radio dial. He found a national news channel. He was traveling in the opposite direction from California, because he thought a change of scenery might be nice. But the news he heard was from Los Angeles.

His ears perked up when he heard the word *fire*. It had been a large one that destroyed much of a huge industrial complex. The announcer said that it had been determined to be the result of arson. He slapped his hand on the steering wheel so hard it stung. He should have been there. That must have been a sight to behold. The thought began running through his head that even though he'd had nothing to do with it, he'd probably be blamed for it.

Then the announcer said that the culprits had been caught, that a shootout had ensued, and that two of them had died. *Amateurs*, he thought to himself. They must have been a stupid bunch.

All the arsonists had been identified, and the announcer proceeded to list their names after first saying that they were all from Utah and that two of them were dead. The person who was believed to be the ringleader had died in the gun battle. He was an ex-con by the name of Lonnie Defollo. Silas jerked the wheel so hard when he heard the name that he almost drove off the freeway.

He pulled off at the next exit and stopped the car in a large parking lot in front of a big, all-night grocery store with only a smattering of cars near it. He was shocked. He recognized the names of all but one of the gang that Lonnie had assembled and led to LA on some kind of foolish mission. One name stood out to him besides Lonnie's. Queen Wise was a close friend of Lonnie, and Silas had met her on several occasions in the past. She was big, mean, tough, and fairly smart.

As he sat in the large parking lot wondering why in the world Lonnie, Queen, and the others had started a fire in LA, the newscaster told him. One of the gang, the one person whose name Silas did not recognize, was apparently singing to the police for all he was worth. To Silas's dismay, the man had mentioned his name! The reason why Lonnie and his bunch had started the fire was in hopes of luring a known arsonist, with whom Lonnie was angry, to come view the fire so Lonnie could get even with him. That, of course, was Silas Villard, who was wanted for many crimes in both Utah and California. But Villard had not shown up, and the cops had surrounded the gang as they were preparing to leave.

Of course he didn't show up. He wasn't in LA when Lonnie had pulled that stupid stunt. He felt anger burning. Lonnie was dead, but Silas was once again in the headlines. That's all he needed. He already had enough trouble. And it was all the fault of Trooper Radford. Once he was finished with Radford, he would slip across the border into Mexico and be beyond the reach, he hoped, of American authorities.

Silas suddenly burst out into an uproarious laugh. Lonnie was no longer a threat to him, and he found that to be hilarious. He finally stopped laughing and began to think about the future. He could no longer risk driving the car he was in. He looked around. He was in the perfect place to steal another one. It took him only ten minutes and he was on his way again, driving another older-model car, one that had been easy to hot-wire.

He'd give it a few weeks, he decided, and then he would find a way to even the score with Radford.

CHAPTER THIRTY-TWO

THE MORNING AFTER CLAUDE'S ARREST, Bentley drove to the hospital with both Evie and Kamryn on his mind. He was anxious to see Kamryn. When he stepped into her room a few minutes later, she sat up and held her arms out to him. He leaned down and accepted a gentle hug. "Ember called. She told me what happened." She grinned. "I'm so glad you were able to catch Claude and that you knocked his teeth out. Did you get some rest?"

"Some. Did you?" he asked.

"As much as is possible in this place," Kamryn said. "I want out of here."

"Not until you've healed a lot more," he said gently.

Before Kamryn could respond, Bentley's phone rang. It was Detective Hank Parker. "Good job getting Claude. You didn't even have to set your trap." He chuckled.

"How did you know about that? I was going to tell you when I got back to Duchesne to pick up Cedrick," Bentley said. "Is that what you're calling about? You probably want to know the details, don't you?"

"I am curious, I admit," Hank said, "but that's not why I called you."

"Really? Do you know something more about Silas?"

"No, but you can quit looking for Lonnie Defollo," he said. "He's dead."

"What! How did that happen?" Bentley asked.

Hank then told him what had occurred in LA. "According to one of the survivors of the gang, it was an effort to lure Silas to the fire and make him pay for whatever grievances Lonnie had against him. Apparently they seemed to think he was in LA. That's all I know, but you may want to see if you can find out any details when you get home."

"I'll do that. Too bad Silas hadn't showed up because he might have been arrested too," Bentley said.

"Or shot. How is Kamryn doing?" Hank asked.

"She's going to be okay. I'm with her now. She's an amazing lady. You'd think she'd be angry with me, but she's not. She's taking it all in stride, but she's scared, not just for herself, but for Ember and for me—Cedric too, for that matter."

"My wife and I are praying for all of you, Bentley. Let me know when you're close to Duchesne, and I'll meet you at your cabin with Cedrick," Hank said. "Then you can tell me how you managed to capture Claude."

A couple of weeks passed. Bentley and Cedrick both worked hard on their little homestead. Cedrick kept up on his schooling, and Bentley made some progress on his second manuscript. His first one had finally been accepted by a New York publishing company, and the lady who was to be his editor told him it should be in print in about a year and a half.

Kamryn was healing rapidly, was out of the hospital, and was recuperating at her apartment. She and Ember were in constant contact with Bentley. Ember was trying hard to keep up on her studies, and Kamryn was hoping to get back to work soon. They were in constant fear that Silas would come after one of them again. Bentley also feared for their safety.

Bentley promised Kamryn when she called early on a Wednesday morning that he and Cedrick would come to the city and install cameras and other security devices at their apartment and even on each of their cars. He had acquired the equipment needed and was anxious to get it in place, hoping that would give the young women some security and peace of mind.

"I realize that you haven't recovered enough to drive yet, but you'll soon be able to, and I want both of you to be safe as possible," he told Kamryn.

"I am so frustrated, Bentley," Kamryn said. "Why can't the cops find Silas? If they could catch him this danger would be over. Claude's bail is so high that he'll never be free, so we don't have to worry about him anymore. I just wish we didn't all have to worry about Silas. I'm sure he's really angry that I got away from him, so he probably wants to get even with me too."

"That's probably exactly how he's thinking. But Kamryn, his luck will run out," Bentley said, wishing he believed that. He wanted Kamryn to believe his reassuring words, however.

***

Silas was an addict. He couldn't go a day without alcohol. And he was addicted to stealing cars. His strongest addiction, however, was starting fires and watching them burn. He got a thrill out of the destruction the fires caused. He didn't care how much it hurt others, because Silas cared only for himself and his constant cravings.

He wandered from place to place, constantly stealing cars and managing to keep ahead of the law. He felt like he was becoming more untouchable all the time. He was certain that the next attempt he made to get even with Bentley Radford would be successful. But in the meantime, he felt the urge to start a fire, a very large one.

Spring had turned to early summer, and a dry period settled over much of the West. So it was not hard for him to start a fire that had the potential to become huge. He started one in the mountains outside of Denver. It spread very rapidly. The authorities ordered evacuations. As houses burned in the flaming holocaust, Silas gleefully watched the fire, moving from one location to another, making sure he wasn't attracting attention to himself. The fire burned for days, but he wasn't satisfied with it anymore. So he ignited another one several miles from the first one. He was happy, except for one nagging problem. Trooper Radford had yet to be punished.

He decided the next fire he started would be at the house Radford was living in, once he figured out where it was located. This time, he would make sure Radford didn't get out of his house alive. As he thought about it, he wondered if it was time to step things up a bit. *Explosives.* The word just popped into his head. Perhaps he could blow up Radford's house. That way, it would be guaranteed that the guy couldn't get out alive, and he'd still get the pleasure of watching it burn to the ground. Yes, that's what he'd do.

He needed to figure out what kind of explosive to use and possibly experiment with it a time or two so he'd be sure to get it right. Inspiration struck his drunken mind again. He knew exactly where he would plant his first bomb, his practice one. Oh yeah, it would be great. It was time to start preparing.

***

Bentley was frustrated. He wanted to spend more time with Kamryn so they could sort out their feelings, but it was hard. Someone else was after his affection, which added to his frustration. An attractive young school teacher by the name of Reese Hall was living in an apartment in his ward. She was around five-ten with long black hair, a dark complexion, and brown eyes. Reese seemed to have decided that she and Bentley would make a great couple. She hadn't known Evie because she came to Duchesne a few weeks after Evie's death to teach at the elementary school. She also knew nothing about Kamryn.

For months, she would smile at Bentley and he'd notice her watching him. He tried not to let it bother him. But a couple of months ago, Reese had begun to make it a point to sit by Bentley and Cedrick in sacrament meeting most Sundays. It was impossible not to talk to her then. And she did like to talk.

Reese was a nice lady, and Bentley hated to be rude to her, but he had no romantic interest in her. She hinted that it would be nice to go out with him sometime. He didn't act on her hint, but she became more insistent. Finally, as Cedrick headed for his deacon's quorum meeting one Sunday morning, she cornered Bentley before he made it to his elder's quorum meeting. She boldly asked him to accompany her to a singles dance at the stake center that coming Saturday. There were other people around, and they all smiled in encouragement. It was awkward for him to say no with all these witnesses.

Reese was not about to take no for an answer anyway, so after awkwardly attempting to turn her down, he finally agreed to pick her up at her apartment and escort her to the dance on Saturday evening. Bentley may have imagined it, but he thought he heard several ladies whisper their approval to each other. He knew that people liked him and felt sorry for him, and he guessed they felt like it was time for him to move on. Again, none of them knew of his growing attraction to Kamryn.

There were a number of young single adults in the stake, but Bentley had not attended any of their activities, despite frequent invites. He had a couple of reasons. First, most of them had never been married like he had and he simply had no desire to mingle with them, feeling like they had nothing in common. Second, he wasn't about to leave Cedrick alone with the threat of danger constantly hanging over their heads. Reese knew nothing about the danger he and Cedrick faced. Having accepted Reese's invitation, Bentley now had a dilemma regarding Cedrick.

Bentley confided in his good friend Hank Parker after priesthood meeting. Hank chuckled at his dilemma. Bentley had not mentioned the growing friendship between him and Kamryn, the girl who had been shot twice because of him. Hank simply said, "It's just a couple of weeks short of a year since you lost Evie. Don't you think it would be okay to start dating a little after this much time?"

"I guess," Bentley said morosely, thinking that dating Kamryn would be okay now, but not anyone else. Even though he and Kamryn talked a lot, and hugged when they saw each other and even occasionally held hands, they had not been on an official date. Nor had they kissed. He had made up his mind that he would not ask her out until a full year had passed from the anniversary of Evie's death. He knew that asking her out would meet Kamryn's approval, because she kept hinting at it when the two of them were together.

Hank spoke again. "Go and enjoy yourself with Reese. She's a really nice lady, very spiritual, and not bad looking either. You don't have to think long term with her, you know," Hank said.

"Oh, it definitely will not be," Bentley said firmly.

"You never know," Hank said with a grin. "My wife and I will take care of Cedrick. So you can't use him as an excuse not to date any time you feel like it."

"Thanks, President," he said, because that was what he was going to ask next.

At home later that day, Cedrick, who was thirteen now and very perceptive, asked Bentley, "Why are you going to a dance with Sister Hall? You told me you wished she wouldn't always sit by us in sacrament meeting."

That was a hard question to answer, but he was honest. "It's because she won't take no for an answer. How in the world did you know that I had a date with her?"

"She was telling some other people about it after church, and I heard her. I think you were talking to Hank then," Cedrick said.

"Oh boy," was Bentley's response.

"Wait, did she ask you to go with her?" Cedrick asked.

"She did."

"But I thought guys asked girls out, not girls asking guys," Cedrick said innocently.

"Well, it's usually that way, but Reese is kind of forward," he said.

"She's pretty, too, isn't she? And she likes you a lot."

"Well, yes, I guess she does, but she's not my type," Bentley said.

With maturity beyond his years, Cedrick grinned and said, "Kamryn is prettier. So was Evie. Bentley, it's almost been a year since my sister was killed. It's okay if you date now. I'm sure she would be okay with it."

Wow! Cedrick had just floored him. But he was glad to hear that Cedrick was thinking that way, because before too long he'd be asking Kamryn out, and he'd worried about how Cedrick would react. Now he knew it would be okay.

"Thanks, Cedrick, that is exactly what Hank said. And by the way, he'll be letting you stay at his house while I'm at the dance with Reese."

"Ah, Bentley. I could stay home alone. We have the dogs and the alarm system, and you told me yourself that you are impressed with how good I am with your guns."

"I am impressed, but until Silas is behind bars, I'm not leaving you home alone. And that is not debatable."

"Okay, I guess you're right," Cedrick agreed, and the discussion ended.

CHAPTER THIRTY-THREE

THE WEEK WAS A LONG one for Bentley. He was constantly thinking unhappy thoughts about his upcoming date with Reese. He was determined to enjoy his time with her even though he wasn't looking forward to it. But he didn't want her to take it the wrong way. And yet he sure hated to hurt her feelings, because she really was a very nice person. However, he guessed it couldn't be avoided, because he was not going to go out with her again. Not if he could get out of it, anyway. His next date would be with Kamryn.

Bentley also continuously worried about Silas Villard. He was aware of the surge of serious wildfires in Colorado and couldn't help but wonder if Silas was responsible for any of them. He thought it was quite likely, but it was possible that he'd gone instead to California.

The man would be coming after him again. There was no doubt in Bentley's mind about that. When or how he might choose to do it was nerve-racking. He prayed often that Silas would not try to use Ember or Kamryn as hostages, but it was always a possibility, and he hated the thought.

He reminded both ladies of that every time he talked to them. They were both worried too, with good cause. He wished he could make the threat go away. But the only way that would happen was for Silas to be arrested.

Saturday night arrived. Bentley dropped Cedrick off at the Parkers' home, and with serious misgivings drove the short distance to Reese's apartment. He was so nervous his palms were sweating. He wiped them on his pants as he approached her door. He took a deep breath before ringing the bell. She must have been standing right there, because she opened the door within seconds.

Bentley stood there with his mouth hanging open when he saw her. She looked absolutely stunning. She invited him in and said, "I'll just be a second, Bentley," and disappeared somewhere deeper in the apartment. She was beaming when she came back, and she took his hand. "I am so excited," she said.

That was obvious. He was not, but he had to admit that she looked really nice, and he decided that it would not be hard to enjoy the evening with her.

At the dance, the two of them attracted a lot of attention. Other women looked on enviously. And that caused Bentley to feel awkward. Guys, on the other hand, couldn't keep their eyes off Bentley's date. One guy looked particularly star struck. He introduced himself to them as a new attorney in town. "My name is Jim," he said. "It's nice to meet you two."

Later, as the dance was in full swing, the attorney cut in, and Bentley watched Reese dance away with Jim. To Bentley, they looked like a cute couple. One guy who was standing at the edge of the room with a young woman on his arm told Bentley not to let that other guy get away with trying to steal his girl.

Bentley visited with the couple for a minute and then found a chair where he sat down by himself and began thinking about Kamryn. He wished it was Kamryn he was with instead of Reese.

He wasn't alone for long. A young lady joined him, sat beside him for a moment, and then asked him if he would like to dance. He didn't turn her down, and as the evening proceeded, he found himself having a surprisingly good time. Before long, he began to dance with Reese again, but after a few dances, the young attorney cut in again. "Sorry," Jim said to Bentley, "but Reese is the best dancer here tonight."

"She really is good," Bentley agreed and headed for the edge of the dance floor.

Before Bentley could even get seated, another young lady asked him to dance. And so the evening continued. Bentley didn't want to be too late picking Cedrick up from Hank's house, but Reese was reluctant to leave while the dance was still going. Eleven o'clock rolled around, and Reese was once again dancing with Jim. He cut in after just one dance, and Jim frowned at him.

"I need to be going soon," he told Reese after a couple of dances. "I need to pick Cedrick up from President Parker's house, and I promised them I wouldn't be too late."

Bentley hadn't noticed Jim approach, but as he tapped Bentley on the shoulder, he said, "If you need to go, I'd be glad to take Reese home."

"That would be nice," Reese said, surprising Bentley.

"No, I brought her, so it's only appropriate that I take her home," Bentley said.

"It's okay, Bentley. It's been fun this evening. But I want to stay longer," Reese said.

Before Bentley could offer to stay longer with her, Jim said, "Seriously, I'll see that she gets home." He smirked at Bentley.

He wanted to argue further but decided it wasn't worth the effort. "In that case, thanks for the evening, Reese. I have enjoyed being with you. You guys have fun. I guess I'll be going now."

"Thank you, Bentley," she said. "Maybe we can do this again sometime." But as Reese spoke, she only momentarily took her eyes off the dashing attorney.

Bentley felt like a fool. Embarrassed by the situation and feeling somewhat used, he hurried to the door before anyone else could stop him and get him back on the dance floor.

He let the hurt simmer all the way to his truck. Hank answered the door when he knocked softly. "Have a good time?" he asked as Cedrick got up from the sofa and stepped toward Bentley.

"It was okay," he said.

"Did Reese feel bad that you took her home this early? The dance couldn't have been over yet. They always go clear to midnight, or so I've been told," Hank said.

"She's still there," Bentley said, unable to suppress a frown.

"You just left her?" Hank asked. "I'm surprised you would do that."

"No, that's not what happened at all. Reese decided she'd rather go home with some new guy named Jim. I can't believe she did that. He offered to take her home, and even though I objected, she accepted."

"That was rude," Hank said. "But I'm not too surprised that Jim would do that to you."

"Do you know him?"

"Sure do. He works for the county attorney."

"Well, I think he's quite attracted to Reese, and she didn't seem the least bit sad when he offered to take her home. Oh well, at least I had a good time until then. And she did say she'd like to go out with me another time. You know what, Hank? I don't think I'm cut out for this dating business. I sure wish I still had Evie."

In the truck, Cedrick asked. "Do you think Reese will sit with us again tomorrow?"

"I guess we'll see." His thoughts turned to Kamryn. It was time to see if she really felt the same way he did. He thought she did, but he had to be sure. He sure couldn't see her treating him rudely like Reese had.

The next morning at sacrament meeting, Reese and Jim walked in together. "She must have invited him," Bentley whispered to his young brother-in-law.

"I know he's not in our ward." Again, there was a moment of regret, but it was only a moment. Mostly, he felt relieved.

***

The anniversary of Evie's death was a difficult day for Bentley. Even though he'd spent more time with Kamryn, the death of Evie was still very painful for him. It always would be.

He'd spoken with Kamryn by phone a couple of days earlier and told her that he and Cedrick planned to put a bouquet on Evie's grave on the anniversary of her death. He and Cedrick planned to buy a beautiful arrangement from a floral shop in town. He didn't even stop at the mailbox beside the highway as they drove out. He didn't get a lot of mail, so he didn't worry about it that morning. His was one of a number of boxes in a cluster there. It didn't have his name on it, but it did have the name he used in his occasional work as a private investigator.

When Cedrick had asked him why he used the other name on the box, he'd responded. "I don't want Silas to see it there."

"Oh, I see. I don't either," Cedrick had responded.

It was after eleven in the morning before the two guys pulled up to the edge of the Indian Canyon Highway and carried the large, fragrant bouquet down to Evie's grave. Bentley had purchased a really nice headstone, and he placed the flowers right in front of it. Tears leaked from his eyes as he kneeled in front of her grave.

Cedrick stood back a ways. There were tears in his eyes, too. It would never be easy, Bentley thought as he wiped his eyes. He prayed for a minute. Then he whispered, "Evie, I will always love you."

It was probably his imagination, but it seemed like he heard her voice whisper, "I will always love you, too."

A few more minutes passed, and still he knelt there. He was aware of footsteps behind him, but he didn't look back. He assumed it was Cedrick coming closer. A hand touched his shoulder. That wouldn't be Cedrick, he thought and looked up. Kamryn was gazing down at him, her eyes full of tears. Without a word she knelt beside Bentley.

Then Cedrick joined them. For a minute or two no words were spoken. When someone finally spoke, it was Kamryn. She said, "You'll always miss her, won't you?"

"Yes, I will," Bentley said.

Cedrick murmured, "Yeah."

"Ember and Brad will be here in a minute or two. They were right behind me." Sure enough, when Bentley looked up, he saw Brad helping Ember out of his car.

They soon joined them, and Ember placed a bouquet beside the one Bentley and Cedrick had brought. Ember's eyes were tearful. She knelt beside the headstone. Brad stood behind her with his hands on her shoulders. For a couple of minutes it was silent at that sacred spot.

Finally, they all stood. "I'm hungry. Are you guys?" Bentley asked.

He knew what Cedrick would say. "I sure am," was exactly what he expected.

"I think I could eat too," Kamryn said softly.

"Let's go to Cowan's Café then," he said.

"You guys go ahead," Ember said, her voice choking. Brad put an arm around her. "I want to spend a little more time here with my sister. Brad and I will meet you over there in a few minutes."

"We'll see you then," Bentley said.

As they walked across the grass, Bentley expected Kamryn to take hold of his hand. But she didn't. He stopped when they reached his truck. Her car was parked right behind it. "Are you okay?" Bentley asked Kamryn. "You seem troubled."

"I'm sad about Evie, and I'm sad for you and Ember and Cedrick," Kamryn said. "But I'm okay."

Bentley shook his head. "There's something else," he said. "I can feel it. Do you want to talk about it?"

Cedrick walked around the truck and got in. Kamryn looked at Bentley, slowly shaking her head. Finally she asked, "It's none of my business, but how was your date with Reese?"

Surprised, he asked, "How did you know about that? It was no big deal. I'd planned to tell you about it. In answer to your question, it was fun in a way, but it was also kind of weird."

"I called to talk to Cedrick that night and he told me he was at Hank's place. I asked him where you were, and he said you had taken a girl from your ward by the name of Reese to a single-adult dance. Is she a nice girl?"

"She is," Bentley said as he began to grin. "Let me tell you what happened." He then gave her a short version of the way she came on to him and sat by him in sacrament meeting each week. He explained that she'd asked him to go to the dance with her in front of other ward members and he found it hard to decline.

"Was it fun going with her?" Kamryn pressed.

"Like I said, it was both fun and weird," Bentley said, and then he proceeded to tell her about Jim and how she ended up going home with him.

"That's what you meant by weird?" Kamryn asked. "Did it hurt your feelings?

"Of course it did, but it's okay. They are an item now, and in a way I'm relieved. Even though several other girls danced with me that night, I mostly thought about two girls."

"Reese and who else?" Kamry asked with raised eyebrows.

"Okay, three. I thought about Reese because I was with her for much of the evening. But the other two are more important."

"Who are they?" Kamryn asked, a look of concern on her face.

Bentley smiled. "Evie for one, and you, Kamryn, for the other." Her face went slightly red, and he asked, "If I were to ask you to go out with me on a real date, would you?"

"Oh, Bentley, you know I would." Her face glowed.

Bentley had not heard Cedrick exit the truck. The young teenager said, "It's about time you asked her out, Bentley."

CHAPTER THIRTY-FOUR

THERE WAS ANOTHER PERSON WHO visited Duchesne on the anniversary of the death of Evie Radford. The man who had caused her death was also in the area. Silas had left Colorado, spent some time figuring out a good disguise, and found someone who would give him some false IDs under the alias of Simon Vernon. He had stolen enough money to give him what he needed to buy an old pickup so he could drive something that was not stolen. It would be safer that way, since the truck was in the same name as that on his forged ID. Then he'd headed west toward Duchesne.

Silas drove by his burned-down house in Myton. He snickered. He didn't care about that house. He didn't ever plan to live in this area again. At some point in the not-too-distant future, he would be leaving the United States behind. Lonnie had got his just dues for burning the house. As soon as Silas had accomplished what he'd come to Duchesne to do, Queen Wise would be joining Lonnie on the other side of the great divide. The house she now lived in, which had belonged to Lonnie, would be going *boom* in a few days. Then, if that worked out to his satisfaction, Trooper Radford's house would be next, with the hated man in it!

He still didn't know where Radford lived other than he believed it to be somewhere in the hills west of Duchesne. He was in town today with a plan on how he might be able to find out where Radford's house was.

He'd started his inquiries that morning at a couple of real estate offices in Roosevelt. They had not been helpful. He was now walking to the door of the second one he'd approached in Duchesne. The realtor was a woman by the name of Rachel Delaney. He walked in, and a lady who appeared to be in her midfifties, looked up at him and smiled. "How can I help you, sir?" she asked.

"I want to buy a cabin in the area," he lied. "My name is Simon Vernon. I am prepared to pay cash if I can find something that is fairly inexpensive. My wife doesn't want us to spend too much."

"Well, Mr. Vernon, why don't you have a seat and I'll see what listings I have that might fill your needs," she said.

He looked at several pictures of cabins but didn't express interest in any of them. Finally, he said, "I have a friend that I believe you sold a cabin to about a year ago. I spoke with him on the phone the other day and promised I'd come visit when I got a chance. He knows I'm looking for a place. He told me where he lived and I forgot to write it down. I want to surprise him, so I don't want to call him again and let him know I'm in town."

"What is the gentleman's name?" she asked.

"Radford, Bentley Radford. He's had a rough time the past year or so. He told me about losing his wife. I'm sorry about what happened. Anyway, if you could tell me where it is, I'd like to drop in on him," he lied with a straight face.

She told him where Bentley lived and then said, "Let me show you a couple more places. They aren't great but you look like someone who could fix a place up."

"I am kind of a handyman at that," he said. "Let's see what you have." He was anxious to leave now that he'd learned what he came for, but didn't want to appear to be in a hurry. He asked her to show them to him.

He expressed interest in one of them. "That might work. Can I take a picture of it to show my wife? She couldn't be with me today, but I promised her I wouldn't settle on anything until she had a chance to look it over. I'll show her the picture, and if she approves, I'll give you a call and set a time that the two of us can come back and have you show it to us. Would that be okay?"

"Of course," she said. "Since she knows you are a handyman, this place just might appeal to her."

"I think it will," he said. "But I need to be sure. We live in Salt Lake, so something in this area would be convenient for us."

Silas Villard, a.k.a. Simon Vernon, left with the picture and the land description. He waited until he had driven away from the realtor's office before smacking a hand on the dashboard. He had what he needed. Radford was in for a massive surprise. He wouldn't, of course, have time to know what hit him. Silas assured himself that he would not fail again. Radford was as good as dead. Just a few more days and his revenge would be complete. Then maybe, before he left the country, he could settle a couple more scores. The names and faces of Piper and Kamryn came to mind.

Silas had not had a beer since before he'd left Colorado early that morning. He hadn't wanted to be drunk when he approached the realtors. That had worked out well, but now he needed a drink real bad. He reached over to the cooler in front of the passenger seat and grabbed a beer.

***

Bentley, Kamryn, and Cedrick were taking their time eating their lunch at Cowan's Café. They had talked about a lot of things, including future plans for Bentley's homestead. After Ember and Brad joined them, they spoke of the progress Ember was making in law school. She told them that she and Brad had spoken to their professors a few days ago. "We asked if we could both be excused from our classes today. When we explained that it was the anniversary of my twin sister's death and that Brad and I wanted to visit her grave, all our professors gave us both some work to study and told us to go ahead. I do have to be in class tomorrow and so does Brad, so we have to drive back as soon as we finish eating because we both have a lot of studying to do."

Their waitress cleared away their plates and asked if they would like some dessert. They all agreed to have ice cream. They had barely begun to eat the cold treat when Bentley's phone rang. He was surprised to see that it was Rachel Delaney calling him. He wondered what she wanted.

"Hello, Rachel," he said.

"Hi, Bentley," Rachel began. "If I remember correctly, today is one year from the day you lost Evie. It must be a hard day for you."

"It is," he responded. "Thank you for remembering me."

"Some of us in the ward thought that you may have been moving your life along with Reese Hall. But I see she's with some other guy now."

"She is, and I'm okay with that."

"You'll find someone," she said.

"Yes, I think I will," he responded, looking across the table at Kamryn and smiling.

"I hope so. Listen, Bentley, I know this is a rough day for you and I hate to make it worse, but I had a visitor today who said he was looking for property west of Duchesne. He left a few minutes ago and I got to thinking and worrying. Something was not quite right about the guy, but it didn't dawn on me until a couple of minutes after he'd left my office."

"What are you referring to?" Bentley asked as he began to worry. "What was the man's name?"

"He told me it was Simon Vernon and even showed me his driver's license as proof. I made a file since he showed some interest in a small, rough cabin I have listed. I got a picture of the license. I also checked my surveillance camera and I can show you what he looks like from two different angles," Rachel said.

Bentley was very uneasy now, and he asked, "Why do you think I should see the pictures?"

"Well, he told me he was a friend of yours and that he wanted to drop in and visit you. I told him where you lived, but now I think I made a serious mistake. Do you know anyone by that name?" she asked.

"No, I don't. But I know who has the same initials," he said.

Before he could finish, Rachel gasped and said. "Oh my word, Bentley, could it have been Silas Villard in disguise?"

"I'll be over in just a few minutes," he said.

"I'm sorry, Bentley. I didn't mean to cause you trouble."

"It's not your fault, but something is definitely not right. Thanks so much for alerting me," he told her. "I'll see you shortly."

After he ended the call, he looked across the table at Kamryn. Her face was pale and her eyes wide. "I'm scared, Bentley. Is Silas in the area?"

"Possibly," he said and told all of them the gist of what Rachel had revealed to him.

"I'm coming with you to see the pictures. If it's Silas in disguise, we all need to know what he looks like now." Kamryn's voice was trembling. He reached over, took hold of both her hands and squeezed gently. Ember was nodding in agreement.

"Let's hope it's not him, but I don't know anyone by the name of Simon Vernon," Bentley said.

None of them were able to finish their ice cream. Bentley paid the check, left a generous tip, and they hurried from the café. "Brad and I need to leave, but let me know what you learn," Ember said. "This scares me."

"I'm scared too, for you guys as well as for myself."

Ember and Brad headed for Brad's car. "May I ride with you and Cedrick over there?" Kamryn asked. "I can get my car later."

"Of course," Bentley said. They waved goodbye to Ember and Brad and then climbed into Bentley's truck. Bentley pulled out his phone and called Detective Hank Parker who answered on the second ring.

"What's up, Bentley? I know this must be a really hard day for you. I'm sorry."

"It is, and it may have just gotten harder. Are you in town?"

"I'm at the sheriff's office. I'm typing a report on a burglary. What do you need?"

"Could you meet me at Rachel Delaney's office? It's very important."

"Of course. I can finish this later. I'll come now."

"Thanks, Hank, I appreciate it."

At Rachel's office, the three of them looked at the copy of the driver's license of Simon Vernon. "It's a good disguise, but I think it's him," Bentley said. "I've studied his picture enough that I know the shape of his face, his eyes, his nose, his mouth, and even his ears."

He was showing Kamryn and Cedrick when Hank strode in. "See how his ears stick out a little? He didn't disguise that well," she said. "I'd know that repulsive face anywhere."

"What's up, guys?" Hank asked.

Rachel answered and said, "I think I may have told Silas Villard where Bentley lives." She quickly explained what had happened. "I got a copy of his driver's license and I have him on video. I'll bring that up and print some stills of him from it while you guys look at the driver's license a little more."

After further study of the pictures Rachel had taken, Bentley, Kamryn, and Hank were all convinced that the man who claimed to be Simon Vernon was in fact Silas Villard. Hank asked Rachel, "Did you see what he was driving?"

She shook her head. "I'm sorry, but I didn't."

Bentley, after the initial shock of learning that Silas was in the area, began to think like a detective. "We need to call some other realtors. This may not be the first place he stopped," he said. "Maybe one of them saw what he was driving."

"I agree," Hank said. "Should we go up to my office and make some calls?"

"You can do that right here, guys," Rachel offered. "I have a list of all the realtors in the basin with their phone numbers and addresses. You can use that list if you'd like."

The two detectives divided up the names and began making calls. "I've got it. He was driving an older either Chevy or GMC pickup," Hank said after ending a call. "I'll broadcast it right now."

Rachel had made several copies of the prints she'd made from the video and of the driver's license. Kamryn's phone rang as she was handing them out. "Kamryn, it's Ember. Have you learned anything yet?"

"Yes, it was Silas who was in Rachel's office," Kamryn reported.

"I was afraid of that. Look, there's something else. I asked our neighbor to call me if she saw anything suspicious while you and I were both gone. She just called. She said she spoke to an officer who was at our door. She asked him what he needed. And he said he had subpoenas for both of us to testify in court against Claude. She agreed to take the subpoenas and signed for them.

I'm not sure why they want you, but I guess now we both have to go. I asked her to open one of the subpoenas and she did. She said the officer told her that both Bentley and Cedrick had been notified by certified mail. It's set for trial on September tenth. I can't believe it's taken this long, but I know that the justice system moves very slowly. That's something I've learned at law school."

"Oh boy, this sounds like fun. I'll text you the pictures we have of Silas. His appearance is altered, but it's him. Keep a close look out for him."

"This is scary," Ember said.

"Especially for Bentley and Cedrick because now Silas knows where they live," Kamryn said.

After Kamryn had finished the call with Ember, she told Bentley about the subpoenas. "Mine and Cedrick's are probably at the post office. They don't leave certified mail in our box out by the highway. I'd better go over there and get them."

"I'm going to get some other officers and go out to your place and check all around the neighboring areas," Hank said. "I'm not sure you guys should stay there tonight."

"I'm not running from that man," Bentley said fiercely.

"I'm not going to stay with anyone but Bentley," Cedrick announced.

No amount of urging by either Kamryn or Hank changed either of their minds. Bentley picked up their subpoenas at the post office and then they took Kamryn back to her car. "You have your Mace with you, don't you?" he asked after a long and tender hug.

"It's in my purse," she said.

"Be careful; you and Ember need to be especially watchful. You should get a hotel room again for a few days. I'll pay for it if you will do that," Bentley said.

"I'm not as brave as you. I think we'll do that. We'll stay at the one that's right there on campus if they have any vacancies. After what that beastly man has put me through, I don't ever want to see him again. But I'll pay for it myself. You don't need to."

"I'd be glad to, but call me when you get home," Bentley said. "And let me know when you and Ember get a room and where it's at."

"I will, and you and Cedrick keep in close touch with me," she said. "I'm worried about you guys."

They were standing on the sidewalk beside Kamryn's car. Kamryn and Bentley were gazing at each other. They hugged again. Then in a minute Kamryn was on her way, Bentley and Cedrick watching as she drove away.

CHAPTER THIRTY-FIVE

When Bentley and Cedrick got home, their dogs came to meet them. After greeting the two dogs, Bentley said, "I think that until Silas is found, we should let these two stay outside, even when we're back home and in the cabin."

"I guess you're right. If Silas tries to get to the house, they'll take care of him, won't you guys?" the boy said as he patted Bolt on the head.

Before they entered the house, they checked all the sheds and the entire property. Most of it was fenced now with four-foot net wire topped by two strands of barbed wire. It was a project Bentley and Cedrick had made a priority for the summer. They now had a bull, a second cow, another pig, and two really nice horses. The first pig was in the freezer in the form of bacon, sausage, and so on. The animals were all fine and acting as calm as usual. The chicks they purchased in March were almost grown and would soon be laying eggs. Bentley and Cedrick loved this place and the animals on it. Bentley was determined not to allow Silas to destroy what the two of them had built.

Hank stopped by a couple of hours later. "We've scoured the area for miles around. We haven't seen hide nor hair of Silas or his truck," he told them.

"That's good to know," Bentley said. "But he's obviously planning something for later."

"You guys can't be too careful," Hank reminded them.

Bentley knew that. He and Cedrick both had pistols strapped to their sides whenever they went outside, even if it was only for a short while. Bentley was not taking any unnecessary chances.

Kamryn called to tell them she was home and that she and Ember were safely settled in the campus hotel. "I'm sure worried about you guys though."

"We'll be okay," he said and explained the precautions they were taking.

They talked on the phone longer than they ever had before. Clearly, the relationship between Bentley and Kamryn had taken a giant step forward. When the conversation was finally over, Bentley sat back in his chair and thought about Evie and about Kamryn. He'd lost Evie, but not forever, and he felt like he'd gained someone who was equally as good. Time would tell, but he had a good feeling about what lay ahead for Kamryn and him.

Several days passed. The late summer continued to be overly warm and dry. There were more wildfires throughout the state, but none in Duchesne County. Silas may or may not have started some of the fires, but the fact that there were none locally gave Bentley some peace, thinking that Silas was likely not in the area.

Bentley stayed busy as several small cases had been given to him by the sheriff to investigate. He enjoyed the time he spent as a PI. But he made sure that he never left Cedrick alone. The two of them worked together.

They made several trips to Salt Lake, where Ember entertained Cedrick at their apartment when she and Kamryn had finally felt it was safe to return, while Bentley and Kamryn went on some dates. Their friendship was quickly turning to love. Loving Kamryn made Bentley worry more about her.

He tried to find out if there was any activity by Silas, but he found none. Apparently the guy was being very cautious. That made Bentley worry even more, because he had no doubt that Silas had something devious in mind. He knew the evil man had every intention of making him pay for what Silas apparently thought of as wrongs he had committed against the guy.

***

Silas had been holed up in the Salt Lake area working on a bomb for several days. He was determined to make one that was large and powerful. He found instructions on the Internet, which he tried to follow closely. Finding the materials he needed was not easy. He was careful to go outside the area for what he needed and to buy no more than one or two items at any one location. He figured that he needed to be cautious, because he didn't want to alert the authorities to his activities. He had to make sure his revenge was a success this time.

He had determined for sure that Queen Wise was now living in Lonnie's house. It seemed she'd taken it over following his death and her release from jail in Los Angeles. She had a trial coming up, but Silas suspected she would likely not show up for it. If he were in her shoes, he certainly wouldn't. He'd missed hearings in Duchesne, but he didn't care.

It had taken some effort to keep track of what was happening with Queen, but a trip to LA had enabled him to learn that she had been released weeks ago on a very low bond. His job, he told himself with a snicker, was to make sure she did not return for trial. He had something better planned for her. If it worked out the way he hoped it would, he had plans to make a second bomb, one that was for Trooper Radford.

He had backed off on setting fires for a while. He was concentrating on the upcoming explosions he was going to cause. He also spent a little time every few days driving past the apartment building where Ember and Kamryn lived. He didn't attempt to make contact with them. He just felt the urge to keep track of them.

He hadn't gone out to the Duchesne area since the day he learned where Radford was living. His next trip out there would be his last, and it would be Radford's last day on earth. Early on a Monday morning, he made a trip past the apartment. He had traded in the truck he'd driven the last time he was in Duchesne and was now driving an old Ford Fiesta.

He was surprised when he saw Bentley Radford's brown Ford pickup in the parking area. He seethed with hatred as he parked a short distance away and watched. It was only a few minutes before Radford, Ember, Kamryn, and Cedrick walked out to the truck and got in. He couldn't help but notice how Radford was looking around as if he were looking for something. "Probably for me," he said to himself with a chuckle.

Silas picked up the pistol he'd concealed under a jacket on the seat beside him. He held it and pointed it toward Radford. It was all he could do to keep from pulling the trigger, but he managed to control himself. There were other people in the parking area, and he didn't want any witnesses. Anyway, he'd psyched himself up to blow the trooper up along with his cabin and whoever else happened to be there when he did.

He put the pistol back under the jacket and waited while the brown pickup pulled out of the parking area. Curious as to where the four detested people were going, he put his little car in gear and followed them. He wondered why they went into the underground parking at the Matheson courthouse, but he couldn't imagine that it had anything to do with him. He drove off to where he was staying to put the final touches on the bomb he planned to use in the late hours of the night. Lonnie's house was going to go *boom* with Queen Wise in it. Then he would start on the next bomb.

***

The day had arrived for the trial of Claude Skeed. Ember, Bentley, Cedrick, and Kamryn met Faye in the underground parking area and they all walked up the steps and into the Matheson courthouse together. They met briefly in a small conference room with the assistant DA who had been assigned to prosecute the case. She was a petite, middle-aged woman by the name of Veronica Newell. She was younger by several years than Professor Aldrich, but both women were super intelligent and highly motivated. Like Professor Aldrich, Veronica had earned a reputation for fighting hard to put the bad guys away, and she was anxious to see justice done for both Cedrick and Faye. Ember took an immediate liking to her. She could picture herself being in Veronica's position sometime in the future.

Veronica invited Ember and the others to sit down, and then she said, "We are going to nail this guy. Make no mistake about it. But success depends more on you guys than on me. So for the next few minutes I want to review with each of you what your testimony today will be. Cedrick, are you willing to testify first? I need to have you lay the groundwork for the case since you are the one he persecuted and stole from first."

Ember watched her little brother with concern. He fidgeted on the hard chair, but he bravely said, "Yes, I guess I'm ready."

"Claude and his attorney won't scare you?" Veronica asked.

"Maybe a little, but I think I'll be okay," he said, his chin quivering ever so slightly.

"You need to know that Claude's attorney will make a motion to keep all of you out of the courtroom except the one testifying, so that means you'll basically be alone except for me. Can you handle that?"

"Why can't Ember or Bentley be there with me?" the boy asked.

Veronica smiled kindly at him and said, "It's so that none of you will know what the other testified to from the stand. I'd prefer to have you all in there with me for the entire proceeding, but I know the defense attorney and the judge won't allow that. You will probably also be instructed not to talk to each other about your testimony once the trial is underway."

"That's not fair," Faye said.

"But it's the way it works, Aunt Faye," Ember, a student of the law, said. "We just have to live with it. Let me ask you this, Veronica; once any of us have testified will we be allowed to stay in the courtroom after that?"

"Only if I can assure the court that I will not recall you for further testimony or to clarify some issue that I think we need to make clearer to the jury," Veronica said.

Faye spoke up then. "Would you consider letting me go first instead of Cedrick? That way I could be in the courtroom where Cedrick could look at me if he felt like he needed to."

Veronica was thoughtful for a moment, and then she made a notation on the legal pad in front of her. Finally, she said, "I think that might work. Would you feel better about that, Cedrick?"

"Yeah, that would be easier," the boy said with a look of relief on his face.

"All right then, that's what will happen," she said. "Ember, you will be third, followed by Bentley. After his testimony I will call the arresting officer. Kamryn, I may not need to use you, but again I might. That's why you are here."

"I don't know what I could testify to," Kamryn said.

"You watched what Ember was going through. I may want the jury to hear that from someone in addition to Ember. That's all. Is that okay?"

Kamryn nodded fiercely. "I can do that. It was all really hard on Ember."

"Okay, then let's move on."

Veronica then went over the questions she planned to ask each of them. "Do any of you have any misgivings about what I'll be asking you?"

None did, so then the prosecutor said, "Now, I may have to insert some questions I haven't planned yet, so be prepared if I have to surprise you. Finally, the hardest part will be the cross-examination by Claude's lawyer. Don't let him make you mad and don't let him make you say something that isn't true. He'll try to do that. If I feel like he's going too far I'll object and hope the judge will keep him in line."

They discussed things a little further, and then Veronica said, "The first thing that will happen today is the seating of a jury. You can all be in there for that. If any of you hear something that concerns you about any prospective juror, slip me a note. Ember, you are a law student, and Bentley, I understand you are a detective. You two are the ones most likely to pick up on anything that I might miss. I'll want you all seated right behind me for the jury selection. Do any of you have any questions?" There were none, so she said, "Then let's get into the courtroom. Oh, and try not to look Claude in the eyes. He'll attempt to intimidate you by looking angry or threatening if he gets the chance. Just try to act like he's not there. I know that's easier said than done, but it's my advice."

The jury was seated before the noon break. It was as good a jury as they could hope for. Ember couldn't help but look at her uncle a couple of times, but he was not looking over at them, so she didn't get any nasty looks. She was disappointed to see that he was dressed in a suit and tie. She'd expected to see him in jail clothes with handcuffs on him. She should have known better.

Cedrick had also noticed and he asked, "Bentley, why did they let him dress nice? He never wears a suit."

Bentley answered by saying, "It's so the jury won't be prejudiced. This way, he doesn't look like the evil man he has become."

"I think he should be in jail clothes," Cedrick said with a frown.

"I do too," Ember agreed. She was sitting beside her little brother, with Bentley on the other side of him and Kamryn next to Bentley. Cedrick was clearly nervous, and seeing Claude all dressed up didn't help. Ember and Bentley both whispered to him from time to time attempting to assure him that it would all be okay.

They all had lunch together, and at one-thirty they were back in their seats behind the prosecutor's table. But they weren't there long, because as expected, the defense attorney made a motion that they be excluded from the courtroom. The only potential witness that didn't have to leave was the lead investigating officer, who was seated beside Veronica at the counsel table.

"So what's going to happen now?" Cedrick asked once they were all out in the corridor.

Ember explained that Veronica would make her opening statement, followed by the defense attorney, and only after that would she call her first witness, which as agreed earlier would be Faye.

A few minute later, Faye was called into the courtroom.

CHAPTER THIRTY-SIX

BENTLEY AND THE OTHERS WERE visiting quietly. He was attempting to help them overcome the nervousness that was understandably bothering all of them. They were sitting near a door to the courtroom on the benches provided there. Suddenly, they heard shouting and screaming coming from inside the courtroom. They all bounded to their feet.

A couple of officers rushed from the next courtroom over and into the room where Claude's trial was being held. In the brief moments the door was open, Bentley could hear pandemonium from inside. A moment later, an officer led Faye out of the courtroom. She was crying, and one eye was going dark. Blood was seeping from her mouth.

"Aunt Faye, what happened in there?" Ember cried out at the sight of her aunt.

"It was awful. Claude jumped out of his chair when I left the witness stand. He got to me and began punching me before an officer could stop him. Then he fought with the officer. More officers came in just before I came out. He's wicked. I'm just glad you guys didn't hear what he was saying to me."

"I suppose the jury heard it and saw what he did," Ember said.

"Yes, I'll say they did," she said.

"Let's find a restroom and get you cleaned up," Ember said gently as she took her aunt by the arm and led her away from the others.

Holding tightly to Bentley's arm, Kamryn asked, "What will happen now?"

"The judge will probably call a mistrial. I expect the prosecutor will be out in a little while and tell us what to expect," he said.

It was an hour before they saw anything of Veronica Newell. When she finally came through the door, she was shaking her head. "Faye, I'm so sorry that he got to you like he did. Are you okay?"

Faye said, "I'll be fine. He's hurt me worse."

"He has?" Ember asked with surprise.

"Yes, but I didn't want anyone to know, not even you, Cedrick," she said as she looked at him.

Veronica spoke again, "The trial is off. None of the rest of you will have to testify. Once Claude was restrained and calmed down, his attorney went with him to the holding cell and talked to him. When they came back in, the attorney moved for a mistrial, which the judge promptly denied. Claude and his attorney whispered to each other for a few minutes, and then they asked to meet with me. It was a short meeting in which I agreed to drop a couple of the lesser charges in exchange for his guilty plea to the more serious ones.

"He and his attorney considered my offer while I explained it to the judge. He asked Claude if he was willing to accept my plea deal. Claude's attorney told the judge that Claude was willing to accept the deal. He pled guilty to the charges I left on the table, and the lesser charges were dismissed."

"Does that mean he'll get less time in prison?" Ember asked.

"Definitely not. Sentencing won't be for a while yet as the judge ordered that a presentence evaluation be conducted by Adult Probation and Parole first. None of you need to be here for that when it happens unless you want to be."

Faye spoke right up. "I don't ever want to see him again."

"Neither do I," echoed Cedrick.

"Nor I," Ember agreed.

"I'm glad I don't have to talk in there," Cedrick said. "I was scared."

Ember put an arm around him. "Me too," she admitted, "and with what happened to Aunt Faye we had good reason to be worried. But thankfully it's over now."

"I just wish it was over with Silas too," Cedrick said. "Can we go now?"

They all headed for the underground parking, where they said goodbye to Faye, and then got into Bentley's truck. As they were driving back to the girls' apartment, Ember suggested, "I'd like to take Cedrick to a movie this afternoon. I think I can persuade Brad to go with us. We'll be really careful."

"Hey, yeah, let's do that," Cedrick agreed.

Ember looked at Kamryn and grinned. "I think you and Bentley should spend a few hours together. You don't have to be back to your cabin too early do you?" That last question was directed at Bentley.

"No, Hank is taking care of our place tonight and in the morning," he said. "What do you think, Kamryn?"

"I think it's a really good idea. After worrying about the trial for the past few days, I'm ready for some relaxation time with you."

***

Silas was ready to take his bomb to Lonnie's house by around two in the morning. He didn't think it was possible to get as excited as he always did just before lighting a fire, but if anything, he was more so. It was like he'd graduated into a newer and better method of destruction. He'd get to see both the explosion and the fire afterward. For Silas Villard, life was great. For Queen Wise, well, not so much.

The only thing that might mess up his night was if Queen wasn't home. But when he drove slowly past the house, he was relieved to see her ratty old car parked in the driveway. He laughed to himself. This was going to be such a rush.

The bomb he'd so painstakingly built weighed fifty pounds. He'd wanted to make sure it was large enough to destroy the entire house. He lugged it for most of a block from where he'd parked the car. The lights were off in the house as well as in the houses on either side and across the street. He didn't think he'd be seen, but just in case, he lugged the bulky bomb around to the back and placed it underneath what he believed was a bedroom window. He set the timer for five minutes, and headed back in the direction of his car.

He didn't go clear back to the car, because he wanted to see the explosion while he was still close enough to enjoy it without risking injury to himself. When he found a spot in the shadows behind a large tree about two hundred feet away, he looked at his watch. If his timer worked, the bomb should go off in one minute.

As he had hoped, right on time the bomb went off. It was spectacular and very, very loud. Flames and burning bits of wood were blown at least a hundred feet into the air. When the burning materials had settled back to the ground, Lonnie Defollo's house was gone. It was great! His bomb had done everything he'd wanted it to.

And More! Houses on both sides of Lonnie's house were burning too. And the heat was so intense that even from his position two hundred or so feet away, Silas could feel the heat. It was so hot that it felt like his face was on fire. He had to move farther back. People came pouring out of houses all along the street. Women and children were screaming, men were cursing. Silas walked right into the crowd that quickly gathered and joined in the cursing. Not one person looked at him suspiciously.

A jacked-up truck drove up from the west and stopped. To Silas's dismay, Queen Wise and a man he'd never seen before stepped out of it not more than twenty-five feet from where he was standing with others who were watching.

"What's going on here?" he heard Queen shout. She was shaking her fists and began cursing like a sailor. "Who did that to my house?" she asked as she looked around.

Silas was slinking away from the crowd when Queen spotted him. "Get that man," she screamed. Surely, she didn't recognize him, he thought, but whether she did or not, he wasn't sticking around.

Nobody but Queen chased after him. She was, however, too slow to ever catch him. Cops and firetrucks raced by as he jumped in his car. Queen was hunched over about a hundred feet or more from him, huffing and puffing. He raced away. That was too close! He wanted desperately to watch as the fire burned the houses on either side of Lonnie's, but he didn't dare risk it. He needed to get away.

Back in his room at the dumpy motel where he'd stayed for the past week, he plopped down on his bed. He shook his fists at the ceiling and cursed as badly as Queen had cursed. The bomb had been perfect, but she was still alive. And she obviously suspected, even if she didn't know for sure, that it was him that had blown up the house.

He began chugging beers. He went through a six-pack before he finally began to calm down. His night had not been a total failure. Queen wasn't hurt, but the bomb had proven to him that he could blow up Radford's cabin and have nothing left of it. He began to laugh. Who cared about Queen anyway? Radford was the one who mattered, and he was convinced that his next bomb was going to work as well as the one tonight had worked. He would make sure his hated enemy—the man who had ruined his life—was in his cabin when the next bomb went off.

He turned on the TV and tuned in to a local channel. As he had hoped, his handiwork in Magna was being reported while the fire was being filmed. It wasn't as good as being there in person; nevertheless, it gave him a thrill to watch the fire destroy the houses near Lonnie's.

He got very little sleep that night, and he consumed a lot of beer. The next morning, he began assembling the bomb that would finally accomplish what he needed to do to complete his revenge.

CHAPTER THIRTY-SEVEN

CEDRICK AND BENTLEY WERE HAVING breakfast in the hotel where they'd spent the night. A television was on, but the sound was muted. What caught Bentley's attention was the brightly burning fire displayed on the screen. He walked over and turned up the sound. What he learned alarmed him. The fire had been caused by a large explosion at a house owned by the late Lonnie Defollo in Magna. It was reported that no one was in the house at the time.

He was surprised when a picture of Queen Wise came on the screen as she was being interviewed. "I'm certain this was caused by a bomb," she said. "And I know who set it off. His name is Silas Villard. I saw a man his size running away right after my boyfriend and I drove up to where a bunch of neighbors had gathered. I tried to chase him, but as you can see, I'm not exactly built like a runner."

She laughed at her own joke. Then she explained who Silas was and that he'd left in what she believed was a white Ford Fiesta. Shortly after the interview with her, the newscaster spoke of Lonnie Defollo, explaining that he had been killed in a gun battle in Los Angeles at the scene of a large fire, which he and his gang, including Ms. Wise, had intentionally started in an attempt to lure Silas there. He explained that Ms. Wise was currently out on bond, pending trial for her involvement in that crime in LA.

The news spoiled Bentley's appetite. Cedrick only picked at what was left of his eggs and hash browns. It was Cedrick who spoke the very words that Bentley was thinking. "He wants to blow us up, doesn't he?"

"Probably, but we won't let him succeed."

"The cops are after him again, aren't they?" Cedrick asked. "They know what he's driving, don't they?"

"I'm afraid he won't be driving that car very long," Bentley said. He didn't have a lot of hope that Silas would finally be caught, even though federal authorities were involved in the case against him. It was up to him to stop him from doing what he now assumed Silas had in mind for him.

"What about Ember? Will he blow up her apartment?" Cedrick asked.

"I don't think so, because it's me he's after," Bentley said. "But I'm not going to take any chances. She and Kamryn need to stay at a hotel again for a while just to be on the safe side," he said as worry knotted his gut.

"Will she do that?" Cedrick asked in concern.

"I think so. I'll call her now."

Ember answered on the first ring. "Is something wrong, Bentley?" she asked.

"I hope not, but do you recall me mentioning a woman by the strange name of Queen Wise?" he asked.

"Yes. What about her?" Ember asked.

Bentley quickly explained about the bomb at the house she was living in and the fact that Queen was certain that Silas had set it off. Ember was a very smart lady, and she immediately said, "Bentley, he wants to blow up your cabin with you and Cedrick in it. What are you going to do? I'm terrified for you guys."

"I can prevent it at my place, but Cedrick and I are worried about you."

Before Bentley could finish explaining why he was worried, she said, "Do you think he might blow up our apartment? Bentley, what are we going to do?"

"You and Kamryn need to go stay in a hotel like you did once before," he said. "And your neighbors need to be warned."

"We could tell them, but they would never believe us," Ember replied.

"I'll call Hank and see if his boss, the sheriff, will call the police chief in Salt Lake and explain our concerns. Then it would be up to the police there to talk to the rest of the people in the apartments. The bomb he set off early this morning was a powerful one. If he sets one off there that's as powerful as the one he's already used, it would be a huge disaster. You and Kamryn get out today, please. I'll call Hank."

Bentley didn't need to call Hank, because Hank called him just as he was finishing his call to Ember. "Bentley, have you heard what happened early this morning in Magna?"

"If you're referring to the bombing of Lonnie Defollo's house, then yes, I have," Bentley responded.

"This makes your situation much worse. If that really is Silas, then he has stepped up his game," Hank said. "From what I understand, it was a powerful bomb. It blew the house apart."

"I've got good security, but my biggest concern is Kamryn and Ember. They will go to a hotel for a while."

"I hadn't thought about that," Hank said. "They live in an apartment building, don't they? That means others are in danger if he plants a bomb there."

"I was just about to call you when you called me. Do you think the sheriff would be willing to alert the chief of police in Salt Lake and let him know about the potential danger?"

"I'm sure he would, and hopefully, they'll take it seriously," Hank said. "I'm at my office now. I think the sheriff is in the building. I'll get right on it."

"Thanks, Hank. Cedrick and I are heading home in a few minutes. I'm so relieved that we don't have to testify against Ember's uncle. Thanks for taking care of my place again. You're a good friend. Hopefully, Cedrick and I won't need to go out of town overnight for a while."

"You'll need to go see Kamryn every now and then, won't you?" Hank asked with a chuckle.

"Yes, I will, but until Silas is in custody I . . ." he paused. "I want to see her, but I also need to make sure my place is secure, and that Cedrick is safe."

***

Silas was uptight. He couldn't believe Queen Wise had told the police that she saw him running from the scene. That had the cops looking for him again. She even told them about the car he was driving. That meant he had to get rid of it and get another one. He seethed with anger over the problems her big mouth had caused. He wanted to get even with her, but he decided that it would be better if he first took care of the man who had started all his problems— Trooper Radford.

He was afraid to purchase another car because the cops were on the lookout for him, and the public was probably watching for him as well. His only option was to steal another car and some license plates so he could switch them from time to time. He accomplished all that in the dead of night. Then he went to work preparing his second bomb. Two days later, he was ready for the big show.

He loaded the bomb into his most recent stolen vehicle, a pickup truck, and was about to head out of town when he had a sinister thought. Before detonating the bomb, he would start one more fire. The apartment complex where Ember and Kamryn lived would go up in flames tonight, and then he'd drive to Duchesne in time to set the bomb off at Trooper Radford's house. Sweet revenge was all he cared about.

He drove to within about a block of the apartments and parked his stolen pickup out of sight. Then he sneaked to the back of the building and splashed gasoline on the walls. He threw a match, then slipped back into the shadows and hid. He watched the flames from a distance, but to his dismay, fire trucks appeared just as the fire was getting fun to watch. He hadn't expected such a quick response. The fire did a lot of damage, but it hadn't destroyed even a tenth of the apartment building before it was extinguished.

He hated that he hadn't been able to watch the front of the building, because there he would have been entertained watching people fleeing from the building in panic. He slipped through the shadows to where he could see the front and was surprised that there were no people standing around. He assumed he must have burned some people in their sleep, but still, some should have gotten out because the fire wasn't that big—to his great disappointment. He wished he'd known exactly which apartment the two girls lived in, and he'd have started the fire close to them. Again, for all he knew, he may have lucked out and started it close to their rooms anyway.

He watched from a safe distance for a while longer, and then he left in disgust. Oh, well, he decided, the girls were either burned or not, but either way, he'd made them homeless. He sneaked back to the truck and drove away. He was disappointed in a way, because the quick response of the fire trucks had ruined his fun.

But his big show was still set for later that night. He needed to get to Duchesne County. He hoped to arrive there at around three-thirty or four in the morning. Then he'd set the bomb on Radford's back porch, retreat into the trees and watch the explosion. He could feel his excitement building.

***

Bentley was awakened by the ringing of his phone. Bleary eyed, he looked at the time. It was one o'clock in the morning. He looked at his phone and came fully awake when he saw that it was Ember calling him. "Ember, are you guys all right?" he asked urgently.

"Yes, Kamryn and I are okay, sort of," she said, but her voice was quivering.

"Sort of? What do you mean?"

"I'm glad you told us to get out of our apartment," she said.

"Did it get bombed?" he asked before she explained further.

"No, but it was set on fire. Only a few of the rooms were destroyed, but ours was one of them," she said. "A police officer called me while another was calling Kamryn. He told me that they were sure it was arson and that it started at the back of the building. He asked me what my apartment number was and I told him. Ours was one of the apartments that was burned the worst. We've lost a lot of our belongings. I'm just glad we did like you and Evie did and made sure all our photos and important papers were backed up or in a safety deposit box."

"What about your laptop?" he asked as anger burned within him. Silas was responsible.

"We both have our laptops and a bunch of clothes and so on. We packed as much as we could and brought it to the hotel with us. I brought all the books and other materials that I need for my law classes," she said. "But now we have no place to live."

"I'll help you and Kamryn figure that out. Don't worry about it. I'm just grateful you're both safe."

"And we are, thanks to you, Bentley. And so are the rest of the people who live in the apartments. Kamryn wants to talk to you," Ember said.

"Bentley, what are we going to do?" Kamryn asked. He could hear her sniffling. He wanted to throw his arms around her and keep her safe.

He said, "Should I come there?"

"Oh, no, don't do that. You need to be there to make sure he doesn't burn or blow up your cabin. We'll be okay." They talked for a little while longer before Kamryn said they needed to try to get some sleep because Ember had a test in a few hours.

Bentley could not go back to sleep. Silas had tried to hurt Kamryn, someone he'd hurt twice before and who had become very dear to Bentley. He'd failed, but who knew what he might try next. Would he come here, or would he do something else first? There was no way to know. He checked all his cameras. There was no activity on them. He stepped out onto the back deck where he was greeted by his dogs.

There was nothing more he could do. Anyway, the chances of Silas coming here tonight seemed very slim. How did he keep avoiding capture? It was making him crazy.

He went back into the house and sat in his recliner. He had no desire to try to sleep in his bed. If he got too tired, he would just let himself fall asleep in the recliner.

CHAPTER THIRTY-EIGHT

SILAS CHECKED HIS WATCH AFTER he pulled to a stop at what he estimated to be about a half-mile from where he now knew Radford's cabin to be. He didn't see any other cabins in the vicinity. He backed the truck out of sight among some trees. He didn't need to shut the lights off because he'd been driving without them for the past few minutes, inching his way along.

He pulled the bomb out of the back seat of the pickup. It was stuffed in a large backpack. He shrugged his way into it after strapping a pistol to his belt. He had a small penlight, which he used sparingly as he hiked toward Radford's cabin. He was feeling pretty good. This was a night he'd looked forward to for a long time. He would not fail.

As he walked, stumbling a little under the extra weight from time to time, he was deep in thought. He was not drunk. He'd limited himself to two beers on his way out from the city. In his mind, he also hadn't been drunk the night Trooper Radford had falsely arrested him. That was why he hated the man so much.

He had planned all along to leave the country by sneaking into Mexico after he'd settled his score with Radford. Foremost on his mind, however, were other people he had sworn to get even with. One of them was the teenaged girl, Piper. If not for her, Radford would have been dead a long time ago. He could easily swing into California as he made his way south to the Mexican border, locate her, and make her pay.

There was still pain in his upper arm from where the deputy had shot him and the dog had bitten him. He'd learned that the deputy's name was Tren Bobbly. The guy was short and chunky. He would be no problem to get even with. If things went as planned here tonight, Bobbly might just show up, and if he did . . . He knew where the deputy lived and if need be, he'd look him up later. Perhaps he'd return after he'd been in Mexico for a while. Silas's thought processes had long since ceased to be rational.

Kamryn, the girl he'd shot twice, was another one he wanted to get revenge against. She'd known her car was low on gas and she should have told him. Maybe she'd been burned tonight along with Trooper Radford's sister-in-law in the fire at the apartment. He would find out, and if she'd happened to live, well, he'd get her too, sometime in the future. He would not forget about her treachery.

Finally, he still had a score to settle with Queen Wise. His anger at Lonnie Defollo had transferred to her. He wasn't sure he would let his revenge against her wait for a return from Mexico in a year or two. On the other hand, he knew that caution was important. He had time to decide what to do with her and when.

Silas approached an unexpected obstacle a short distance ahead of him. He shined his small light toward it. There was a net wire fence, topped by two strands of barbed wire, a fair distance from Radford's cabin. That made Silas very angry. Did Radford really think he could fence him out? He set his backpack down about fifty feet from the fence and walked all the way back to his truck, seething with anger. He had pliers in the truck. He could easily enough cut a hole in the fence and go through to the cabin. It was the extra time and trouble that angered him so much.

***

Bentley had fallen asleep briefly, but he woke up when he heard his dogs growling on the back deck. Something had disturbed them. He quickly checked all his cameras and saw nothing to alarm him. A large, graceful buck had jumped the fence east of his house a short while before. Perhaps it was wandering around near the corrals. If so, its presence would not go unnoticed by the dogs.

He put his phone away after making sure there was nothing on any of the cameras to worry about. He stepped out onto the deck. Both dogs were staring into the area of his corrals. It was a dark night, so he grabbed a flashlight from his kitchen and went back out again. He shined it toward the corrals and sheds. He heard the door open behind him.

He glanced back as Cedrick who was rubbing his eyes as he walked over to the edge of the deck and stopped beside him. "What is it?" the teenager asked.

Before Bentley could answer, the large buck stepped into the light of his beam. The dogs both looked like they wanted to go after the deer. Bentley spoke quietly and grabbed Twy's collar. Without needing to be told, Cedrick grabbed

Bolt's collar. Then they watched as the beautiful animal wove its way through the corrals. They'd seen both deer and elk on their property many times, but they had never seen one come this close to the house.

They both watched, fascinated. It finally disappeared to the west. "Wow, that was cool," Cedrick said.

"It was a beautiful animal, that's for sure," Bentley agreed.

They stood there together for several more minutes, still holding the dogs. Bentley had tried to teach them not to chase animals without his order, but it was clear that both of them wanted to do just that. They tugged against the guys, looking to the west where the deer had faded into the darkness.

A warning buzzed on Bentley's phone. He looked at it. "The buck just reached the fence and set off one of our alarms," he said to Cedrick. The dogs were still tugging in that direction. "I really don't want them to go after the deer, although I think he jumped the fence already."

The alarm went off again. "He must have come back," Cedrick said.

"Probably. Or maybe now he's just grazing along the other side of the fence. Maybe we're going to have to take the dogs inside for the rest of the night. That pretty buck seems to have distracted them."

"Were you on the phone with Ember and Kamryn a few hours ago?" Cedrick asked as soon as they were back inside with the doors locked.

"I was. Did I wake you?" Bentley asked.

"I heard your phone ring. I'm having a hard time sleeping," the boy said.

"You and me both," Bentley said with a grin. "I'm just going to sit here in my recliner for the rest of the night."

Cedrick looked at Bentley and began shaking his head. "Ember doesn't ever call this time of night. Is she okay?"

"She's fine, and so is Kamryn."

"Bentley. Something must have happened. Why did they call?"

Bentley had always been honest with Cedrick. The boy had a right to know, so he told him about the fire at their apartment building and explained that the ladies weren't there and why. Cedrick listened, wide-eyed. "It was Silas."

"I imagine. Now, let's turn the lights off. I'm staying here, but you can go back to bed," Bentley said.

The boy shook his head. "I'm going to sleep on the sofa."

"That's fine," Bentley agreed as he turned off the lights and closed his eyes. But after a moment, he picked up his phone and started checking the cameras again.

"Can you see that big buck?" Cedrick asked from his position on the sofa.

"No, he must have moved on. Wait, there's something moving. Maybe it's him after all," he said and started scrolling through each of the other cameras.

***

Silas had clipped a hole in the fence. He'd left his backpack with the bomb in it where he'd set it down when he went after the pliers. It was about fifty feet away. He couldn't see the cabin from here because of some large pinion trees, so he didn't know how much farther it was. However, he knew exactly in which direction he had to walk to reach it.

Silas thought about the large buck that had jumped the fence when he first reached it after going after the pliers. As he walked back and grabbed the bomb, he was still thinking about that buck, thinking about how much food it would have provided back in those weeks when he was trying to survive in the hills. He stood for a minute and listened to the sounds of the night. Darkness was his friend, and the sounds of the night out in desolate places soothed his nerves.

He could hear crickets somewhere near. In the distance, a coyote howled. Closer, an owl hooted. He was feeling content. He moved toward the fence and the hole he'd created. Just as he reached it a cow mooed, soft and long. Radford must have a cow. *How sweet.* Well, after a few minutes, someone else would have to care for the cow, because Radford would be in a million scorched pieces.

He shoved the backpack through the fence ahead of him. He stepped through and shrugged the backpack onto his back. At that point, Silas cleared his mind of the deer and the owl and the coyote and all other distractions. He had a cabin to blow up. That's all he could think about now.

He crept through the trees, and soon the dark shadow of the cabin loomed in front of him. An evil grin of anticipation split his bearded face. Just a few more minutes and he would have his explosion and the most anticipated fire of his arsonist career. More importantly, he would have his revenge, his long awaited revenge. He licked his lips, adjusted the heavy backpack, and picked his way forward. He came to a corral fence and veered north around it. He could see other shadowed buildings.

***

Bentley had started to drift off when both dogs growled. He sat up in his chair and heard Cedrick do the same on the sofa across the room. Bolt's growl was not like the one they'd heard earlier when the large buck had passed them. It was deep throated, giving Bentley chills.

"Bentley, Bolt hears something. Should we let him outside?" Cedrick asked as he quietly approached the recliner.

Bentley got to his feet. "I think we should," he said. Twy didn't have the same kind of threatening growl, but he was giving it his best effort. "Be silent," he said, a command both dogs knew well and always obeyed. He stepped to the door. As silently as possible, he unlocked it and then turned the handle. He'd never noticed the door squeak before. It was a very soft sound, and he guessed that was why he hadn't noticed it earlier. Also, it wasn't usually as quiet outside as it was now when he opened it. He paused and listened to whatever was beyond the door after opening it just a crack. All he could hear were crickets and the hoot of an owl. Good sounds. Safe sounds. But Bentley didn't feel safe, and his chills grew in intensity.

***

Kamryn was wide awake. She could hear Ember's gentle breathing on the other bed. She had apparently fallen asleep again after they'd talked to Bentley. Kamryn was thinking about Bentley. She thought about calling him just to hear his voice. But he'd probably gone back to sleep after her last call.

She thought of Evie and how Bentley's heart still ached over her loss. Evie had loved Bentley with all her heart. So, Kamryn reminded herself, did she. And in her heart she knew Evie was okay with that. She would want Bentley to be happy. She wished she was with him right then, so he could hold her tight and tell her everything was going to be okay. She needed to hear him say that. He was so strong and so fearless.

"Kamryn, are you awake?" Ember said from the other bed.

"Yes, I thought you were sleeping."

"I can't sleep. I'm so afraid of what Silas will do next."

"So am I," Kamryn admitted as chills ran down her spine.

CHAPTER THIRTY-NINE

BENTLEY HEARD WHAT COULD BE footsteps. Was the big buck back? No, it had walked almost silently when it passed by a short while ago. He shoved the door open, grabbing the rifle he kept there for just such a moment as this, and then he said, "Attack," hoping he wasn't dooming some poor animal to vicious bites from Bolt.

The big German shepherd lived up to his name, bolting through the doorway and across the deck like a streak of lightening. Twy was right behind him. Moments later, there was a shout of terror and then a gunshot. Bentley's heart leaped in fear for his dogs. If it was Silas out there—and nothing else made sense—then one of his dogs may have been shot.

There was a second scream, a man's scream. Then another shot. One of the dogs started yipping, and a moment later, Twy limped onto the deck and then collapsed at Bentley's feet. Cedrick, who had been standing behind Bentley, switched on the deck lights. There was the sound of running footsteps fading into the distance as whoever had been here fled west toward the fence.

"Do you have your phone?" Bentley asked Cedrick.

"It's in my pocket," the boy responded.

"Call 911 and then call Hank," Bentley said urgently as he dropped down beside Twy. His dog was bleeding from a wound in one front shoulder. It didn't look too bad, but there could be another bullet somewhere else on his body. Or there could be a bullet in Bolt, and he might be lying out there mortally wounded. He prayed that was not the case.

"Take Twy inside," he said to Cedrick. "Check him over carefully and try to stop any bleeding you can see."

"Be careful, Bentley," Cedrick said as his brother-in-law leaped off the deck and ran into the darkness, dialing a number on his phone. "Hello,

Hank. We need help. Someone shot our dogs. Bentley's chasing him. I called 911 already."

"I'm on my way," Hank said.

***

Bentley had his phone in his hand with the flashlight app on so he could see where he was running. He feared he would see Bolt lying there on the ground. But he didn't see him so he kept running. He hoped that Silas—it had to be him—was hurt badly, that Bolt had managed to rip into him with those powerful jaws and sharp teeth of his.

Bentley turned the light off, suddenly realizing he might give his mortal enemy a chance to spot and shoot him, notwithstanding the darkness of the night. He came to the fence, and despite the darkness could see that a hole had been cut in it. He stooped and went through, because it seemed that the top strand of barbed wire had not been cut.

He decided that Bolt must be injured but not enough to stop him from pursuing the trespasser. Bentley was gaining on whoever he was pursuing, because he could now hear running footsteps and occasional curses. Several minutes ticked by, and the running stopped. A car door opened and then he could see something lifted into the back of a pickup truck. He could see Silas in the dim glow of the interior light as he attempted to climb in.

Bolt grabbed a leg and Silas pointed his pistol and fired, but Bolt dodged the bullet. However, in doing so, he lost his hold on the man's leg. Bentley raised his rifle. "Silas, throw down the gun. I have a rifle and it's aimed right at you. I would love to fire it. Just give me a reason."

Silas fired a wild shot past Bentley. Bentley called his dog. "Bolt, come."

The ever-obedient German shepherd moved slowly toward Bentley. Silas gave up shooting into the dark and fired up the pickup. Spinning its wheels, the truck flew backward toward Bentley. He and Bolt both dodged, and the truck stopped, and then started forward, picking up speed fast. Bentley raised his rifle but did not shoot. The truck was weaving crazily and he might or might not hit it. If that was a bomb that Silas had put in the bed of the truck, he might hit it, and if he did, it might explode.

If the bomb was as powerful as the one that had blown up Lonnie Defollo's house, both Bentley and his dog could get killed in the blast. He lowered his rifle and watched as the truck sped down the rough road. The lights of the truck came on when it was a couple hundred yards away, but it was apparently too late for Silas to see where he was going. Even at this distance, Bentley could tell that the truck was off the road. A moment later, it struck a large tree, and at that moment, the bomb in the bed of the truck went off.

It blew the truck and all the surrounding trees and bushes apart. The blast was so powerful that it knocked Bentley to the ground. Bolt whimpered and lay beside him. It took a moment for Bentley to get his bearings. When he finally did, he sat up and looked at where the truck had been. The forest was burning now, but there was no sign of the truck. It had been obliterated.

Silas's final fire was torching the pinions and cedar trees. It was bound to be a bad one. Silas, however, was not able to watch it. Silas Villard, arsonist, kidnapper, killer, and all-around bad guy, would not be igniting any more fires. Bentley pulled his phone from the pocket where he'd put it when he turned the light off. He turned the light on and shone it on his courageous dog. He was bleeding from his abdomen. Chances were the dog was mortally wounded, but Bentley was determined to help him if he could.

After putting his phone back in his pocket, he lifted the big dog up in his arms. He left the rifle on the ground and headed toward his cabin, flames from the surrounding forest lighting his way.

***

Cedrick had the bleeding stopped. Twy had only been shot one time, and he would live. But he worried about Bentley and Bolt. For a long time he'd sat on the hardwood floor beside Twy, tears of sadness, frustration, and fear streaming down his face. Suddenly there was a very loud explosion.

He ran to the door, unlocked it, and stepped onto the deck, his heart beating wildly. In the distance, flames were leaping high into the dark night sky. Cedrick knew what was happening. Silas's bomb had gone off. "Bentley!" the boy cried, dashing from the deck and running toward the distant flames.

He stumbled and fell, picked himself up and ran again, only to trip once more. He slowed to a walk. He reached the fence and spotted the hole. He went through it, determined to find Bentley, if he hadn't been blown up.

Cedrick's phone rang in his pocket. He pulled it out, praying that it was Bentley. It was Hank. He fell as he attempted to answer it, dropping it. He searched and found it a moment later and said, "Hank, the bomb went off. Bentley was chasing someone. I'm afraid Bentley and Bolt are dead. I don't know what to do."

"Are you in your cabin?" Hank asked, his deep, steady voice calming the frightened boy a little.

"No. I'm looking for Bentley."

"Cedrick, listen to me. Go back to the cabin. Wait for me there," Hank instructed him.

"But I've got to find Bentley," the boy sobbed.

"Cedrick, go back to the cabin. There are a lot of cops on the way. We'll take care of finding Bentley."

"Okay, I guess," the sobbing thirteen-year-old said. "But the trees are on fire. It's a big fire."

"I'll call for firefighters. Go to the cabin."

Cedrick, who was still on the ground, started to get up when he saw someone coming past a tree. He cried out, "Bentley! You're alive."

"I'm okay, but we need to get help for Bolt. He's hurt bad," Bentley said.

Bentley did not stop walking nor did he put the dog down when Cedrick rushed up and threw his arms around him and then let go after being dragged for a few steps. But he stayed right with Bentley. "Do you still have your phone?" he asked Cedrick.

"Yeah. I just talked to Hank. He's coming and so are a lot of others."

"Good, turn on your flashlight. Even though the flames behind us are lighting things up a little bit, I don't want to stumble and hurt Bolt worse."

Cedrick did as he was directed. The two of them reached the hole in the fence. They both ducked and passed through. "Will the fire burn our cabin?" Cedrick asked a moment later.

"Remember how hard we both worked to clear things around the cabin, sheds, and corrals?"

"Yeah, that was hard work."

"It was, but the fire won't reach the cabin. I hope it doesn't even reach our property."

"Is Silas dead?" the boy asked next.

"Yes, he got blown apart by his own bomb."

"Good!" Cedrick said. "He deserved it."

When they reached the deck, Bentley laid Bolt on the floor. "Get the first-aid kit and some water," he instructed. "Bolt's still alive and I want to make sure he stays that way. How is Twy?"

"He's going to live," Cedrick said over his shoulder as he rushed to do Bentley's bidding. He loved Bolt and he'd do anything to help save him. Both dogs would need a veterinarian, and for Bolt, every minute of delay mattered.

Hank arrived a few minutes later. "Sorry about all this," he said. "I sure wish we could have caught that guy before he did this to your dogs. Are they going to make it?"

"Twy's not too bad. But Bolt worries me. He looks better now than he did out there by where Silas died," Bentley said.

"There are fire crews coming, I don't believe they'll be too long. Hopefully they can stop the fire before it burns too much of the area," Hank said. "So tell me what happened. I'll have to do a report on this even though Silas is dead." Hank paused. "Are you sure he's dead?"

"No doubt about it, Hank. He crashed his truck into a tree. He did not get out of it before it blew up. That truck disintegrated. So, I guess, did Silas."

"At least the threat is past," Hank said. "Okay, I'm going to record this so we don't have to go over it again. Start right from the first."

"It all started with a very large, four-point buck," Bentley said, speaking rapidly as he was anxious to get his dog to a vet. "I was sitting in the recliner. Ember had called and I didn't feel like going back to bed."

"I know about the fire at their apartment building. Did it do much damage to the girls' belongings?"

"It sounds like their apartment was one that was damaged the worst. Ember thinks they pretty much lost everything. I guess they'll learn more later today."

"I'm sorry. Okay, so the buck came in and set off an alarm. Then what happened?" Hank asked.

Bentley was tending to his dog, bandaging and doing what he could to make him comfortable. It took almost ten minutes to tell Hank the story. Hank shut off his little recorder, and then he said, "I suppose this will make the news. You will probably want to call Ember and Kamryn before too long. If they hear it on the radio or TV, they're going to think the worst."

"I'll call Kamryn as soon as I get these dogs in the truck. I'm going to head to Ballard and then call the vet so he can meet us there. I pray this dog lives," Bentley said, gently stroking Bolt's head.

"I wonder how bad he hurt Silas," Hank commented as Bentley picked the big dog up.

"I think he hurt him pretty bad because Silas was running slowly. I still can't believe that Bolt kept after the guy even after being injured so badly himself. This is one brave dog."

A minute later, both dogs, Cedrick, and Bentley were in the truck and headed down the lane. Cedrick was in the back seat holding Bolt, talking to him and praying out loud. Bentley added his own prayer to the boy's.

CHAPTER FORTY

"Hi, Kamryn," Bentley said when he answered her call around nine that morning. He had been planning to call her but so far, he hadn't done it since he knew she needed her sleep. She was clearly awake now. He asked "Were you able to sleep last night after we talked?"

"Not very much. Neither did Ember. She has an exam in an hour. I hope she doesn't flunk it. She called Brad and he's coming here. Ember and I are faced with having to find a place to live," she said. "We'll stay here at the hotel until Silas is captured—if he ever is."

Bentley took a deep breath. "I have good news," he began. "Silas is dead, so you can look for an apartment without worrying about him."

For a moment, Kamryn said nothing, but Bentley could hear her breathing hard. He waited for her reaction. She finally said, "Bentley, are you and Cedrick okay?"

"We're fine. You don't have to worry about us," he said.

"Okay, mister, something has happened. Do you care to tell me about it?" she asked in a pseudo-stern voice."

"Okay, but it isn't pretty," he said.

"It never is if Silas is involved," she responded.

"That's for sure. He came here a couple of hours after I talked to you and Ember, but he failed to blow us up. On the other hand, he did succeed in blowing himself up," he said.

"Details, Bentley. This sounds pretty drastic, but I need details, and I need them quickly because I want to tell Ember as soon as she gets out of the shower."

So Bentley gave her a rapid but fairly complete recitation of the events of the early morning. She gasped several times, but the worst was when he told her about how badly injured Bolt was.

"Is he going to live?" she asked with a trembling voice.

"I don't know. Cedrick and I are sitting in the waiting room of the veterinary clinic in Ballard. We've been here for a couple of hours now. I hope to hear something soon," Bentley said with a catch in his voice.

"What about Twy? I love that dog. He saved your life, yours and Ember's and Cedrick's," she said.

"Yes, he did, and he was part of saving us last night. He's here too, and the vet already told us he'll be fine, that his bullet wound wasn't very severe."

"Oh, good. Bentley, I'm going to shower when Ember leaves. Then I'm coming to see you. I don't have to work until after the weekend. I need to see you," she said.

Bentley realized that he also needed to see her. She was filling a huge hole in his heart, and he admitted to himself that he loved her. He had not forgotten about Evie. He would love her for eternity, but he would also love Kamryn that long.

An hour after the call from Kamryn, the vet came out and told Bentley and Cedrick that the surgery went very well and that Bolt would fully recover. He did tell them they would have to leave him at the clinic for several days, but they could take Twy home.

In the truck a few minutes later, Cedrick said, "Can we say a prayer?"

"I was about to suggest that too," Bentley said. "Do you want to say it, or do you want me to?"

"I will," the teenager said. He gave a beautiful prayer of gratitude for the lives of their dogs. He surprised Bentley when he said, "Heavenly Father, please bless Bentley and Kamryn that they can get married so we can be a family."

He closed his prayer on that note. Bentley said, "Thanks, Cedrick. That was a beautiful prayer. Kamryn is coming out in a little while. I think your sister will come too after she finishes her exam. I'm glad for what you asked in your prayer, because I would like very much to marry Kamryn. I hope she feels the same."

Cedrick looked over at him and grinned. "She does. She told me so."

Ember called before they got home and announced that the exam hadn't been too bad. "Kamryn is on her way to see you now. Oh, and guess what? Brad has asked me to marry him. We want to do it right away. You should ask Kamryn. We could have a double wedding."

"I will do that, and I hope she says yes," he said, smiling at Cedrick.

"Bentley, I can't believe how peaceful I feel. With Silas dead and Uncle Claude in jail, it seems like the weight of the world has been lifted off me."

"I feel the same," he said. "I think Kamryn does too."

As soon as Kamryn arrived at the cabin, shortly after Cedrick and Bentley had returned from the vet's, she bounded toward him. Cedrick was a grinning witness to the kiss they shared. "I love you Kamryn. Will you marry me?"

"Of course I will. I love you too."

Cedrick said, "I guess we need to get another horse." They all laughed.

ABOUT THE AUTHOR

CLAIR M. POULSON WAS BORN and raised in Duchesne, Utah. His father was a rancher and farmer, his mother a librarian. Clair has always been an avid reader, having found his love for books as a very young boy.

He has served for over fifty years in the criminal justice system. Twenty years were spent in law enforcement, ending his police career with eight years as the Duchesne County Sheriff. For nearly thirty-two years, Clair has worked as a Justice Court judge for Duchesne County. He retired from that position in November of 2021. Clair is also a veteran of the US Army, where he was a military policeman. Clair has been personally involved in the investigation of murders and other violent crimes in his career. He has served on various boards and councils during his professional career, including the Justice Court Board of Judges, Utah Commission on Criminal and Juvenile Justice, Utah Judicial Council, Utah Peace Officer Standards and Training Council, and an FBI advisory board.

In addition to his criminal justice work, Clair has farmed and ranched all his life. He has raised many kinds of animals. He is also involved in the grocery store business with his oldest son and other family members.

Clair has served in many capacities in The Church of Jesus Christ of Latter-day Saints, including full-time missionary (California Mission), bishop, counselor to two bishops, Young Men president, high councilor, stake mission president, scoutmaster, High Priest group leader, Sunday School teacher, young single adult adviser, and ward missionary.

Clair is married to Ruth, and together, they have five children, all of whom are married: Alan (Vicena) Poulson, Kelly Ann (Wade) Hatch, Amanda (Ben) Semadeni, Wade (Brooke) Poulson, and Mary (Tyler) Hicken. They have twenty-six grandchildren whom they both cherish, and they love spending quality time with them. They also have two great-granddaughters and a great-grandson with two more on the way. Clair and Ruth met while both were students at Snow College and were married in the Manti temple in 1969.

Clair has always loved telling his children, and later his grandchildren, made-up stories. His vast experience in life and his love of literature has always contributed to both his storytelling and his writing of adventure and suspense novels.

Clair has received many awards and recognitions during his criminal justice career, most recently having been awarded the Lifetime Achievement Award as a Justice Court judge. He also received a Lifetime Achievement Award from his publisher, Covenant Communications.

With this book, Clair will have published over forty-five novels.